To Stick.
I hope you enjoy
the story.
Best wishes,
Dave

David McCulloch

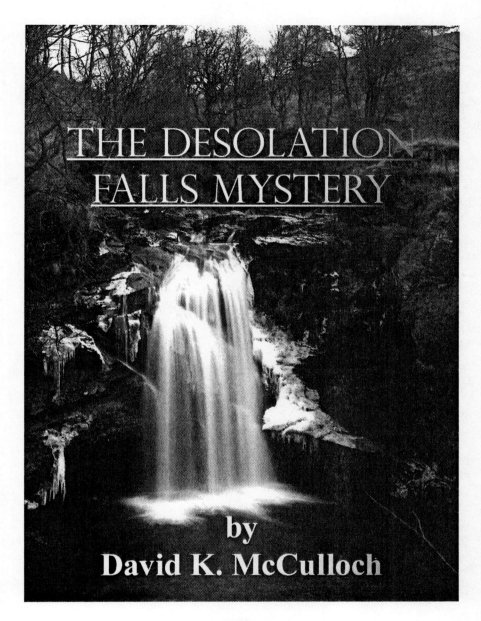

THE DESOLATION FALLS MYSTERY

by
David K. McCulloch

authorHOUSE™

1663 Liberty Drive, Suite 200
Bloomington, Indiana 47403
(800) 839-8640
www.AuthorHouse.com

This book is a work of fiction. People, places, events, and situations are the product of the author's imagination. Any resemblance to actual persons, living or dead, or historical events, is purely coincidental.

© 2005 David K. McCulloch. All Rights Reserved.

No part of this book may be reproduced, stored in a retrieval system, or transmitted by any means without the written permission of the author.

First published by AuthorHouse 11/07/05

ISBN: 1-4208-9436-6 (e)
ISBN: 1-4208-9095-6 (sc)
ISBN: 1-4208-9096-4 (dj)

Library of Congress Control Number: 2005909129

Printed in the United States of America
Bloomington, Indiana

This book is printed on acid-free paper.

Author's Notes

This story would never have been written without the love and support of my wife Kathryn, who not only encouraged me to try, but also freed up the time for me to write. Thanks also to the family and friends who gave me advice and encouragement. I especially thank Lewis who has been a tireless help and a major supporter. Thank you for never doubting that we would get to this point, Lewis.

I would also like to thank Adele Clark, Dick Rubin and Ake Lernmark for reading every word and making constructive comments. I am indebted to Ake for giving me an education about aspects of the Swedish character, and for his detailed knowledge of the world of molecular biology and academic laboratory life.

My admiration of those who toil in forensic crime labs is immense. This story benefited greatly from the wit and wisdom of several of the forensic scientists at the Washington State Patrol Crime Lab in Tacoma, especially Terry McAdam, Jeff Jagmin, Ron Wojciechowski, Chuck Vaughan, Terry Franklin, and Matt Noedel. They are an impressive team. I am glad that they are all on the side of the "good guys."

I would never have got this far without the boundless optimism and friendship of Randy Platt, a gifted writer. I am deeply grateful to Ruth Cohen of her sharp professional eye that has improved my writing mightily.

This is work of fiction. All of the characters in this story are products of my imagination. Any resemblance to persons living or dead is coincidental. There is no Combined Criminal Investigation Facility on Delridge Way. Although there are many wonderful natural hot springs in the Pacific NorthWest, none is called Kamagutz. There is an excellent nursing home on Vashon Island but it is not called Goldentide and is not located on the Burton peninsula.

CONTENTS

SUNDAY

I	Valentine's Day Gloom	3
II	A Grand View Ruined	14
III	Old Wounds And Open Sores	35
IV	Snake Oil Devotee	46
V	Pretentious Bohemian	67
VI	Tater Tots and Fiddle Tunes	82

MONDAY

VII	The Dell	95
VIII	Dead Useful Information	108
IX	Hostile Possibilities	121
X	Not So Innocent Victim	138
XI	Roadside Revelations	149
XII	Locked in Hell	160
XIII	Late Night Feelers	172

TUESDAY/ WEDNESDAY

XIV	Imperfect Symmetry	187
XV	An Elegant Discussion Of Death	205

THURSDAY

XVI	Fight Or Flight	223
XVII	Stir-Fry Emotions	237

FRIDAY

| XVIII | Pressure From On High | 253 |
| XIX | Scouting Party | 270 |

SATURDAY

XX	Frosty Atmosphere	283
XXI	Bloody Indictment	291
XXII	Straggling Hound	301
XXIII	The Culb Hut	313
XXIV	Red Water At Kamagutsz	325
XXV	Desolation Falls	340

SUNDAY

| XXVI | A Bitter Road To Follow | 349 |
| XXVII | Something To Celebrate | 360 |

Prologue

Tami Stillwell shivered with anticipation in the cool February air. The spicy dampness of the deck's cedar planking filled her with excitement. The haunting moan of the foghorn that drifted across the water on the wind from the Southworth ferry seemed to play for her alone. An impudent robin perched on the railing in front of her and cocked its head to inspect her before flitting into the shelter of the rhododendrons that flanked the deck. Frost-kissed leaves sparkled and danced in the pale morning sun where the bird had entered, and kept moving with the gentle on-shore breeze. Down below, beyond the bulkhead, mist still hung over the tide flats. Two herons stalked the shallows like sacrificial priests performing ritual executions to bless the day. Tami spread her arms wide and did a slow pirouette, like a flamboyant conductor drawing every nuance of pleasure and beauty from the scene.

"This is so awesome."

The young man didn't look up. All his attention was focused on rolling the perfect joint. He didn't want any of the buds to blow off and roll between the slats of the deck. This was the good stuff. B.C. Bud – high potency hybrid all the way from Canada. He wouldn't get this again unless the band went on the road. He shepherded every last leaf crumb onto the paper, rolled it tight, licked and sealed it with satisfaction. Only then did he raise his head complacently to see what had got the girl so excited.

Looking west over Colvos Passage the white tips of the Olympic Mountains peeked above the steep tree-lined slopes of the Kitsap Peninsula. The sky above them had the steel gray of rain in it. The view was totally familiar to him. It wasn't such a big deal. Besides, it would look so much better in a few minutes after he took his first few hits of weed. Still, the girl seemed impressed, like he thought she would. This was good.

"Yeah, it's a pretty spot," he said.

"Not the scenery, Aaron. I mean this place. They have their own private beach and like a gazillion feet of waterfront. I can see three kayaks and a sailboat lying on the bulkhead down there like they're just beach toys. Do you think they have servants to keep the place cleaned up?"

"I know they have a really cute gardener who keeps their garden well tended, don't they?" Aaron said.

"When he's not stoned, that is." Tami walked over to a totem pole towering twenty feet above the deck, and slowly inspected the stack of carved characters. "Get a load of this thing. It must have cost thousands to have it carved. The deck's been built around it. Is that one at the top the Thunderbird or the Raven or what?"

Aaron sat, cross-legged and grinning, on the cover of the hot tub. He moved his arms and head like a lanky string puppet.

"Thunderbird Five ready for take off, Mr. Tracy. Thunderbirds are go!"

x

Tami's face was blank.

"You never seen re-runs of that seventies puppet show?" Aaron said. "It's so cheesy it's cool."

He pulled a box of matches out of his khaki pants and prepared to light up. Tami noticed his sparkling teeth and shiny tanned skin. His blond dreadlocks stuck out at cute angles from his head, like one of her mother's cactus plants. Even his toes were handsome, long and thin, curling with pleasure as he held the smoke inside for several seconds before exhaling.

"Are you sure no one's going to come by?" Tami asked.

"No way, man. The house to the north is a summer-only place. No one's been there for months. And the old lady through the trees will be at church for the next hour. She usually has lunch with her daughter down by Tahlequah after that. No, make that always has lunch with her daughter after church. She won't be back till around three."

"How do you know all this stuff?"

"I've been doing the Covington's garden for over a year, man. The folks who live around here are mostly rich retirees. They live to a strict schedule, in case they forget to wipe their butts or something."

"You've met the Covington's then? I didn't think they were that old, are they?"

"I see them every once in a while. Mostly Mrs. C. She's pretty cute. Has an accent. A bit too old for me, maybe, but she'd be experienced, wouldn't she? She'd know what a guy likes."

Tami turned away.

Aaron gazed off across the hazy water and imagined what sensual pleasure he would ask for first. If the band got one good break this summer, like maybe opening for Toad Kill at Bumbershoot or going on the road with Wasted Bombshells, they'd have it made. There would be plenty of fawning and exotic women around them to take his mind off the strain of a big national tour. King-sized hotel suites. Complimentary room service. Full service massage. Massaging the system. That was it. Perfect irony. Headline news – Skunk Bucket trashes hotel rooms while massaging the system. He could turn that into a new song. "Full System Massage."

He gave Tami a proprietorial gaze as she moved gracefully around the deck running her hands over every surface. The tank top and jeans clung to her small supple frame. She had small tits, but her energetic willowy body was a turn on, and so were those big brown eyes. He held out the joint to her.

"Want a couple of hits?"

Pungent marijuana smoke curled and hung in the still air. Tami waved it away with distaste. "Makes your throat burn. I don't like it."

"Suit yourself. I thought you wanted to warm up."

Aaron unbuttoned his shirt and took it off. His cargo pants were not baggy enough to hide the stiffness in his crotch.

"You are so cute, Tami. I have been wanting you ever since I first saw you. You make me feel so horny."

Tami made a face and inspected his chest. It was fun to make him wait. He had thin muscled shoulders, nice pecs with a few wisps of hair in the hollow by his breastbone. She recognized the multicolored tattoo over his heart - the skull and lightning bolt of The Grateful Dead.

"You like the Dead? Now I know why you wanted to borrow my jacket. That's the kind of crap my folks listen to. Them and the Rolling Stones, for God sakes. Those old guys look like dried up corpses with all that makeup on to cover up their wrinkles. It's disgusting."

"The Stones and the Dead are classics, man. Icons. It's on their shoulders that we build our own riffs. So are you not wrinkled underneath your clothes? Are those goose bumps I can see?" He stared at her nipples, standing out in relief against the halter-top flattened against her body by the wind.

"I am not taking off one thing unless I can get warm in a hurry. We don't even have towels."

Aaron leapt off the tub cover and pulled out a large grip bag from behind the bench. He extracted a striped bath towel with a flourish and laid it on the deck.

"You only get to use this once we've been tubbing," he said.

Aaron unzipped his pants, stepped out of them and began prancing naked on the deck. His semi-stiff penis waggled comically as he pretended to play a guitar and mimed his best stage moves. Then he stood with his back to the totem pole, opened his mouth and held his arms out wide.

"Me Thunderbird."

Tami giggled. "Oh my God, I can't believe you, Aaron. You could hang Frank's Stetson on that thing."

"On what?" Aaron looked around in mock puzzlement before letting his eyes settle on his crotch. He faked an English army officer accent. "My God, Miss Stillwell, how did that get there? You're going to have to help me deal with that in a moment. It has become something of an emergency, what! But first we need to warm you up. Let's hit the jets."

He pressed a button on the outside of the hot tub, setting off a deep throaty rumble from inside. The vibrations on the deck planks made Tami's feet tingle.

Aaron unclipped the clasps at the corners of the hot tub cover and yanked it clear above his head.

"It'll be so toasty in there," he said.

Tami's scream shattered the stillness and sent birds squawking for shelter. She stumbled back to the railing. Her hands covered her mouth, stifling the screeching wail that rose into the sky and hovered there with the mist, suspending time and reality. Aaron followed her petrified gaze to the bright blue water of the hot tub where a bloated naked body twirled a slow pirouette amid the carefree bubbles of the jets.

xvi

SUNDAY

2

I

Valentine's Day Gloom

Canyon walls of salad dressing disappeared towards the distant horizon as far as the eye could see. I don't think I'll ever get used to American supermarkets.

"This whole aisle is salad dressing? How can anyone need this many choices? I don't think I'll eat enough salad in a lifetime to try a quarter of these flavors."

"That's because you're forty-five and Scottish, dad. To you, salad means two bits of limp lettuce lying beside a couple of hard-boiled eggs, stale cheese, and a few slices of cold pickled ox tongue."

I examined the bottle, which my daughter had selected and tossed in the cart. "What's this - organic low-fat raspberry, kiwi and ginseng vinaigrette? Are you planning to eat this stuff? It's interesting how human fashions change. In the nineteen eighties that kind of combination would show up on bottles of shampoo. Raspberry and ginseng, pH-balanced, protein-enriched for greasy, problem hair. Maybe when people finally rebelled and refused to slabber it on their hair anymore the big companies started putting it in bottles of salad dressing instead. The power of advertising, eh?"

Jennifer put two youthful hands on resolute hips and favored me with a look of reprimand. The furrowed brow spoiled her radiant nineteen-year old face. I could tell she was enjoying the exchange, though. It was good to see her smile. She hadn't smiled enough in the past year.

"I see it contains extra virgin olive oil, Jen," I said.

"No virgin jokes, dad. It's Valentine's Day."

"Don't I know it? Callum was telling me he has to come up with three "friendship words" for every single person in his class."

"They're still doing that in fourth grade? I don't think I had to do that beyond second grade," Jennifer said.

"Mrs. Henley treats everyone as if they're in second grade, including the parents. Apparently Callum asked if he could be excused from doing friendship words for Erica Jarvis. Mrs. Henley was not amused. She left a message on my machine at work expressing concern at the cynical and antisocial atmosphere that must exist in Callum's home life. Had I considered family counseling? What a bloody cheek she's got!

"It's Social Engineering, so it is. Land Of The Free, indeed. They're just conditioning all the wee fourth graders into being obedient little conformists and well-behaved consumers. America turns everything into tacky commercial excess. Valentine's day has become pink hearts and chocolate day, just like St. Patrick's day is green beer and daft hat day. They've even turned Superbowl Sunday into a national holiday."

"You mean beer and flab day."

"Or nachos and glitzy TV-ad day."

Jennifer loaded a dozen cartons of unfamiliar yogurt in the cart, ignoring my suspicious look.

"We need more yogurt, dad. It's good for your creaking old bones. This stuff's pesticide-free. Trust me. So how did they celebrate Valentine's Day in the dark ages back in Scotland?"

"The only people who cared about Valentine's day were spotty adolescent boys like me who were too scared to talk to the girls they really fancied. Instead we'd send them anonymous Valentine's cards filled with dirty jokes or sappy poems."

"Anonymous? What's the point of that?"

"That was the whole point. You could be suave and witty if they didn't know who you were. Actually you were supposed to hide your true identity somewhere on the card by writing it in a cryptic code or hiding it under the stamp. Half the fun for the girls was trying to guess who'd sent them."

I lost my train of thought as we passed the produce section of the store and Jennifer began piling Bok Choy and red-leafed chard on top of the yogurt. Was I going to be expected to actually eat this stuff?

"I don't see you writing poetry, dad," Jennifer said.

"True, but I'm a dab hand at plagiarism. Wordsworth or Shakespeare were my favorites. You know:

Shall I compare thee to a summer's day?
A box of chocolates, a roll in the hay,
Naw! I'd rather lie here and look out the winda,
In hopes of seeing my lovely Linda."

"Is that your idea of being suave and witty? And who's Linda? I thought it'd be mom you wrote Valentines to."

The humorous twinkle left my eyes. "No, I didn't meet your mom till I went to Edinburgh University. Linda Munro was my high school heart throb."

"Sorry, I didn't mean to spoil your day by mentioning mom."

"It's okay. I need to get used to it."

We were at the checkout stand when my pager went off. Nearby shoppers were immersed in the shocking front-page scandals of the tabloids. "Bloated divorcing rockstar caught in love tryst with two-headed cocaine-crazed alien – exclusive photos on page 9." I glanced at the phone number and decided to take the call outside. Sex-starved aliens were one thing. Hearing one end of a forensic pathologist's phone conversation might be a little too much reality for my fellow shoppers.

The QFC parking lot was surprisingly busy and noisy for a Sunday morning in Seattle. I had to raise my voice to be heard above the traffic pounding past on Forty-fifth.

"McLure here."

"Donald, I'm glad I caught you. Hope you're enjoying this lovely morning."

I pulled my jacket collar up against the damp chill of the drizzle. The sky was gray and threatening rain. The false bonhomie from the dispatcher could mean only one thing – that my quiet Sunday had just been cancelled.

"Have they moved your office to Arizona overnight, Jim? It's pissing wet where I'm standing. And isn't Jepson meant to be on-call?"

"Yes he is, but he's in bed with the 'flu."

"The 'flu? He seemed fine on Friday."

I was suspicious, to say the least. This had been a bad year for the 'flu and the staff at the King County Medical Examiner's department had been hit hard. But I happened to know that Keith Jepson had a

7

hot new romance in his life. He might well have company in bed this morning but her name wasn't "Flu." Still, it wasn't worth venting my spleen on the dispatcher.

"So where's the body?" I said.

"It's floating in a hot tub on Vashon Island."

"And they don't think that it is an accidental death?"

"The sheriff on Vashon is not sure. They've asked for crime scene techs and homicide."

"Who's been assigned to the case? Hold on a minute," I said.

Jennifer was beside me with the grocery bags and had a pleading look in her eyes. She put the bags on the ground and did steering wheel mimes with her hands.

"You promised me the truck today," she whispered.

The dispatcher said, "Katy Pearson's the homicide flavor du jour. You still there?"

"Okay, I'll call her. I'll figure something out."

• • •

The house was silent when Jennifer and I got back, a sure sign that Callum is either asleep or outside of a half-mile radius. The living room was a bombsite of discarded sleeping bags and pillows, pizza boxes and pop cans. Ten-year-olds can truly redefine the word entropy. Jeffrey had been here for a sleepover – a Star Wars marathon where they had watched all the movies in chronological order while eating enough junk food to satisfy Jabba-the-Hutt.

Callum and Jeffrey were dead to the world when Jennifer and I left for the store so I had left them a note and asked my neighbor, Harley, to keep an eye out. In keeping with McLure Family training, Callum had written me a note in reply. The back of a large piece of his art work dangled from the kitchen door frame, suspended by half a roll of Scotch tape:

Hi dad and Jen,
Jeffrey's mom came and took him home (Booo!). I'm round at Harley's to eat waffles and play with Taffy. I'll clean up later,
Luv Callum (smiley face)

Callum has picked up the smiley face trick from Jennifer. It can be added to any request or statement as a talisman to ward off evil responses from grumpy fathers. I asked Jennifer to nip round to see if Callum had outstayed his welcome, while I went to gather my stuff.

Some people keep boxes of lingerie or love letters in their bedroom closet. Me? I keep a murder bag. It's an occupational technique I learned from Professor Alan Campbell at Edinburgh University. Murphy's Law of murders is that they always occur at inconvenient times, today being a case in point. It is a good idea to have everything you need in one handy place. I use an old backpack

9

I once bought at Graeme Tiso's in Edinburgh. I used to tramp the hills with it brimming full of insect repellent, dehydrated packets of chow mein, pipe tobacco and Scotch. Nowadays it contains plastic gloves, test tubes, needles, syringes, paper bags, scissors, cameras, coveralls, hood, goggles and facemasks. I try not to let the contrast linger in my mind. Instead of lying on a grassy mountainside puffing my pipe and reading a book I spend my days wading among maggots in some urine soaked basement trying to examine a putrefying corpse. It is just one of Life's little jokes at my expense.

I changed into my scruffiest walking shoes and rummaged in the bottom of the closet for my rubber boots as a back up. Some of Elspeth's clothes were still hanging there – the ones she had moved beyond but I hadn't. A hint of perfume disturbed my equilibrium – a fresh, flowery innocence from the days before she discovered the heavy musk and patchouli sophistication of her new friends. A hint of how life used to smell and feel before she left me behind.

It was six months since she had walked out on us, although six years was probably a more accurate estimate. By the time Callum had started kindergarten Elspeth's interest in all things domestic had steadily waned. Her interest in all things Donald had evaporated too, if only I had recognized it.

Twelve years ago Elspeth Paterson and I flew in from Scotland to conquer America and take on the world. I was going to transform the field of forensic medicine through the techniques of molecular biology. She was going to put a dent into worldwide famine and injustice. But our paths had quietly diverged. Mine meandered into obscure back alleys of science, sniffing among the garbage in the endless quest for research funding. Elspeth's quest led her to the front porches and back bedrooms of a succession of adventurous and exciting young American men. She found more and more reasons to spend weeks and months abroad. Africa mostly. I'm not sure when I stopped being adventurous and exciting.

The axe finally fell last August. She arrived back with a young man in tow and didn't even try to hide it. She moved out that night and had only returned to collect her favorite things. We had exchanged business-like voice mails in the past six months, and e-mails or notes about coordinating Callum's schedule anytime she was in the country and was back in town. It was all very civil and mature and emotionless. And then yesterday the fat letter had arrived. I knew it was trouble the moment it appeared in the mail with its postmark from Nairobi and the contents to tear away at the gossamer foundation I was building under my new life. Familiar phrases came back to me as I checked the contents of my backpack.

Things aren't working out with Jack. He's too bossy and self-centered. Moody and arrogant. He's got very different values, really, when you get to know him. I miss Andy's sense of humor, feisty arguments with Jennifer, Callum's laughter and your calm stability, Donald...

It's a testimony to my own insecurity how much that last sentence hurt. Andy is our eldest son. He's twenty-four going on forty. Medical school will do that to you. Elspeth's cryptic summary of the family characteristics had needled me more than it should have. I wondered angrily whatever happened to my humorous, feisty, laughing personality. Apparently boring, predictable, solidity was my only remaining virtue.

I'm planning to come back to Seattle soon. Might even stay for a while, get a desk job, use my skills and experience to help organize it for others to go on Third World Field Trips. The travel thing is getting old. I need my own space; time to reflect on where I am headed...

The whole nine yards of clichés.

I want to be living closer to Callum, too. Maybe I could rent a place nearby, if I can afford it... or even move back in unless you've already replaced me...

This was followed by double exclamation points and a smiley face. Everyone is using the magic talisman to get their way with Donald these days, it seems. I can hardly blame her. It works every time.

I buried my face in the hem of an old summer frock and inhaled hungrily. I was back on the slopes of Beinn Dubh, twenty-five years younger, showing off the beauty of the Western Isles to a laughing, playful Elspeth. I was watching her lift that dress over her lithe sweaty body, feeling her push me back into the heather with urgent breaths. She was backlit by the summer sun, her tousled head framed by scudding clouds and a sky the color of bluebells dancing in the breeze. She sprained her ankle on the way down the hill that day, as I recall, and had to be carried. I don't remember complaining. She felt as light as my heart. I would have carried the ambulance up the mountainside to meet her, if she'd asked me.

"You about ready, dad? You okay?"

Jennifer was framed in the bedroom door, playing nervously with her hair. Her youthful posture and mannerisms were so like her mother's. The very cadence of her voice rubbed salt in my memories.

"I'm fine. How's Callum doing?"

"He's having a blast. They're trying to catch Taffy to clip his nails. That dog can crawl into the tiniest of places. It's a hoot."

"And it's okay for him to stay for dinner? I'm not sure when I'll get back."

"It's fine, dad. I'll be back by six anyway. Is that a letter from mom?"

I grabbed the letter off the pillow and stuffed it in my jacket pocket.

"I've barely looked at it," I lied. "I'll maybe have a chance to read it on the ferry."

Maybe. Reading it again would be the easy part. Making sense of it was going to take some doing.

II

A Grand View Ruined

From the front of the car deck I watched the Klahowya carve a dirty arc of foam through the water towards the north end Vashon dock. I could hardly see the mainland through the drizzle. Endless soggy trees lined the shore as far as the eye could see. A few drab boats rusted quietly on their moorings and clanked in complaint as the wake from the ferry disturbed them. Diesel and seaweed fumes tugged at my consciousness with unwanted childhood memories. A thin slick of oil with garbage floating on it got churned as the engines reversed to slow our progress. Pigeons shivered on the cables high above us, dropping shit on the ferry workers as they lowered the ramp. A picture postcard day in Puget Sound it was not.

I had only managed to get through half of Elspeth's letter before crumpling it violently and tossing it into the trash. In the six months since she breezed out of my life with young, hip, sinewy Jack dangling on her arm like a charm bracelet, I had been through the usual stages of ego-plummeting self-flagellation. How could I compete with Jack Bolton of the dry wit, rugged physique and wild unpredictable spirit? I obviously hadn't tried hard enough to stay fresh and interesting. I had become a clumsy unimaginative and insensitive lover, a dull predictable housemate. I was pathetic and inadequate. I was a diet of porridge and cold toast when Elspeth wanted smoked salmon soufflé washed down with champagne.

I circled the drain for three weeks after she left, sinking slowly under the weight of my flabby gut and mountainous self-pity. I can't remember what event actually jerked me out of my funk but something finally changed my perspective. Maybe champagne and soufflé was what Elspeth Paterson needed in her life but Callum, Jennifer and Andy needed porridge and toast-wholesome, reliable and sustaining. A catatonic drunken lush for a father wasn't going to be much help to them. I threw out the pizza boxes, cut out the alcohol and started pushing weights again and pounding the streets every day, no matter what the Seattle winter threw in my face. The colder and dirtier the better. My muscles ached, my lungs burned and my joints complained but it felt great to be doing something to jump-start my dying ego. Besides, it took my mind off the fact that I hadn't had sex in almost a year and hadn't connected emotionally with anyone except my kids for longer than that.

With the first reading of the fat letter my insecurity and longing had resurfaced but this morning I had more sense. For Elspeth the crown of her soufflé had collapsed and the champagne was flat. This particular vintage-chateau de Jacques, Extra Brut-was no longer doing it for her. She wanted to come back for a few weeks of porridge and toast before sniffing around for another exotic menu item. Well no thanks. Callum and Jennifer needed boring reliable old dad. And they didn't need him to get his fragile equilibrium disturbed again.

I needed to maintain my new positive go-getter approach to life for their sakes as well as my own.

A swarm of foot passengers swept past me up the ramp demonstrating the endless variety of organizational structure that passes for "Family" these days. Unattended kids with downcast eyes were met by excessively cheerful adults, in various same-sex or opposite-sex groupings. For some this would be Sunday visitation for the non-custodial parent. For those who portrayed the traditional nuclear family, I saw tight-lipped couples scrutinize their squabbling offspring before having them inspected by the in-laws for Sunday brunch. One bawling tantrum ahead of me watched her heart-shaped balloon float away while bickering seagulls deftly avoided it as they wheeled and dove to dislodge a fish head that another was carrying. The infuriated child parked her pink-flowered butt in a muddy puddle to the angry shrieks of her mother. I was glad that stage was behind me.

I wasn't sure I would recognize Katy Pearson, although her name was familiar enough to me. The word around the department was that she was newly promoted to homicide detective. Enthusiastic and confident. Thorough but not pushy. Intense but thoughtful. And really good-looking. That part was usually added in there somewhere. She had attended a recent autopsy I had done and asked relevant, perceptive questions. Bumfled up under a mask, hood and gown her physical appearance was a blur. All I could remember was that she was fairly tall, had intelligent blue eyes and wore very little makeup.

The woman standing beside the King County Jeep Cherokee had

to be her. I'm not good at guessing women's ages; mid to late thirties, I'd guess. She looked slim, fit, around five foot eight and a hundred and thirty pounds. Her short brown hair was cut in a fuss-free, no-nonsense style. Dark olive slacks hugged supple attractive legs. The sturdy brown ankle boots were elegant as well as practical. A rust-colored fleece under maroon anorak completed the northwest earth tone look. A bright yellow silk scarf acted as a counterpoint. It was wrapped loosely round her neck with one end flung over her shoulder like an airforce pilot, giving her a hint of reckless daring beneath the calm, controlled exterior. She looked anything but enthusiastic and confident, though. I could tell she was registering details about me and I hoped the impression was favorable.

I tried to walk purposefully and fast but without the athletic swagger that some women interpret as arrogance. On the other hand I didn't want to walk like a guy who hadn't been laid in over a year. Actually I'm not sure exactly sure how to cover that up. I think women can just tell. I sucked in my gut, and slung the backpack over my shoulder. At least my leather jacket looked good, neither biker-scruffy nor Nordstrom-slick. My hair was washed, the mustache neatly trimmed. According to my neighbor I have a nice smile, and okay teeth for a Brit. And my handshake is warm and firm, I'm told, not what you'd expect from a pathologist. Oh what the hell, I wasn't going out on a date.

"Officer Pearson? Thanks for picking me up. My daughter said to tell you a big thanks from her, too."

"No problem, and just call me Katy, by the way. Do you go by Doctor or Professor?"

"Donald is fine."

"Is this all your stuff?" Her delivery was wooden and distracted. She looked preoccupied and unhappy. I decided to inject a little energy and good humor into the day, test out my charisma and scrape the rust off my chat-up skills.

"Yes, everything I need is in the backpack. It reminds me that I used to have the kind of life where I filled a pack with books by Jean-Paul Sartre and cans of McEwans Export beer and headed for the hills. I've never fancied the leather briefcase look. A bit too slick and corporate for my taste."

I opened the passenger door to find a shiny new leather briefcase lying on the passenger seat. Katy Pearson lifted it over onto the back seat.

"Let me get this offensive, slick, corporate item out of your way, then, shall I?"

"I'm sorry, I didn't mean to imply..." I began.

She shrugged, did a quick U-turn on the dock and roared off up the hill, leaving me to wriggle awkwardly at her side. Great job Donald. Your sensitivity, witty repartit and smooth-talking chat-up lines are a wonder to behold. Here's someone you're going to have to work closely with for days or weeks and you've managed to offend her within five minutes.

"Been to Vashon before?" Katy asked, going through the motions of small talk.

"Only once. I've a friend with a waterfront place at the north end. I was at a party there once. It was dark, though. I didn't see much. Look, is something bothering you, Katy. I'm sorry if I offended you back there at the dock."

She looked me over, establishing her advantage with the ghost of a smile. "It takes more than that to offend me. It's this death that bothers me. The local sheriff bothers me. He has already tainted the crime scene. I hope he hasn't screwed anything else up since I left."

"What happened?"

"Apparently the kids who found the body called nine-one-one and didn't make it clear that the victim was long dead. Dispatch sent an Aid Unit as well as the nearest uniformed officer. The paramedics rushed onto the deck and by the time they realized the kid was dead they had smeared their fingerprints everywhere and kicked a marijuana joint down a crack in the deck. Sheriff Pitman went blundering underneath to retrieve it. He didn't wear gloves. He didn't sketch exactly where he found it. He didn't use his brain at all, in fact, and now he's trying to make up for it by acting like my deferential great-uncle."

"You think it's murder?" I said.

"It will help a lot when you give us the cause of death. She was found lying in a hot tub with the cover latched down on top of her.

Looks like murder to me but Gary Pitman thinks maybe a bunch of teenagers were partying there, doing drugs and using the tub. He thinks maybe one of them passed out and drowned. The others panicked, put the cover back on and split."

"Without calling nine-one-one?"

"Doesn't sound likely to me, either," she said.

We cut off the main highway and wiggled through a somber forest of hemlock and Douglas fir, wet and dank, untouched by the sun. A few tendrils of mist reached across the narrow ribbon of asphalt ahead of us. On a rare straight stretch of road we passed a row of country mailboxes. They were mounted on posts or suspended from branches, some painted all cutesie-dootsie to look like cows, salmon or Orcas, complete with dorsal fins. Several of the boxes had major dents in them and one lay uprooted on the verge with its lid hanging off.

Katy said, "Like the rural vandalism? Drive-by baseball bats. They like straight stretches of road where they can hit a bunch one after the other and keep driving before anyone can catch them. You got kids?"

"Yeah, but none that would do that. At least I hope not."

We turned through a wrought iron gate with the name "Grandview" scripted in black. The driveway was long and sloped down towards the water through large established fruit trees and camellias. The rear entrance to the house was unprepossessing but the multi-peaked roof protruding well out into the air suggested that a substantial house was built into the bluff. The popping-eyes of a totem pole glared at me above the rhododendrons and gave me a jolt. Could this be Linda's house? Surely not every waterfront house on Vashon boasted one of those?

Several cars were parked under the carport. A Medic One ambulance, a green and white cruiser from the King County Sheriff's Department, an unmarked station wagon and two other sedans. I nodded at them.

"Wow, who do all these belong to?" I said. It was the wrong thing to say.

"Don't you start. Pitman's already giving me a hard time, hinting that I'm overreacting. I called out the Crime Scene Response Team from Delridge Way. I thought you'd approve of that. Using the Total Station Crew to mark out the scene is perfectly reasonable, especially if it is a murder. I know we don't know that yet but by the time we do know it would be too late to use TSC. It was my call and I'll justify it to anyone."

"That's fine, I only asked."

"And even if your techs have some experience lifting latent prints, with an outdoor crime scene on a wooden deck with rain threatening any minute, I thought bringing in experts from the Finger Print Lab in Olympia would be a smart move. The reason there are so many cars here already is because you were the last person to show up."

Her cheeks flushed to match the color of her anorak but only briefly. The challenging look in her eyes was accompanied by logical, well organized, carefully delivered responses. If this investigation was going to be a marathon I needed to pick up my pace. I was still doing my warm-up stretches while this formidable woman was in full stride.

An older uniformed officer approached us as we got out of the car. Katy sucked in her breath through tight lips. "Here, let me introduce you to Pitman, the sheriff. He lives on Vashon and knows one of the families involved."

Gary Pitman had the haunted look of cancer about him. He had waxy gray skin like cold oatmeal, sunken eyes and the posture of someone who had given up the fight. He looked wooden, a stick figure inside the perfectly creased brown uniform shirt. He was probably close to retirement age. I wondered if he realized he might not make it. He shook my hand obsequiously and unleashed a flood of flattery about hearing me lecture once.

"It's a terrible business, Professor McLure, just terrible. When will young people learn the dangers of drugs? Just a girl, she is. I've probably addressed her class at school in the DARE program in recent years, for all the good that has done. A tragic accident."

"We don't know it was an accident, Gary." Katy Pearson didn't hide her exasperation. "We haven't even determined the cause of death. Let's give Donald a chance to do his job."

I asked, "Do we know the identity of the victim? Is she someone who lives here?"

Pitman pulled out his notebook, anxious to make a professional contribution. "The deceased is an eighteen-year-old high school student by the name of Myra Garfield. She was seen at school on Friday afternoon, acting normal in every respect. Her parents are on their way back from Reno/Lake Tahoe, where they were skiing. Myra was supposed to join them yesterday but didn't show up."

"Have they been notified of the death and the circumstances?" I asked.

"We contacted the local police there and had someone talk to them in person. They know she's dead but not the details."

I said, "The kids who found the body – do they live here? What's their connection to the owners?"

"They're both local kids. Beyond high school, though. The young man, Aaron Klein, says he works here as a gardener and odd job guy. I still have to confirm that with the owners. He hangs out with the druggie music crowd. My guess is that they use this place for partying. I have warned some of the off-island homeowners that it is a bad idea to leave a hot tub plugged in and turned on when they are not in residence. I'd check the victim for signs of sexual activity and drugs, if I were you, Professor McLure. Well, I'm sure you'd do that as a routine in a case like this."

Katy pulled me away. "Let me show you where the body is. We

can go through the house and onto the deck through the French windows."

She led the way through a porch and into the kitchen. Water skis, kayak paddles, croquet mallets, sandals, life jackets, coolers and other expensive beach toys lay around in a careless jumble. A wet suit buckled limply in the corner looking vaguely obscene, like a decapitated pornographic blow-up doll. The place smelled musty and damp. My feet slipped and crunched on sunscreen, potato chips and sand - the discarded remains of last year's summer.

The kitchen windowsill was thick with dust and dead bugs. Faded postcards with curled edges leaned against a vase of withered flowers. Some shells, bleached-white sand dollars and a few rusty nails lay undisturbed. In the sink a plastic container overflowed with the slimy pellets of moisture retardant, which had failed its attempt to thwart the dampness of a Northwest winter. To prevent the pipes from freezing green ethylene glycol stains were visible in the sink drains giving a faintly medicinal smell. Between the fridge and the breakfast bar I saw a glue trap which held several dead spider carcasses but no rodents.

My discomfort was growing. I knew exactly what I would see in the main living room before I walked through. There would be elegant cane and basket weave chairs and a couch on a Persian rug over hardwood floors, a solid walnut coffee table, massive stone fireplace to the right and a solid wall of glass giving unobstructed views to the west. I stepped through and congratulated my memory like the echo of an old Boy Scout Kim's game. Only the painting above the fireplace was new.

"The deck's over this way," Katy said.

"I know. I've been here before, Katy. About three years ago. I wasn't certain until I came into this room. That painting there is a recent addition but I have sat in that very chair drinking Talisker beside a fire roaring in that grate. If I'm not mistaken I have even been in the hot tub we're about to inspect."

"You know Sebastian Covington?"

"No, but his wife Linda is a ghost from my past."

Katy Pearson gave me another look that was uncomfortably cool and calculating.

I pulled on a pair of latex gloves and walked through the French windows without touching the doorknobs, which were covered with dark gray fingerprint powder. Half a dozen people picked their way carefully around the deck engrossed in their own specific professional tasks. I didn't recognize the nerdy guys using the TSC equipment but it is always impressive to watch. Gone are the days when forensic scientists or homicide detectives sketch out the crime scene on the back of an envelope. For most serious crimes in well-funded metropolitan areas, crime scenes are drawn and catalogued using the Total Station Crew. Based on the technology of the global positioning system a central unit is placed in a fixed location at the scene. The techs then use laser pens to mark the position of other objects at the scene in exact relation to the central unit. The precise location and orientation of cigarette butts, bloody knives, half-eaten sandwiches or dead bodies is recorded electronically while a computer builds up a complete picture of where everything is in relation to everything else. When the job is done the computer can print out a perfect map of the scene in laser quality print. It can then be enlarged, rotated, viewed from every angle to be displayed later in court. Every piece of evidence is carefully labeled and numbered, its location marked on the printout. Most juries are impressed, as well they should be.

The two finger print folk from Olympia were new to me, also, but Rusty Bellagio, one of the techs from our lab, looked up briefly and waved at me before returning to the task of dusting the hot tub cover for more latents. The other person from the Crime Scene Response Team was a woman I vaguely recognized - a large cheerful Hispanic woman whose laughter filled the corridors of my workplace. Crime scene techs usually work in pairs, both signing and witnessing any pieces of evidence. These two made an odd pairing but seemed to enjoy working together.

The deck had been built off the south wall of the house to catch all the sun. It was roughly octagonal in shape and about twenty feet across, solid cedar construction with a clear stain to preserve the golden warmth of the wood without hiding the grain and knots that gave the wood its character. Built-in bench seats lined the edge on three sides towards the back, surrounded by massive rhododendrons. The side opposite the house contained wide stairs stepping down to the grass. The other three sides to the front of the house faced west. The hot tub was raised above the deck so that bathers could have an unobstructed view of the Olympic Mountains above the railing. In one corner of the deck, next to the stairs a massive totem pole towered up. Embarrassing memories filled my head. I remember receiving glowering disapproval from the totem characters for that ill-advised dip I'd taken into the forbidden pool, three years ago.

My eye was drawn inevitably to the young female body lying face down in the tub, steam rising from her exposed rear end. It is hard to remain objective when you know that the dead body you are examining is lying in your friend's back yard, but I tried to push it from my mind. As a professional routine I always try to ignore the details of the victim for a few minutes to take in the broader circumstances of the crime scene. I walked carefully across the deck towards the stairs that led down to the lawn. A plastic identification placard had been placed over a small pile of ash on the deck.

"That's where the paramedics kicked the marijuana joint through the crack in the deck," Katy said.

On the lawn beside the steps some deep tire marks had chewed up the wet grass. The female crime scene technician, was busy mixing up Dental Stone beside them. Her name came to me. Gina Fernandez. She was in her mid-fifties with a chain-smoking husband and ten kids, as I recall. What right had she to be so cheerful and good humored all the time? She was humming a tune to herself as she worked. I knew the routine. She had already taken measurements and photographed the tire tracks. Now she would take plaster casts of the treads.

"Could these be from the Medic One van, Gina?" I asked.

She spilled some plaster onto the grass. "Doctor McLure you

startled me. Now I making a mess. No, the medics they parked up by the driveway. It's possible the tire tracks are from the perp's vehicle, I think."

The hot tub cover lay discarded on the deck beside the totem pole. The duo from Olympia methodically dusted the plastic snaps and vinyl surfaces for more fingerprints.

I approached the hot tub and noted the temperature. One hundred and four degrees Fahrenheit. Estimating the time of death from the core body temperature would be a lost cause. It would have equilibrated to a hundred and four by now, maybe even a little higher if decomposition had got going.

Death is never a cheerful sight but is particularly depressing when the victim looks as young and unblemished as this one did. Her firm young rump protruded from the water with arms and legs hanging below the surface. I reached for my notebook to catalog some of the details. Rusty or Gina had probably taken photographs already and the Total Station Crew would produce three-dimensional wizardry with their computer drawings but I had brought my own camera anyway. The techs don't always realize which details are the most significant.

The distribution of skin color was telling. A dark pink line had formed at the water surface due to hypostasis; the redistribution of blood in the body after death due to gravity. There was a large blanched white area on her buttocks, which looked for all the world like the coastal outline of Australia. This would be where the lid of the hot tub had pressed against the flesh and pushed away all the blood. There were no visible signs of violence or injury on the back surface of the body. Her face was obscured by long hair, in multicolor shades of purple and blue. It swayed back and forth, looking for all the world like an exotic sea anemone from the Great Barrier Reef.

Pitman helped me get the gurney out of the CSRT van. I spread out a white cotton sheet on top of it, staying well away from the identification tags on the ground and other important areas of the crime scene, and called Rusty over to help me lift the body out.

"It's so weird, Donald. She's warm and not even stiff. She doesn't seem dead at all."

"On her back please Rusty."

I hoped my matter of fact tone would help soften the fear and horror in his eyes. In his mid-twenties, Rusty was at his happiest finding fingerprints in obscure locations to help nail "bad guys." He had a hard time looking at victims, innocent or otherwise.

He was right, though. It was disconcerting to handle a body that was warm and supple. Rigor mortis was long past. Her face and neck were a dark crimson. Of course this was because they had been hanging deepest in the water and so gravity would have pulled more blood there, but it was easy to imagine that she was just angry and indignant at being stared at while she was naked and defenseless. Her lips pouted with scorn. The opaque lifeless eyes seemed to look right through me the way the eyes of all teenagers are oblivious to anyone over the age of twenty-five.

Rusty shivered. "Oh God, Donald, I think the skin's coming away from her heel. You know how your mom blanches peaches in hot water so the skin will slip off. That's what it feels like. God, that's awful."

I pushed him away and examined her left heel. Skin slippage is a common occurrence if a body has been submerged for several days. Putrefaction in the subcutaneous tissue does break the bonds to the tougher epidermal layer causing the thick keratin to peel away. But Myra Garfield had been seen alive less than forty-eight hours ago. Even in hot water it would be unusual to see skin slippage so soon.

There was an area of raw flesh the size of a quarter over the left Achilles tendon with some central bleeding and a few ragged tatters of skin attacked to the edge. A similar but smaller lesion was present on the right heel. The surrounding area was red and inflamed, suggesting that this was an antemortem injury; one that had occurred before death.

I said, "It's just a couple of blisters, Rusty. I think the lassie was wearing new shoes in the day or so before she died."

The skin on her hands and feet was crinkled in the fashion described in pathology textbooks as having the classic "washerwoman's" appearance. I don't know where pathologists get their penchant for using homely comparisons to describe disgustingly serious conditions. It must come from spending hours and years in dark rooms on your own squinting down microscopes at sections of cancerous tissue and diseased organs. You lose all sense of reality and begin seeing comforting similarities between what you are looking at and objects in the more mundane world. So the unraveling of the lining of blood vessels due to catastrophic high blood pressure gives it the classic "onion skin" appearance. And when blood dams back into the liver so that it is ready to explode, the appearance is said to resemble a freshly cut nutmeg. It is all a bit sick.

There were no signs of serious violence or injury on the front of her body, no stab wounds, gunshots, no bruising from ligatures or strangulation. But the soft curve of her breasts and stomach were blemished with some odd linear abrasions. They were scrape marks, a whole series of them in two parallel sets of six or eight. Each scrape was pencil thin and ten to twelve inches in length. Five or six scrapes close together like a bar code. There was a four-inch gap and then another set of six.

I pulled out my reading glasses and peered closely. There's a crack in the right lens where Callum stood on them. Sherlock Holmes may have used a magnifying glass but I find that squinting through the left lens of my reading glasses from two inches away gets the job done, even if it doesn't look quite so suave and impressive. There were a few tiny pink fibers embedded in one of the scrapes and a tiny gray sliver of metal and grit in another. I drew a sketch and took several photographs using my macro lens. I parted her legs gently and inspected her external genitalia and anus. Apart from signs that she shaved and groomed her pubic hair there were no signs of trauma.

"Rusty, when we're done here let's verify the temperature of the water in the tub, then turn the power off and drain the water out through a very fine filter. And bring the filters from the tub itself back to the lab, too. It looks like her body was dragged or scraped over something. There are some fibers and debris stuck in the wound."

"Did that happen before or after she died?" Katy Pearson was looking over my shoulder.

"I'm not certain but I think before. The skin around the scrapes is raised and red suggesting that there was time for her body to begin to mount an inflammatory response."

"Any guess to the cause of death?"

I placed a hand on Myra Garfield's perfect stomach and pressed firmly. A grayish mess of foam extruded from her mouth like ghoulish toothpaste from a tube. Rusty shrank back but Katy Pearson leaned closer to inspect. I caught a faint whiff of perfume, light, flowery and understated.

I said, "It's not an infallible test but I'd say she drowned. I'll have a better idea when I open up her chest."

"Has she been raped?"

"There were no signs of blood or trauma around the perineum. No semen, dirt or blood on the labia or the outer part of the vagina but the hot tub jets might have washed that away. We'll check the hot tub filters and do a more extensive examination back at The Dell."

Gina Fernandez yelled from behind the deck. "Officer Pearson, there's a pile of clothes over here in the bushes. Girl's clothes. Looks like maybe they fell off the back of the deck."

"If there are shoes among them I'd like a look," I said.

There wasn't much more to be gained from a visual inspection of Myra Garfield's body. I wrapped her hands and feet in clean paper bags and took some blood samples from the femoral blood vessels in her groin. I don't always do this but I knew the body would be taken back to the mortuary long before me. I wouldn't get to the autopsy until tomorrow. This way the toxicology lab could do an initial screen.

Rusty and I had the body bagged up for transport back to the morgue by the time Katy came back holding the pile of clothes. Clean pressed pedal-pusher denims, pale green mohair sweater, white cotton brassiere, underpants and socks. They were neatly folded and pressed. The shoes were white tennis shoes without the laces, well kept but certainly not brand new. There was no sign of blood in the heel area. The most notable item of clothing was a battered buckskin jacket with a fringe across the back and down both sleeves. The skull and lightning bolt logo of the Grateful Dead was embossed onto the back of the suede.

"The clothes certainly could belong to the girl," Gina said. "We'll bag them all separately and you can show them to her parents when they get back from Lake Tahoe."

"I should ask the woman who lives here if they're hers, first," Katy said.

There was a short humorless laugh behind me. "There not mine. It's been a few years since I would have looked good in that outfit."

I turned to see Linda Munro staring out through the French windows looking sad and lost and needy. She was the last thing I needed to see, right then.

III

Old Wounds And Open Sores

I had never been in a long term or intimate relationship with Linda Munro but she had been in the periphery of my life for thirty years. I had observed her lustily across the science lab in Ayr high school with her short skirt and throaty laugh. We had sat up all night, cross-legged on the floor of incense-filled college rooms in Edinburgh, and had lain on our backs, looking up at the stars from Salisbury Crags discussing Dylan Thomas or Erich Fromm. Despite the mutual attraction, it seemed we were always with other partners and so unavailable to each other. We acknowledged this with the stoical fatality that comes so easily to the Celts. As a race the Scots are much more comfortable with poignant self-denial and tragic failure. It is easy success and unabashed pleasure that makes us uncomfortable. I always held back. I was already committed to someone else. Elspeth, for the most part. But that might have been an easy excuse. It might have been that I always recognized some subtle signs and cues in Linda Munro's behavior that told me I wouldn't like what I found deep inside. On the day I found a dead body in her hot tub I recognized them still.

We sat on opposite sides of the fireplace. At Katy's suggestion I had put on a fire while she and Pitman made some phone calls from their cars. Linda cradled a cup of tea and struggled to find the most appropriate persona to display in this situation. For some people stark tragedy peels away their protective layers of bullshit and allows the true self to be laid bare. Others just hunker down and curl up like a hedgehog, daring anyone to get too close. I waited to see whether Linda would fall into platitudes about shock, horror and revulsion at the death of a stranger in her backyard or whether she would feel compelled to connect with me over our shared past. My mind drifted in the silence, mulling over inconsequential details of the room. The antique pendulum clock on the wall stood motionless. Raindrops turned to rivers on the window branching and dividing chaotically under the pull of gravity. A yellow-jacket interrupted the silence with its faint buzzing, so odd to hear this early in the year. Maybe there was a nest in the house that had got awakened when they turned the heating on.

"I guess I should be grateful to those kids," Linda said.

"Why's that?"

"Because if they hadn't found the body, chances are I would have found it when I went to check the spa and add the chemicals."

"What chemicals?" I said.

"You obviously don't deal with the joys of spa maintenance, Donald. You have to check the hardness and acidity of the water and adjust it from time to time. We buy our spa chemicals in bulk at Costco. It's just as good as the name brand stuff. I was putting the stuff in the car this morning when the phone rang. It was bad enough to get a call from the police saying what had happened. It would have been far worse to see the body."

That's another response that some people have to tragedy. They focus on some trivial or irrelevant detail and go on about it in tedious detail.

Linda Munro's own body still hovered on the cusp between voluptuous and overweight. She had an expensively tousled mop of tinted hair giving herself a look that was supposed to be wild, carefree and spontaneous but was anything but. The black Cashmere sweater and white silk pants were tight fitting and pricey. She wore just enough makeup to allow her Health Spa tan to shine through and to accentuate her perfect heart-shaped lip pout.

When I looked past her slumping shoulders I could see sheets of rain moving across the water and battering against the plate glass window. I felt lucky to have dealt with the crime scene and the body before rain washed away crucial evidence.

"Were you planning to come over this weekend, anyway?" I said. "I'm surprised the hot tub was on. Do you leave it on all the time?"

"No, as I was telling Detective Pearson, we usually have our gardener turn it on a few days before we're going to come out."

"Was that the young man who found the body?"

"Yes, Aaron Klein. Sheriff Pitman seems to think it is stupid to have that arrangement, that it is just inviting schoolchildren to use the place but I don't care. I actually get a kick out of imagining some high school students getting high, letting things go, being spontaneous, screwing each other in the tub. It's not something Sebastian would ever be interested in doing. At least not with me."

She stared bravely off into the logs. Perhaps it was my imagination but I thought she changed position in her chair to make sure she was striking the best pose of noble tragedy, while presenting me with her cutest profile.

"Have things not improved with Sebastian?" I said.

"Status quo, really. He's busy a lot, of course. Busy, busy busy. There are always so many critical timelines and great opportunities, aren't there? Idle hands would make Sebastian a dull boy, wouldn't they? No, that's not right. It's supposed to be all work and no play that makes for dull boys, isn't it? I forget what idle hands is supposed to do."

I didn't interrupt. She was obviously finding it therapeutic to keep prattling on.

She gave a brave theatrical laugh. "Oh, we have fun sometimes, I suppose. We travel to exotic places. I have lots of nice things. There's not a lot of passion, Donald, but you can't always expect that, can you? You can just hope for it now and again." She gave me a direct, challenging look. I returned it with enough controlled neutrality to provoke a hollow laugh. "I'm sorry, Donald. Did I offend your Presbyterian morality and integrity when I came on to you in the tub that night? I guess I miscalculated your availability. Or maybe I just underestimated my own need. Let's just blame it on alcohol, shall we? That's the lame excuse that people usually give. So how are you and Elspeth doing?"

Katy Pearson and Gary Pitman appeared outside the window, dressed in hooded rain jackets with their backs towards us. Pitman was pointing down at the beach explaining details about something. Whatever it was it would be more palatable than the torture I was going through in here. Discussing Elspeth was the last thing I was inclined to do with Linda Munro right then.

"Have you given your statement to the police already?" I said.

"Yes, of course, let's not talk about personal stuff, Donald. Heaven forbid that we face up to the fact that we made some personal mistakes. Sorry, did I say "we?" I meant that I, me, personally am prepared to admit that I made some bad personal choices."

"Linda…"

Her hands quivered as she struggled to keep the tremble from her voice. "Sorry, I'm rambling onto irrelevancies. Yes, I've given my statement to the police. No, I didn't know Myra Garfield or her parents. The first time I ever heard their name was today. I have no reason to think that Sebastian knew them either, although the police will need to talk to him separately. Actually that's not true. Now that I think about it one of the regional sales guys might be called Garfield. I don't think he lives on Vashon or has kids though. Sebastian would know. He and I were planning to come out together this afternoon to air the place out. We were going to have our annual staff party here next weekend but I don't suppose we'll do that now."

I stayed silent. She flicked at some imaginary dandruff or dust that might have fallen onto her Cashmere-covered breast, then looked up quickly to see if I was staring.

"I suppose you think I'm shallow and selfish, Donald, thinking of how inconvenient it is to find a dead girl on my deck when I should be thinking of how awful it must be for the girl or her family. Do you think I'm cold and heartless, always thinking of myself? Not passionate and caring like Elspeth. Maybe if I had wanted to save the world you would have been more interested in me."

When psychiatrists let their patients ramble on they call it "therapeutic listening." I'm not sure what it's called when dour uncommunicative Scotsmen do it. Whatever it is called I'm good at it. There was no way I was going to bite on any of the barbed hooks she was casting before me. I'd learned my lesson the last time I was here.

• • •

The view from the deck was perfect that night. The warm summer sun was turning red as it dipped to kiss the Olympic peaks.

Even the mosquitoes didn't seem too bad for August, although three large glasses of Scotch whisky is a pretty effective anesthetic. I called in through the open French windows.

"When do you think Sebastian and the other couple will show up?" I said.

Linda called from the kitchen. "Anytime now, I should think. Why don't you go ahead and try out the tub?"

"Och, I don't think so Linda. I didn't bring any shorts or swimming trunks."

Actually the original invitation made no mention of hot tubbing. It was to come for an informal barbecue with her husband and one other couple they knew. The Lagerbergs were billed as a vivacious pair of academics who were planning a sabbatical in Scotland and wanted to pick my brains about who to contact and where to stay in Edinburgh. Elspeth was gone on a trip. Callum was off at summer camp. Reminiscing about Scotland with some well-educated couple sounded pleasant enough. Getting into a hot tub with perfect strangers was another thing entirely.

Linda appeared in the doorway to mock me. She was wearing a gaudy Hawaiian print frock and sounded slightly drunk.

"Donald, you're on the West Coast of America, now, not the West Coast of Scotland. Nobody cares if you're naked in the tub. Suits are totally optional. But if you'd rather cover up your crotch I can get you a pair of Sebastian's shorts. On you go, Donald, just

41

get in. I'll toss you the shorts with my eyes closed if you want to preserve your modesty."

Ten minutes later, against my better judgment I had stripped and got into the tub. I was looking up at the glowering totems when Linda reappeared. She was wearing a bathrobe now, her face flushed with mischief.

"I couldn't find any of Sebastian's shorts or trunks. That was him on the phone, by the way, saying that the Lagerbergs had to cancel and Sebastian's going to stay late at the office. Sorry, it's just you and me, I'm afraid. I thought this might make you feel more comfortable."

She threw off her bathrobe and let the rosy glow of the sunset play over her naked breasts, and thighs. In her hands she held two empty whisky tumblers and the rest of the bottle of Talisker.

I got out of that tub faster than the proverbial scalded cat, waving away her entreaties as I scrambled into my pants and shirt, dripping wet. I made little effort to conceal my anger and embarrassment at being duped and caught the first available ferry back to Seattle.

It had become known as "The Hot Tub Incident" whenever it was brought up in arguments with Elspeth after that. She surprised me by saying she wished I had slept with Linda Munro that night. It would have done me good, she said. At the time I couldn't understand what she meant. Now I think she really meant that it would have done her some good. It would have made Elspeth feel less guilty about her own infidelity.

• • •

"Do they think it was an accident then?" Linda's question brought me back to the surface. "Alcohol and drugs, I suppose. That's what Sheriff Pitman was saying to the paramedics when I arrived."

"It's too early to say. I'll have a better idea once I do the post mortem and get the lab results."

"Always so careful and sensible, aren't you, Donald? You don't overreact or overinterpret. You just keep weighing the evidence for and against, then make the most prudent decision. I guess I could just never pile enough positive attributes on your scales."

I let that one pass.

"How long before we can get the place back to ourselves and can clean up?" she asked.

"It will depend on what we find and how quickly they can make an arrest. The area surrounding the deck will be kept off limits as a crime scene for a few days at least, I would think."

"I do care about the girl and her family, Donald. I can hardly imagine the grief her parents will feel. Makes me glad that Sebastian and I decided not to have children." I barely flinched an eyebrow but she picked up on it. "Did you think that our childlessness was not an active decision, then? That we couldn't have any? That I was infertile? No, it's just that I didn't want to turn into a dumpy little housewife like my mother. And I was afraid of becoming unattractive to Sebastian and losing him. I wanted to travel the world with Sebastian and do adventurous things with no encumbrances. We used to talk vaguely of having kids someday but we haven't mentioned it for years."

"Are you still teaching psychology at the University of Washington?" I said.

"Yes, two days a week. We don't need the money but I enjoy the energy and altruism of the students. And their company. It's not just passion and sex I keep looking for, Donald. It's companionship and support. You know mother's in a nursing home now?"

"Your mom? I thought she had moved out here. Didn't you buy her a house here on Vashon?"

"Yes, she still has the little bungalow over on the Burton peninsula but she hasn't lived there for over a year. She's dementing fast. I suppose it's Alzheimer's disease. That's what they seem to call all dementia these days. She was getting pretty forgetful in Prestwick when we last visited and it got worse rather than better when she came out here. I should have realized, I suppose, that with all the cues of her familiar environment taken away she'd become even more disoriented. She began leaving the stove on, burning things, losing her keys, leaving doors wide open, wandering around in her underwear trying to hitch a ride to the airport. All sorts of things that seem amusing if they weren't so tragic."

"Is she doing better in the nursing home?" I asked.

"They're nice enough to her. At least most of the staff are white. Some of these places in Seattle are staffed by Asians and Mexicans who barely speak English. It must make the old folk even more confused."

"Is the nursing home not in Seattle, then?"

"No, it's here on Vashon. It's that new place down in Burton. You hear it advertised all the time on KIRO. Goldentide it's called. Caters specifically for psychogeriatric cases like mother. It's expensive but Sebastian was happy to pay. Frankly, I think he was pleased to get her as far away from Seattle as he could. He and mother never got along, even when she was sane. Do you know he won't even come and visit her now, Donald. He leaves it all to me. It's just awful. There are some days she doesn't even recognize me." She wiped away a few tears and looked over at me with longing. "She still talks about you, you know, Donald. Mother, I mean. She always said I married the wrong person. God, I wish I'd managed to bed you when I had my chance back in Edinburgh. Before Elspeth Paterson spirited you away."

Katy Pearson coughed politely from the doorway. "Can we go now, Dr. McLure?"

Linda covered her face with her hands, leaving me to face the brunt of Katy Pearson's inscrutable gaze.

IV

Snake Oil Devotee

Neither Katy nor I spoke as we drove away from Grandview and headed south on Vashon highway. It was a relief to get out into the open air and away from the oppressive atmosphere of the house. I have to admit that at this stage of the investigation my depression was due more to the juxtaposition of The Fat Letter and meeting Linda Munro again. Yes, it was disheartening to see a dead girl but that's hardly unusual in my line of work. Myra Garfield's death was sad. She was younger than Jennifer and should have had her whole life ahead of her. But the death of someone young is no great surprise nowadays. Many of the cases of unnatural death that I see are in teenagers. Irrational invincibility meets unexpected reality. Accidental drug overdoses, choking on vomit, snow-boarding into trees, skidding cars off cliffs, home-made bungee jumps using cord that's too long into water that's too shallow. The variety of human stupidity is impressive.

And then there are the suicides born out of despair and a soulless sense of futility; self esteem so low that daily life is torture with future prospects looking worse. I have stood in many a garage or bedroom to catalogue the results of botched hangings. I saw them when I was training in Edinburgh and I see them today. They don't look so different whether they are in Leith Walk or Lake City Way. Scruffy little rag dolls dangling from rafters. Cherry-red swollen heads, shit and urine dribbling down their legs onto the floor splattering the explanatory note left behind as a last defiance. A faltering poem or a stream of invective directed at a parent or girlfriend. Some personal slight or trivial omission on someone else's part is held up as being the final unforgivable insult that precipitated the deed.

The hardest deaths to take are the ones where the personification of downtrodden misery strikes out at innocent bystanders with no remorse. Like the rash of school shootings that this country has suffered through in recent years. Wanton violence that poisons whole communities. Teens killing teens. Not that the callous disregard for life is restricted to troubled teens. There are a lot of older creeps out there who kill for no reason, or who may even target young people, jealous of the perfect bodies and good health that they flaunt. I hadn't made up my mind about Myra Garfield's death yet. Nothing felt particularly creepy although the skin scrapes were curious. I decided to postpone wild speculation until I had done the autopsy and evaluated some of the other evidence. As we drove through the damp February air it was Elspeth Paterson and Linda Munro who occupied my thoughts.

A watery sun broke through the clouds as we stopped at the four-way flashing red light that indicated the center of Vashon town. We passed through the entire downtown area in about fifteen seconds but it was long enough to sample a little social biopsy of the variety of human life that shared the island. A teenager scowled at us from the street corner. With cell phone clamped to metal-studded ear, skateboard under tattooed arms and cigarette dangling from unsmiling lips he was flaunting all the current symbols of "cool" in one impressive display. A well-coifed poodle lifted its leg and left an editorial comment on the wall next to him. Its owner was from the blue-rinse-hair, rosy-cheeked retiree brigade, striding past and defying the drizzle with a neon smile and about a thousand dollars' worth of breathable, insulated, waterproof, high-tech body armor from REI. Her cheerful greeting was ignored by a couple of unshaven men who slouched across the road into Bishop's Pub with grim determination.

"You think she could be involved in the girl's death?" Katy asked.

It took me a minute to realize that she wasn't referring to the dog-walker. I said, "Linda Munro? I don't think so, although I don't suppose I am the most objective person to ask. I've seen her on an occasional basis for thirty years but I don't really know her."

"Sounds to me as though you used to know her rather well," she said. Indignation flushed my face. How much had she heard of my conversation with Linda?

Katy hurried on before I could respond. "You know her husband?"

"Only be repute. I've never met him. Linda thinks he may have an employee called Garfield, by the way, but that might not mean anything. It's a common enough name."

"How soon can you get me the time of death?"

"That's going to be tricky. We can't use the drop in body temperature because she's been lying in the tub. I'll check the stomach contents when we do the post mortem. That may tell us how long it was since her last meal and what she ate. It would help if we knew who last saw her alive. Maybe who she had her last meal with."

We cut off the main highway and weaved our way into the heart of the island. Katy clutched a scrap of paper on which Gary Pitman had sketched directions to Tami Stillwell's house. Generic country roads surrounded us with endless trees and no landmarks. Katy skidded to a halt, reversed with a frown and plunged into a long rutted gravel lane that descended into nondescript woods. Driveways branched off every few hundred yards marked with thick chains strung between trees and hung with No Trespassing signs.

"It's supposed to be the last driveway on the right," Katy said. "I think I'll park here where we can turn around. I don't want to have to reverse all the way out of here."

The clothes we had found in the bushes by the deck lay on the back seat, individually sealed in plastic bags. Katy bundled them in a large Nordstrom's sack and stepped out into squelchy ooze that came over her shoes. Feigning nonchalance, she held the bag of clothes in front of her and picked her way between the muddy puddles. I pulled the rubber boots out of my backpack and stepped out of the Jeep a few minutes later feeling smug. I hadn't needed my boots at the crime scene but at least I would have dry feet when I got to the house.

The leafless canopy above us did little to hold back the rain, which disappeared into rotting piles of leaves and toadstools, pruned branches and uprooted stumps, lying like discarded corpses after a battle. Stiff brown stalks of last year's blackberry canes stood tall and erect, their wicked thorns dripping as if with saliva. Withered tendrils of moon vine and poison oak were halted in their upward climb. Shriveled nettles and horsetails hung limply, their energy spent. It was Nature-on-hold, the dormant season during which gardeners get a chance to draw a few breaths of respite in their battle with noxious weeds. As far as I can tell the dormant season in the Pacific Northwest lasts about two weeks.

We emerged into a clearing where humans had left their tasteless marks. All the native plants and trees had been bulldozed to the square edges of the property forming unnatural ridges now choked with dense swaths of alder saplings. A dilapidated barn dominated the scene. It had the kind of double pitch to its roof which is referred to as Dutch-style around here, though I don't recall ever seeing any like it in Holland. It may have looked grand when it was built but half a century of drizzle and damp had worn it down. With a sagging roof and one door hanging off it leaned slightly to one side like a staggering drunk who realizes he doesn't recognize anyone at a party and wonders how he got there in the first place.

In front of the barn was a pale lilac Cadillac with peeling paint and failing suspension. It was one of those flamboyant nineteen-sixties models with the shark fin extensions on the trunk to hold the taillights. Next to the barn was an Airstream trailer, one-time symbol of space-age chic with its sleek aluminum hot-dog appearance. Today it looked out of place and dejected like a large gray turd. Some modern construction had been built on to the back of the trailer. Between this and the barn was a fence and beyond that a muddy paddock. Behind the paddock, at the very back of the property I could see the concrete foundation for a house. It was a recent construction. Some of the wooden boards and strings to mark out the concrete mould were still visible.

The rain was more noticeable here in the clearing. It fell with relentless blandness, challenging the stamina of anyone trying to stay cheerful. Katy marched straight to the door of the Airstream but I hung back to glance into the barn. It was a jumble of furniture, boxes, broken pottery, paint cans and assorted junk. There did seem to be some method to the madness, though. Things in frequent use were placed closer to the front door. Several rolls of pink fiberglass insulation were piled against the front wall. There was a power sander and paint dust everywhere. A discarded piece of green carpet flopped over some oxyacetylene welding equipment. Maybe that was to protect it from the dust. Two bales of alfalfa hay were stacked on one side of the door smelling slightly moldy. They weren't getting enough protection from the dampness. There was the thin rancid smell of rodents about the place, too.

At the back of the barn an old boat was up on blocks for repairs. It looked to be a substantial cabin cruiser with a deep rounded keel; an unattractive craft looking embarrassed to be seen like this, like a fat pregnant woman up in stirrups. The hull of the boat was sanded down to a shiny pink undercoat. That was probably the source of all the paint dust.

A snort made me turn. Two llamas leaned over the fence looking down their imperious noses at me. Their coats were shaggy, mud-encrusted, and had that sickly wet-dog smell that stays with you for hours. I straightened up and brought my eyes level with the smaller llama. It moved away nervously but the other pushed its head towards mine and shoved its large teeth and bad breath in my face.

"Down Dally! Go on, git!" A woman's voice shouted from the door of the trailer. "He's all bluster, that one. He'd run a mile if you climbed the fence."

"I'll take your word for it," I said. Katy glared at me. I wasn't sure what her problem was. Was I undermining her authority, holding her back or making the people she wanted to interview nervous? I couldn't tell, but I cut short my snooping and made my way over to meet the owner of the Dally Llama.

Sonya Stillwell was not one of God's more perfect creations. With sallow skin, sloping shoulders and furtive shifty eyes, she reminded me of the runt in a litter of kittens that my Uncle Harry once tried to drown. Her eyes showed the same indignation, fear and betrayal. Even her voice had a feline whine.

"Tami said it was Myra Garfield they found in the hot tub. I can hardly believe it. She was over here just last week."

Katy said, "Over here? Did you know the girl then? Was she a friend of Tami's?"

The woman stiffened. She lifted the corner of a grubby smock and dabbed her mouth. A toddler appeared at her side, his cherubic face smeared with jam. He clutched the hem of the woman's smock with one hand and crammed a jelly sandwich into his mouth with the other. Sonya Stillwell patted his haystack of blond hair affectionately and stroked the long tassel that went down his back.

"You'd better come inside. Mind your head. It's pretty messy I'm afraid. I've been working."

It was dark inside the trailer. Sonya Stillwell scurried around removing toys and clothes from the couch, mumbling apologies as she went.

"What a mess the place is. I wasn't expecting any visitors of course but you'd think I could keep the place tidier than this. Frank would be mad if he knew I'd let people see the place in this state. This is only temporary, you know. Frank's going to build us a big new house this summer."

Katy said, "That's quite all right Mrs. Stillwell. This is not a social call. There's no need to apologize. I'd just like a word with Tami."

"Me get my own room!" said the toddler.

"That's right sweetie. You'll have your own room," his mother replied.

"I sleep in my own bed!"

"That's right, hun."

"Not need diapers!" The toddler tugged at Katy's sleeve. "I not need diapers!"

If Katy Pearson has any warm, gushy mothering instincts they were not on display that day. I think she would have made creative use of a large roll of Duct Tape if she had one on hand. As it was she ignored the child's self-important smile and pulled out her notebook.

"I understand Tami found the body and called the police. She gave a brief statement to Sheriff Pitman but I'd like to get a few additional details."

Sonya Stillwell stood to leave. "You stay here, Starflame, and I'll go get Tami, okay?"

She had to be joking. Starflame? They had named the wee boy Starflame? I think I once lost five pounds betting on a horse called Starflame at the Ayr races. A hapless nag with no coordination and little heart. It was not a pleasant memory. I looked over at Katy to see if the name had made the same impression on her but she had withdrawn inside her thoughts as if no one else was in the room. The child gave a running commentary as he bounced and skipped around us in the tiny living room. He carried a stick, which he poked in my direction from time to time, accompanied by explosive sound effects.

"Not a gun," he announced. "Guns are bad. This not a gun. This my kill stick."

I made noncommittal grunts and scanned the room. The walls were covered in a teak veneer that was coming away in places. It was dark and gloomy. The aroma of mildew and unwashed dishes caught my nostrils. A sagging gray couch with broken springs took up one whole wall. A foreign-looking blanket in drab earth tones covered some of the bare patches in the upholstery. On the wall above the couch was an out of date map of the world which still showed the USSR. It was ripped, with the USA hanging off. I wondered idly if this was some kind of political statement. Other wall decorations included a poster of medicinal herbs, various astrology symbols and a signed photograph of some unprepossessing spotted bird peering out from the crook of a branch on a massive old growth tree.

Cinder blocks and planks created a makeshift bookcase crammed with volumes on homeopathy, herbal medicine, aromatherapy and colortherapy. There were also several selections from the Adult-Children-Of-Screwed-Up-Parents section of the self-help library. Don't get me wrong. I'm open-minded about all sorts of naturopathic, holistic, herbal, Ayurvedic remedies for life's cruel surprises. Some of them probably even work. Let's just say they weren't a major part of the medicinal landscape when I was growing up in the industrial backwaters of Ayrshire. I'm prepared to believe that three thousand years ago in the mountains of Tibet some old fat guy discovered amazing healing properties in junka-weed root. I just have a hard time believing that the benefits will be the same from the little capsules of junka-weed powder being sold in bottles of thirty for $49.95 at Bartell's drug store, next to the cans of cherry Coke and Britney Spears CDs.

The variety of alternative medicines seems to have increased exponentially in recent years. Their elevation to multibillion-dollar respectability is baffling to me but I'm always interested in educating myself. I picked up a well-thumbed book on "The Miracle of Homeopathy – why less is more." That was certainly true if you looked at the rich, beaming author on the back cover bragging about how many millions of copies had been translated into foreign languages.

Most of the window ledges and other horizontal surfaces in the trailer were cluttered with feathers, rocks, shells, incense holders and some homemade pottery of the Moon/Sun/Ying-Yang motif. An alcove separated the living room from the kitchen area. A string of red hot peppers and garlic dangled beside several potted cacti. Some of those were large and phallic, like nightmarish porcupine penises. They looked incongruous with the dripping moss outside.

"Any thoughts?" Katy asked quietly. I'm not sure how long she had been watching me.

"Nothing very specific or helpful," I said. "It seems to be a depressing set up, full of unfulfilled hopes and endless searching for alternative solutions. They are practicing an odd approach to aromatherapy and colortherapy, though. I wouldn't think that stale fat and drab grays would be very likely to balance a person's psychic center very well."

"There you are! Please come and sit down." The loudness of Katy's voice gave me the clue that I should shut up.

Sonya Stillwell stood with her arm around the slumped shoulders of a young woman. I couldn't tell if they had overheard me. One glance at the girl brought out all my fatherly protective urges. She was bundled up in a quilt and kept her head bowed. A curtain of lank brown hair fell across her face. Pale, fragile hands poked out from the edges of the quilt. She stared at them through red-rimmed eyes as if the hands were strange alien objects, not part of her body. She rubbed the dark gray tips of her fingers together with an abstracted concentration.

"God, Tami, have you not washed that stuff off your hands yet?" Sonya Stillwell said.

The young woman wriggled away from her mother's arm and snapped at her. "It might help, Sonya. The police said it might help catch whoever did it." She began sobbing.

"I don't see why they couldn't have waited until you weren't so upset. But what do I know, eh? I suppose they know what they are doing."

"I volunteered, Sonya. Nobody harassed me. The fingerprint guy was really nice. Said if they knew what Aaron and my prints looked like they could ignore those and try to find others that belonged to whoever..." She shuffled over to the couch and curled up in the corner. "I should never have gone there. I never would have if I'd known it was Miss Munro's house. I'm so ashamed."

Katy held out her a business card. "Tami, my names is Katy Pearson. I'm a detective with the King County Police Department. I know you're upset and I know you've already given a statement to Sheriff Pitman but it's important that I ask you a few more questions. We don't even know for sure if Myra Garfield was murdered or not but the sooner we investigate the better. This gentleman is Dr. McLure. He is the medical examiner and he'll help us figure out how Myra died. Do you think you can tell me what happened this morning?"

Tami Stillwell looked up at Katy and then me. Katy's hand still dangled the business card in front of the young woman's face. She extended her hands and gently clamped the card with the edge of each hand, keeping her dirty fingertips from touching it.

"Don't want to get it covered with ink," she mumbled.

Katy said, "Tell me what happened when you were on the Covington's deck this morning. Had you ever been there before?"

"No of course not. It was Aaron's idea. I'd never have gone if I'd known Miss Munro lived there."

"You know her?" Katy asked.

"Kind of. I'm sure she doesn't know me, though. I didn't even know she lived on Vashon. She teaches psychology at the U. I'm taking the basic set of introductory classes this semester. Two

58

lectures, one lab and a small group discussion. There's like about five hundred people for the main lecture. I'm sure she doesn't know me from a banana slug. She's great, though. Makes it kind of fun. Tells stories about when she was growing up in Scotland and stuff. All the weird guys she dated. When she showed up at the house today I just about died. I am so embarrassed. I had no idea she lived there. Aaron said the house belonged to people called Covington. I didn't know that was her married name. I was leaving when she arrived. She didn't recognize me or anything. We'd already given our statements. I could not believe it was her house."

She buried her head onto her knees and sobbed silently. Starflame scowled and poked at her with his stick. She grabbed it fiercely and stuffed it in the couch cushion behind her back.

"You're not meant to play with guns," she said.

"Not a gun. Mine. Give it."

Starflame began a furious stamping routine, prancing up and down in a useless display of energy that was unpleasant to witness. He reminded me more and more of that knock-kneed pony I lost money on in my gambling youth. I think the horse was a three-year-old, too.

Katy said, "Would you mind taking the child away Mrs. Stillwell? I need to ask Tami a few more questions."

Katy asked her questions quickly, unsure how long we'd have before a disruptive Starflame would re-enter our orbit. Tami seemed

59

less tense and defensive with her mother and brother out of the room, but she continued to sit dazed and motionless.

"Did you know Myra Garfield?" Katy said.

"A little, I guess. Hardly at all, really. We'd hardly ever spoken. I'd see her at dances or concerts on the island, like, but most of my social life is in Seattle, in the U-district. On the Ave., mostly."

"But your mom said Myra was over last week."

"She comes over sometimes to baby-sit Star. I do it sometimes, of course, but there's times when I've got other things to do. He's not my real brother, anyway."

"So you didn't speak to Myra last week?" Katy asked.

Tami shook her head.

"When was the last time you spoke to Myra?"

"I can't rightly remember," she said, a trace of southern drawl showing through. "I'd usually be gone when she was over here. Sonya or Frank would arrange it. They can tell you more about her than me."

"Is Frank your dad?"

"Stepdad. I'm adopted."

Katy said, "How long have you known Aaron Klein?"

A look of warmth and pride came over the girl. She sat up straighter and ran her fingers through her hair as she thought about her answer.

"Three weeks and two days. His band was doing a gig on campus. Well, near campus. Up by Greek row actually. I don't usually go up there but I wanted to hear them play. Aaron kept smiling at me between songs and I went up and talked to him afterwards. He didn't know that I was from Vashon, too. Most of the band's from West Seattle. Except Mosh. He's from like Mars or something." She giggled.

"Had you dated Aaron in the past three weeks?"

"Dated?"

Muted squeals were approaching from the far end of the trailer. A Starflame eclipse seemed imminent.

"Had you had sex with him, Tami?" Katy said.

"What's that got to do with anything?"

Katy's expression softened. She squatted down on the floor and looked up at the young woman with warmth and concern. "I'm sorry for all these intrusive questions, Tami but we need to try to understand details about the people who knew Myra. I am trying to find out if anyone might have had a motive for killing her. Do you know if Aaron Klein was having sex with Myra?"

The girl looked offended. "You'd need to ask him that. He was really nice when he was with me. Gentle and funny. We'd gone out a couple of times. In a group with the other guys in the band. We had a barbecue on KVI beach last weekend. Made a bonfire in the rain. It was pretty cool." She looked up to inspect Katy's face. "I hadn't had sex with Aaron. Not yet, anyway. This morning was going to be our first time. He said he knew this really cool place where he works as a gardener. Said they had a deck with a hot tub. Totally secluded. He said the neighbors would be gone and the owners were cool about it. It sounded like so much fun. But it was awful."

She covered her head with the quilt and curled up into an even tighter ball. Sonya and Starflame returned, the boy clutching what looked like a hairy piece of brown rope dripping in syrup.

"Sugar cane dipped in honey," Sonya explained proudly. "All organic. We don't do candy in this house. You okay, Tami?"

Katy took the articles of clothing out of the Nordstrom's sack and laid them on a plastic sheet on the couch beside Tami.

"We found these clothes near the deck and wondered if they were yours or if they belonged to Myra Garfield."

Tami mumbled her answer from under the quilt. "I didn't take off any of my clothes this morning. I already told you that. I came back wearing everything I went with."

"I'd like you to look at them, just the same. You too, Mrs. Stillwell. Do you recognize any of these as belonging to Myra?"

Tami thrust her head out from under the quilt, picked up each bag in turn, and shook her head quickly before dropping the bag back onto the couch. The denim pedal pushers, the mohair sweater and the underwear produced no response but when she lifted the bag containing the buckskin jacket she froze. Sonya moved closer.

"Isn't that Clayton's jacket?" she said.

"It's mine," Tami snapped. "It's mine, now. He's gone."

"Who's Clayton?" Katy asked.

"Tami's stepdad."

"I thought that was Frank."

A trace of embarrassment came over Sonya Stillwell's bland face. "Clayton was her stepdad before Frank."

Tami's shoulders sagged, her voice filled with betrayal. "I can't believe he let her wear my jacket."

"But he couldn't have, sweetheart," Sonya said.

"Not Clayton, mom, Aaron. I let Aaron borrow my jacket last weekend. He's really into the Grateful Dead. Said he wanted to wear it on stage. I can't believe he gave it to Myra Garfield."

Tami rose and stumbled from the room. After she had gone, we all stayed silent for some time, even Starflame. I was grateful for the sugar cane. I expected Katy to ask Sonya Stillwell for some explanation of her daughter's behavior but Katy stayed calm and unreadable. She let the tense silence build to see if it would precipitate any response. Sonya was the first to crack.

"She's really upset. You'd best leave your questions till later."

Katy said, "We'll see the Klein boy next but we may need to talk to Tami again."

"It must have been a shock for her seeing another drowned girl." Sonya Stillwell bit her lip. "I just thought of that. It probably brought some of those bad memories back."

"Excuse me," Katy said. "Could you please explain yourself, Mrs. Stillwell?"

"Her best friend was drowned in Texas. Tami found her. In their swimming pool. We were neighbors."

"How long ago was that?"

"About four years ago. We'd lived in Houston since Tami was an infant but she hated the place after her friend's death. That was part of the reason we moved up here. To get away from it all. Make a new start."

64

"I'm going to the nursing home."

Tami stood in the kitchen alcove. The change in her demeanor was striking. She wore a clean pressed sweatshirt, black slacks and sneakers. Her hair was brushed and her face washed. She had not put on any make up and the signs of her recent crying were still obvious. It gave her a noble, stoical appearance.

Sonya said, "Oh honey, are you sure you want to go? I can call in. I'm sure they'd understand. You should just go and lie down. I could make you some Chamomile Tea. Or maybe some Moon Cycle tea. The Dong Quai should help balance your internal harmony. You want to try the Moon Cycle?"

"No, I want to go. They're counting on me. Especially Mrs. Ahearn. Besides, it'll take my mind off it all."

Sonya explained, "Tami works part time at the new nursing home down by Burton. The Goldentide. Cleaning out bedpans, doing bed baths, reading to the old ladies and men. Those that aren't gaga, anyway. I don't know how she can do it."

Tami smiled. "I like it. Old people are cool. They have these amazing stories."

"How long have you worked at Goldentide?" Katy asked.

"Almost a year. It's helping me pay for school. I can only manage one evening during the week because of my class schedule but I work more on Saturdays and Sundays."

"Do you know a Mrs. Munro?" I asked. Everyone turned towards me. I had kept quiet during Katy's interview so as not to be a distraction.

"He talks funny," Starflame announced.

"Linda's mother stays at the Goldentide," I said to Katy. "She moved over here from Scotland a few years ago so that Linda could look after her. She still has a house somewhere on Vashon, but she was getting so forgetful that Linda had to move her into the nursing home. I thought you might have noticed her Scottish accent, Tami."

Tami shook her head. "Maybe she's new. Mrs. Burley has me work with the same ones most of the time. That way they get to know you. It's reassuring for them to see a friendly face. Someone they know." She moved towards the outside trailer door.

"We won't keep you then," Katy said. "You've got my card. Please call me if you think of anything else that might help. We can get the rest of our information from Mr. Klein."

Tami turned back, her face strained. "You don't think he had anything to do with it, do you? He couldn't have done it, Detective Pearson. I just know he couldn't. He's not like that. He's not like that at all. He's really nice. He'd never do anything like that. Not Aaron. He's great."

Kids sometimes repeat things that they want to believe. Over and over again. If you say it often enough then it must be true.

V

Pretentious Bohemian

"What do you want? If you're looking to buy, she's not at home. Call the FarWest office."

The door was shut in Katy's face before she got a chance to show her ID or get her introductory remarks out. I heard a woman's voice from inside the house. The sullen young man opened the door again and gave us a sarcastic smile.

"My mistake. She is at home. But she's not on duty for the real estate vultures. Some other schmuck is out selling up chunks of the planet to rich off-islanders, today. So call the-"

Katy thrust her badge in his face. "We're not here to talk to your mother about real estate. I'm Detective Pearson from King County homicide. Assuming that you're Aaron Klein, I'm here to speak to you."

That got rid of his smirk. There was a quaver in his voice that bespoke fear below the bravado. "I already gave a statement to the goddamn police." A phone rang deep inside the house, making him jump. "I'll get that, mom. Mom, I said I'll get it. Shit, mom, listen for once why don't you. If that's Mosh I need to talk to him right now."

A woman appeared at his side. "It wasn't Mosh, Aaron, and there's no need to shout. Don't leave these nice people standing out in the cold." She turned to us with an expression of earnest concern and overdone sincerity. "Hi, I'm Patricia Klein. Patricia, remember, not Patsy. I may be a little crazy and I have been known to fall to pieces now and again but I don't sing about it."

The rude young slob rolled his eyes. This was obviously one of his mother's oft-repeated little jokes. Standing side by side the two were so different in appearance that I doubted if they were from the same species, let alone the same family. He was tall, slouching and surly. His clothes looked as though he had slept in them for a week. In a sewer. I'm surprised his mother was prepared to stand that close to him. Fleas can jump several feet. Mind you, she had covered herself in so many chemicals that no self-respecting flea would have recognized a potential home anywhere on her body. She was probably a foot shorter than her son but looked taller because of perfect posture and about eight inches of sculpted blond hair. I use the word "hair" loosely. Those strands had been steeped in so much chemical soup, had been broiled, basted, frizzed and stretched so often that they looked even more plastic than the gleaming smile with which she favored us.

"Are you here about the awful accident that happened to Myra Garfield. Aaron was telling me. He's really devastated. He's still in shock. He just has a funny way of showing it." She stepped past Katy and brought her face a fraction closer to mine than was socially appropriate. Her perfume could have cleared a room full of skunks. I would have stepped back but she gripped my forearm earnestly. "I can hardly imagine how Mr. and Mrs. Garfield are feeling, officer. I shall go over and offer whatever help I can, although it's hard to think of anything that would help, isn't it?"

"Detective Pearson is the officer in charge, Mrs. Klein," I said, breaking free from her grip.

Patricia Klein looked quickly between us, assessing the extent of her faux pas.

"Of course. I didn't mean to imply. Come on inside, Officer Pearson."

Sitting beside Katy Pearson on a white leather love seat might have felt comfortable in a certain setting but this wasn't it. We faced spotless plate glass windows giving an unobstructed view of the Burton marina. Gusts of wind chased ripples across the surface of the water and made the boats shiver. The room itself was bright and airy but lacked warmth or life. A sparkling glass and chrome coffee table stood on a cream-colored carpet. There was a Chihuly-knock-off vase on the coffee table, all blue and green swirls. On the wall hung a bland abstract painting chosen because its colors matched the carpet and the vase. Mrs. Klein perched on the edge of a high-backed cane chair on one side of the window with perfect posture. Aaron slouched in an armchair on the other side faking boredom and disinterest.

Katy seemed unfazed. "Mr. Klein, I am aware of the statement you gave Sheriff Pitman. However it leaves out several important details. Your eyes look distinctly bloodshot to me, and while your mother might believe that it's from heartsick tears and grief I was wondering if it had more to do with the marijuana joint we found at the crime scene."

That got his attention. Katy held up a hand in a preemptive move to silence his mother. "It was Aaron I came to talk to, Mrs. Klein. I expect he can put a couple of coherent sentences together if he concentrates really hard."

The young man blushed. "What the hell is this? Pitman said it was an accident. I was helping out, for Chrissakes. All I did was find her body. Are you accusing me of…"

"No one is being accused of anything at this point, Mr. Klein, but a young woman has died under very suspicious circumstances. I'd appreciate it if you'd give me your full attention."

Aaron Klein pulled himself into a slightly more upright slouch, moving slowly, conceding as little as possible.

I was seeing a whole different side of Katy Pearson now. She had been so warm with Tami, and now so tough with Aaron Klein. Was this a man-hating thing, or just good professionalism; adapting her interview technique to the situation? It was fascinating to watch her in action. She had her notebook out to emphasize that she meant business. Her fingers were slim and elegant, the nails nicely manicured. She wrote with a noisy, confident scrawl that seemed at odds with those delicate sensual hands.

"I understand you work as a gardener for the Covingtons," she said.

"I do some stuff for them. It's not like it's my real job but it pays the bills."

Bills? I was itching to ask him which particular bills he paid, since it looked to me as though he sponged off his mother. He was easy to dislike. His sneering face looked like a perfect target for the back of my hand but I kept that thought to myself.

"So what is your real job, Mr. Klein?" Katy said.

"I'm lead singer in a band."

"One I'm likely to have heard of?"

"I doubt it," he scoffed.

"The name of the band, Mr. Klein?"

"Skunk Bucket."

I burst out laughing. I couldn't help it. Sitting in that sanitized living room where every speck of dust was wiped away with scented feather dusters, the name struck me as funny. Was this his blow for freedom? His statement of personal rebellion? Judging by the pride in his voice, I think so.

"What's so funny, Dr. McLure?" Katy's eyes told me that she didn't appreciate the interruption but I couldn't help myself.

"It's nothing. It just struck me as an odd choice of name."

"What's so damned odd about it?" Aaron said.

"It just reminds me of something. I think Skunk Bucket is what my neighbor calls his dog when it has been rolling in dead seagulls at Golden Gardens beach."

No one laughed. It wasn't my day for impressing people with my helpful, insightful remarks. I squeaked my way farther back into the corner of the leather love seat and shut up. Katy wanted to keep Aaron Klein on the run. I could understand why she didn't want my distractions.

"Did you have permission to use the Covington's hot tub, Mr. Klein?" she asked.

"Kind of," he said.

"Explain that."

"Mrs. C. asked me to turn it on last week. I'm sure she wouldn't have minded. I was just like testing it out for them." He smiled at that.

Katy sounded incredulous. "Did they say they wouldn't mind? Have you done that before?"

"What is this? I thought you guys would be pleased that Tami and me found her body. I thought we'd be like heroes."

"Is Tami Stillwell your girlfriend?"

"Did she say that? I'm a musician, man. I know a lot of girls." He looked over at me, hoping I'd be jealous or impressed, no doubt. Katy certainly wasn't.

"Did you know Myra Garfield?" she said.

"Yeah, a bit."

"Had you ever taken her to the Covington's hot tub?"

"Who told you that?" Aaron shot an angry glance at his mother.

"I haven't told them anything, darling. I only just met them."

"Mosh then. I should have told him to keep his mouth shut."

"Who's Mosh?" Katy asked.

Patricia Klein replied. "Jan Mossandrian. He's the base player in Aaron's band. A nice boy. From Holland, you know. Mosh is his nick name."

73

"His stage name, mom."

"Oh all right, Aaron, his stage name. Nick name, stage name, I'm sure it doesn't matter to Officer Pearson."

Katy's voice was cold. "I'd like Mr. Mossandrian's address and phone number please. I'd also like you to answer my previous question, Mr. Klein. Have you ever taken Myra Garfield to the Covington's hot tub and if so, when?"

He looked at the floor for several seconds, weighing the implications of his response. When he spoke his answer was barely audible. "Friday night."

"I beg your pardon?" Katy said.

"Friday night, I said. I took her there on Friday night before the gig. She was fine when I left. I mean like totally fine. Laughing, happy."

"Is that the only time you've taken her there?"

"Yes it's the only time!" He glared at Katy but seeing that self-righteous indignation wasn't going to advance his cause, he softened his tone. "The tub was drained and turned off most of the winter."

"And was Friday night the last time you saw Myra Garfield alive?"

74

Aaron nodded. "She was leaving on Saturday morning to do the family skiing thing with her folks. At Tahoe or somewhere. She said she didn't have time to come to the concert. Had to go home and pack. The flight was at some ungodly hour."

"So you left her there alone in the tub?"

"Yeah. So what? I mean she's not a kid. She had her car there. She said she wanted to sit in the tub for a bit longer."

Katy raised her voice. "Give me more details. When did you go to the Covington's house? How did you get there? Did you travel in separate cars?"

Aaron Klein perched on the edge of the armchair like a dejected Raggedy Andy in a macabre puppet show. He leaned his skinny elbows on gangly knees and cradled a guilty looking face in his hands. Dirty blond dreadlocks fell across his brow.

"We went together in her car. Her mom's car, that is. It's a white Toyota. A Camry, I think. That'd be about six o'clock, maybe a little after. The band was meant to be playing in the high school auditorium, but not till ten. They had some high school kids' band for a warm up. I left around nine so I could change and help carry the gear and tune up."

"How did you get to the high school? Didn't you say her car was still there when you left?"

"Mosh swung by to pick me up."

75

"At nine o'clock?"

"Yeah. I'd told him to come around eight thirty but he's always late."

"What kind of car does he drive?"

"A VW bus. It's an old rig but it runs pretty good."

"And were you and Myra in the tub when he arrived?"

He nodded.

"Naked?" Katy asked.

"Of course we were frigging naked. Do you want me to spell it out for you?"

"No, but I'd like to know as much detail as I need to find out how and when Myra Garfield died. Did you have sex with her on Friday night?"

He glanced over at his mother.

"I can ask your mother to leave if you'd like. You can also have a lawyer present if you think you need one."

"I don't need a goddamn lawyer and I don't care what she hears. I'm my own man. I live my own life."

"Then answer the question."

"We'd fooled around some. Had sex a couple of times."

Katy wrote in her notebook very deliberately. "Now does couple of times mean twice or did you lose count? And was there just the two of you fooling around and having intercourse or did Mosh or anyone else join in?"

He tried another glare of moral indignation but couldn't really pull it off. "I'm not into that, man. It was just Myra and me."

"But did Mosh come up onto the deck? Did he see both of you naked in the tub?"

"I was already getting dressed by the time he came up onto the deck. I heard him coming. You can hear that damned bus a mile away. I was half dressed when he got there. I knew we were late for the gig."

"Was Myra still naked in the tub when Mosh came onto the deck? Did he see her there?"

"What's that got to do with anything? Yeah, he saw her. Hell, she didn't care. She was loving it. Giving us both the full frontal show. She was a little drunk by then."

"And stoned?" Katy said.

"I didn't say that. We'd had a bottle of wine. Nothing else."

I sat up and touched Katy's arm. "Can I ask a couple of questions?"

"If they're relevant," she said coldly. It was clear I hadn't scored any Brownie points with Detective Katy Pearson so far.

"Did you and Mosh leave together then?" I said.

"I already said that."

"How did Myra's body look when you left?"

He gave me a look of disgust. "Are you some dirty old English geezer who gets off on talking dirty? You should try these one nine hundred numbers sometime, buddy. Ninety-five cents a minute. Satisfaction guaranteed."

Apparently no one had ever told Aaron Klein that if you really want to piss off a Scotsman just call him English. I exercised admirable restraint and stared him down until he continued.

"She looked great, man. Crispy. Totally fortified. A full hundred percent of the Surgeon General's recommended daily allowance."

I said, "Really? She didn't look very crispy or fortified when we pulled her body out of the water this morning, sonny. She looked like a pathetic wee girl who came to a premature and unnecessary demise after getting mixed up with the wrong crowd. She looked about the same age as my own daughter." Anger was rising in my throat. Katy raised a hand to silence me but I ignored it. "I'm not asking because I 'get off on talking dirty.' I want to know if there were any blemishes on her body? Did you rough her up at all or scratch her while you were screwing her? Did you come in her mouth, her vagina, her anus or all three? I want details, son, and I want the truth. I'll match up your statements with what I find when I have to cut up her poor wee dead body during the post mortem tomorrow."

That silenced the room. Patricia Klein looked prudish and offended. Her son looked pale, scared and tearful.

"There was nothing kinky, man. She sucked on me for a bit and then she sat on the edge of the tub while I…" He took a deep breath before finishing. "I came inside of her."

"Her vagina?" I said.

"Yes."

"And her body had no scratches on it anywhere?"

He shook his head. "It was perfect, man. I'll never forget how she looked when I left. She looked awesome, man. I can still hardly believe she's dead."

Katy cleared her throat. "But you did believe that she had gone to Lake Tahoe on Saturday. You're quite sure you didn't see her between when you left her at nine o'clock on Friday evening and this morning when you discovered her dead body in the hot tub?"

"That was the last time I saw her. I thought she was skiing and having fun all weekend."

Katy said, "So you decided to take Tami Stillwell, another young woman, to the hot tub this morning. Is this a regular thing, Mr. Klein? How long have you known Tami?"

"No it's not a … regular frigging thing." He sighed with exasperation. "I met Tami at a concert. I've known her for a few weeks but we haven't been like going out. I mean not just the two of us, anyway. This morning was the first time we'd done that."

"What was Myra Garfield wearing on Friday night?" Katy asked.

The abruptness of her question seemed to surprise him. It puzzled me a bit too. I noticed that she had left the Nordstrom's bag in the car but I had assumed this was just an oversight on her part.

Aaron shrugged. "I don't remember."

Katy rolled her eyes. "Oh come on, Mr. Klein. You drove together in her mother's car, all horny and full of anticipation, I'm sure. I bet you hardly kept your eyes off each other. What was she wearing? Don't tell me you didn't watch her strip before she got into the tub. Did you help her get undressed?"

His face flushed with anger. "She was wearing a checked shirt. One of those red and black flannel things like lumberjacks and worker dudes wear. With a wifebeater underneath. No bra."

"A wife beater?" Katy said.

He gave her a pitying look. How did straight stiffs like her get through life? He drew lines on his chest as if explaining something to a child.

"One of those white cotton tank top things but cut lower. Like what fat beer-drinking morons wear." His eyes lit up. "Like Homer. On the Simpsons. A wifebeater."

I tried to help. "It's a man's undershirt, Detective Pearson. In Scotland we'd call them semmits."

Katy nodded, poker-faced, keeping her eyes on Aaron Klein. "What else was she wearing?"

"Black jeans, green sandals."

"Underwear? I'm sure you noticed that?"

"They were red. Kind of a high cut thong deal. Shiny. Satin or silk or something."

Katy stared at him for several seconds. "I'm going to want blood samples from you, Mr. Klein. We'll want a genetic comparison with any semen or blood we find on the dead girl's body. You are not being charged with anything at the present time, but I'd advise you to get a lawyer."

VI

Tater Tots and Fiddle Tunes

The lights were on in the house as Katy pulled up behind my truck at the kerb side in Fremont. Smoke rose from the chimney at a good clip so Jennifer must have been home for a while and got the fire well established. Sounds of laughter and music emanated from the open window next to the front door. It made the constant rain seem a bit less inhospitable.

"Do you want to come in for a minute?" I said. I don't know why. Katy Pearson looked lonely and sad. I felt I hadn't shown myself in a very good light. I wanted her to see me with my happy family around me. I could tell she was hesitating. "I know Jennifer would love to meet you and thank you for being so accommodating today."

We hadn't spoken much on the way back. We left the Kleins' house in Burton and drove straight to the north end dock. The line of cars snaked its way well up the hill as families returned to the mainland after Valentine's day festivities. Katy used the privilege of her law enforcement status to pull in at the head of the line. We were waved on first, right down the center of the ferry to be first off on the other side. Katy got out immediately and went upstairs to the passenger deck. I took the hint and stayed put. I felt I hadn't created a great impression with my flippant remarks and blunt approach to the case. I wished she hadn't overheard the end of my conversation with Linda but that was that. As we drove off at Fauntleroy I tried to make some amends.

"That was a good idea asking the Klein boy to describe her clothing rather than showing him the clothes we found," I said.

"Was it? It has got me more confused than ever. Maybe the clothes we've got aren't Myra Garfield's at all."

"You think somebody murdered her, took her clothes and left these instead?"

"I wouldn't go that far. We don't know for sure it was murder. You said so yourself. Maybe you'll be able to tell me tomorrow. But I can't think why Aaron Klein would lie about what she was wearing. His description of her clothing sounded authentic to me. Her folks will be back tomorrow. I'll go talk to them and show them the clothes we found at the scene. The thing that bothers me about the clothes we found is that, apart from the buckskin jacket, they look clean, pressed and unused."

"Maybe she's just neat. Folds her clothes when she takes them off," I offered.

"They looked and smelled like they just came out of the drawer. Do you think the lab boys could tell if they'd ever been worn since they were last washed and dried?"

"They might. We could look for tiny traces of urine or sweat on the panties or under the arms of the T-shirt. If we found something positive it would prove that they had been worn since they were last cleaned. But if we can't find anything I doubt if it would stand up in court as proof that they were fresh out the closet."

Katy's face was strained. "I'm wondering if some voyeuristic perp saw the two of them making out in the hot tub. Maybe he was watching from the bushes, waited for Klein to leave and then murdered her. Maybe he gets off on women's clothing that have already been worn. Maybe those red silk panties are under his pillow right now. I don't know. I'm too tired to think. Do you think the scratches on her chest could have been the result of a struggle while she was raped?"

"She would need to have been forced onto her front on a gravel path or something while she was raped from behind. I couldn't see any sings of violence on her neck or arms or perineum. I'd expect those if she was raped. Unless she was unconscious by then. I'll know more tomorrow."

We drove the rest of the way home in silence. Although not overtly hostile to me, Katy Pearson gave me the impression that she had had more than enough of my company for one day.

She said, "I won't come in, thanks. Hopefully you'll have your own transportation tomorrow. When were you planning to do the autopsy? I'd like to be there."

"I should get to it around eleven. We have an interdepartmental meeting first thing and I've got some desk work to attend to but this case will be my top priority after that."

I watched wistfully as her taillights and my ego shrank into the distance. My head and back ached as I walked up the path. The cure I needed was the comfort and normalcy of my own house and family, but my heart sank when I saw what was lying on the porch. A nine-by-thirteen glass casserole dish covered with aluminum foil may not put a chill in the heart of most men but it has that effect on me. The warm greasy smells rising from the edges of the dish and the pink scented envelope sitting on top confirmed my worst fears.

As I picked up the casserole the front door flew open and Callum stuck his head out. Jennifer bounced past him to greet me, her face flushed with good-humored energy.

"Is she gone? Was that the angel who drove you around all day? I wanted to meet her and say thanks. I hope you weren't too cynical and obnoxious, dad. Be sure and thank her for me." She made a face at the casserole and held her nose. "Oh God, is that from Gaylene Jarvis next door? I don't even want to touch it. Let me hold the door open so you can dump it in the kitchen."

Callum grabbed my hand, causing greasy drips to dribble onto the porch. He tugged me into the living room. "Hey dad, come on inside and get your guitar. Harley and me are working on The Rakes of Mallow but we need you to strum the chords to make it sound really good."

The warmth and vitality of the living room almost knocked me over. A golden fur ball shot across the room and jumped up to my knees, wheezing happily. Taffy is a Welsh Corgi rescue dog that my neighbor, Harley, got from the pound. Taffy's last owners couldn't stand his barking so had his voice box removed. Then they couldn't stand his wheezing so they abandoned him. Harley took him in, recognizing a kindred spirit in the dog, another plucky survivor who keeps bouncing back against the odds. Dogs don't forget that kind of thing. Taffy is always eager to see me, especially if I am carrying food. With meaty grease on my hands he was all over me. I put the casserole on the kitchen counter then bent down to rub behind his ears.

Harley was sitting on the piano stool cradling his mouth organ. He gave me his usual blunt assessment.

"You sure don't look like you had a good day. Come on in and get your guitar out. It'll improve Callum's day even if yours is beyond recovery."

Harley D. Wilson is more than a neighbor. He is my psychologist, confidant, philosopher, baby-sitter and maybe the least likely best friend that a middle-aged, middle-class white Scottish guy could have. He brought his family to Seattle from Mississippi during the nineteen sixties to escape the violence of racism engulfing them. I'm not sure how old he is. Black skin weathers the ravages of time much better than white skin. His rugged features and quiet eyes shine with a timeless patience. Strong callused hands tell of a lifetime of labor. With his kids gone and his wife dying the year before we moved in next door, Harley has adopted us as a second family.

The pendulum clock above the fire struck nine. That is bedtime on school nights. Callum slammed the door shut causing smoke to billow into the room, a clumsy diversionary tactic on his part.

"I know it's late, dad, but you've got to hear this, okay? You stay here and talk to Harley while I get your guitar down."

Jennifer called from the kitchen. "Take a look at this, dad. It's like toxic waste."

"Taffy doesn't seem to think so," I said. He was sitting at Jennifer's feet doing that inquisitive, head-bobbing "aren't-I-adorable" movement that dogs do to get your attention.

The pink envelope contained a traditional card of pink roses and hearts. The message read, "A heart-y meal for a sex-y man!! Happy Valentine's day, Gaylene."

Harley looked over my shoulder. "She's making a play for you, boy. She's trying to fatten you up for the kill."

Jennifer said, "Kill is right. Does any of the stuff in here qualify as a food item?"

I'm no gourmet chef but I recognized this genre – the quick and easy family meal, circa 1955. Ingredients: extra fatty ground beef, macaroni, and a tin of condensed cream of mushroom soup. Method: mix together into a glop, dump into a casserole dish, top with a bag of frozen Tater Tots and cook at 375 degrees for one hour. Voila! A whole-week's supply of cholesterol and salt in one nifty plateful.

Jennifer held up the kitchen garbage can. "Be my guest, dad."

Harley said, "You're getting too picky, you two. This smells pretty good to Taffy and me. You let me know if you're going to throw that out. I believe I'd enjoy a little of that, although it might put a strain on my old heart."

"You mean because of the cholesterol?" I said. "Since when have you ever cared about that?"

"Never, but I'm betting Gaylene will have laced it with aphrodisiac. Ginseng or yohimbine, maybe."

"You-what-bean?" Callum had returned with my guitar.

"Never mind, Callum. Let's play a couple of quick tunes before you go to bed. What key do you play The Rakes of Mallow in?"

Celtic folk music seems to cut across all boundaries of age, gender, race and culture. The up-tempo, foot-tapping Scottish country-dance tunes washed away my concerns of the day and transported me back to my own childhood. I was about Callum's age when I took up the piano, then switched to guitar during college. I'm no great shakes on the guitar but I can strum the chords and do a few simple base runs. Callum has been playing the fiddle for less than two years but has the memory, agility, dexterity and poise to pick up new tunes and deliver them with instinctive rhythm. It's in his genes. Harley played Mississippi delta blues in his youth but can vamp and harmonize wonderfully on his harp. The overall effect was glorious. Callum stood in front of the fire swaying back and forth as the rhythms of twenty generations of Scottish fiddlers coursed through his body.

We transitioned from The Rakes of Mallow into The White Cockade, Kate Dalrymple then finished with a stumbling attempt at The Irish Washerwoman. That one is in 6/8 time and goes at a breakneck pace. I usually love playing it but tonight the title of the tune reminded me of the crinkled skin on Myra Garfield's dead fingers. The contrast to Callum's nimble warm digits flying up and down the fiddle neck got to me.

While Callum got himself ready for bed I scooped a generous portion of Gaylene's casserole for Harley to take back to his house. Jennifer gave me a hasty goodnight kiss and disappeared to her room.

I said, "Want to stay for a night cap, Harley? Let me go tuck Callum in first."

Callum was sitting up in bed reading one of the Redwall books, and surrounded by a gigantic rubber rat, a furry headless troll and a bobble-head horned devil. He spends most of his allowance in

Archie McFee's gag store in Ballard. I regard it as a minor victory that he is not yet into rap music and hair gel. I'm sure that's coming. I tiptoed carefully across the minefield of Lego spaceships and soccer cleats that covered the floor. He laid down the book and talked to me in an earnest whisper.

"Dad, what's a cold frame?"

Mental agility is helpful for raising kids. "It's a kind of mini-greenhouse thing that gardeners use to protect plants from the frost in winter time. Why?"

"Harley says his spinach and kale are no good this year because his cold frame is rotted and broken. So I was thinking. We have to do a practical math project where we have to measure and build something. We've got to show all the calculations and plans and everything. Most people are doing boring old birdhouses or doghouses but I was wondering if you could help me make a new cold frame as a surprise for Harley. Taffy wouldn't use a doghouse anyway. He sleeps on Harley's bed."

"I would think a cold frame would be easy enough. Why don't you get my tape measure from the basement and take some measurements from the rotted cold frame tomorrow without letting Harley see you. We can sketch out a plan after school, okay? That's a great idea, Callum. You're very thoughtful."

The fire was low when I returned to the living room. I fixed Harley a bourbon and soda, got myself some scotch and put another log on the fire. The flickering flames cast shadows on the wrinkles of his forehead as he fixed me with a quizzical look.

He nodded towards the kitchen. "You've got woman problems, I can tell. You're not getting enough attention from the one you're interested in and getting too much attention from some others. Is that it?"

I said, "Gaylene Jarvis was the last straw. It has been a confusing day, that's for sure. Elspeth sent me a letter saying that she's discovered thorns on her new rose, so she thinks she might want to move back in with us. The next thing I know I bump into an old flame who still wants to connect with me. And then I meet a fascinating woman working the case today and I make a complete fool of myself trying to be suave and interesting."

I gave Harley an abbreviated account of my day, focusing on my inept conversations while glossing over the gory details of the case. Harley knows what I do for a living but shows no prurient interest in the particulars. He is not squeamish but has lived through enough pain, cruelty and violence himself. Nowadays he tries to focus on what goodness he can find in humanity.

He sipped his bourbon slowly and stroked Taffy's neck as I told my tale. "You want my opinion, Donald, you trying too hard to be suave and interesting. You're forcing things. That might work for teenagers trying to show off, testing out a new image of themselves every couple of months. But the women you're around don't want that. You're still blaming yourself for Elspeth leaving. You're thinking there's a problem with you. Like you're not interesting enough. You're not enough fun when you get down and dirty. That you got to be more wild and unpredictable. But that's not you, Donald, and it wouldn't of kept Elspeth anyway. I've watched her ever since you guys moved in next to me. She's got this need to keep moving on, to have new men keep reassuring her that they find her attractive. It's not going to make her happy in the long run but there ain't nothing you can do about it. You need to let go of her and move on.

"The strain's showing on you, buddy. You got the look of a hunted man, unsure which way to turn, forgotten how to stand tall. Makes you vulnerable. Women can sense when a man's lost his confidence. Some of them, like Gaylene Jarvis, wants to scoop you up and mother you but that's not what you need. Maybe your old girlfriend picked up on those things, too, but she sounds like one to avoid.

"I like the sound of this Katy, though. A detective, you say? She's got some fire in her belly, that one. Maybe she already got a man but maybe not. You should find out. Maybe she's looking for one. If she is, she don't want some troubled woose pretending to be what he ain't. You're a good man, Donald McLure. I just got to look at how well Callum and Jennifer are doing to know that. And Andy, too, except he's gone. You already launched him and you're a big part of why he's such a fine young man. But you're no gigolo. Trying to be suave and worrying about three or four women at once is not your style. You need to keep your life simpler and good things will happen.

"Now is there a world shortage of bourbon or something or do I have to enlighten you on the subjects of politics, religion and baseball before you'll give me another hit of this stuff?"

MONDAY

94

VII

The Dell

I usually look forward to Monday mornings more than most folk. My work is stimulating, varied, worthwhile, and I have great colleagues. Heading south on the Alaskan Way Viaduct after a pep talk from Harley and a good night's sleep I should have been in a great mood. I even have an easy commute by Seattle standards. It's a straight shot over the Aurora Bridge, under the Battery Street tunnel and onto the viaduct, which snakes along the downtown waterfront and past the football and baseball stadiums.

There's always talk about tearing the Alaskan Way Viaduct down. The argument is that it is so old and cracked that it won't be able to stand another earthquake. The lobbyists are mostly rich condo owners who think it spoils their million-dollar view out across Elliott Bay towards the Olympics. I hope they don't succeed. The elevated roadway gives impoverished romantics like me a breathtaking vista on our way to work. At least on most days it does.

This morning, looking out from the lower level of the elevated roadway, the view to the west was a study in depression. It was like a vast canvas painted by Mark Rothko on a day when he had a hangover and was contemplating suicide. A gray featureless monochrome extended from the drizzling clouds above to the flat oily water below. Horizontal slabs of pavement and crumbling concrete columns broke the vista into rectangles of drab uniformity. It was not a scene to cheer the soul for the week I had ahead.

I crossed the West Seattle Bridge and stopped at Tully's for some caffeine to jolt me into a better humor. If I was chairing the interdepartmental staff meeting in less than an hour I would need to fake it better than this. I cut through some side streets onto Delridge Way and pulled into the rear parking lot of the four-storey glass and concrete cube that has been my place of work for the past several months. The small sign above the public entrance says, "State of Washington Combined Criminal Investigation Facility," but everyone who deals with it refers to it as "The Dell." Its unprepossessing public façade belies its political significance. This building was what won the election for the current governor of the Evergreen State.

The hot button issues during the governor's race that year included fears about rising crime, worries about police corruption, and suspicion that police crime labs were biased and sloppily run. Radio talk show hosts produced statistics showing that the solve rate for major crimes in Washington State was among the worst in the nation. Candidate Ron Eckhart upstaged his rivals by saying he would fund a bold initiative to fix all these problems in one elegant move. His administration would build the CCIF to symbolize the new approach to major crime. It would combine state-of-the-art forensic science laboratories and a medical examiner's suite in the same building. It would be staffed by the best and the brightest, including forensic pathologists with affiliation to the University of Washington and paid for by state dollars. Coordination with Efficiency. Integration with Integrity. Those were the rhyming couplets, which peppered his campaign stump speech.

The facility was built in the first two years after his election and had been up and running for only a few months. But with re-election only fifteen months away, pressure was growing for Governor Eckhart's office in Olympia to produce a report showing how successful the CCIF had been.

I had been successful in applying for the new position as scientific director at the Dell just four months ago. After eight years of bench research in molecular biology I had tired of the grant-writing treadmill that dominated my life at Pacific Northwest Research Associates. The brutal murder of my colleague Balfour Dalgetty at Slate Creek Lodge was the final straw. I felt soured with academic life. I hungered to get back to the gritty day-to-day reality of forensic pathology where I could apply my knowledge to help solve crimes. It was a decision that I did not regret.

I managed to get to my office before anyone saw me. Jogging up the back stairs two at a time I slipped through the halls soaking up the comforting cacophony of science. Whirring centrifuges mingled with laughter and whistling. The air was redolent with organic solvents and fresh-brewed coffee, floor polish and the smell of new vinyl. The clean hard edges of the lab benches contrasted with the soft soothing splash of the water baths. Blinking lights from automated analyzers flickered in my peripheral vision. The hum and vacuum suck of freezer doors vibrated across my skin. All around me I heard throats clearing and chairs scraping as weekend adventures were recounted.

I closed my door quietly and moved over to the window. As scientific director, I get a corner office on the fourth floor. It gives me a distant view of the West Seattle golf course. Even at eight thirty on a dreary February morning I could see a few masochists duffing and hacking their way up the fairways. Watching their hunched shoulders and angry gestures while I cradled my warm latte had me feeling better in no time.

The staff meeting was at nine, which gave me less than half an hour to skim the surface of my e-mail and voice mail. I booted up the computer and found the neat pile of papers which the temporary administrative assistant, had placed on my chair. She was not long out of college, and I had already determined that the young woman was not cut out for this line of work. She didn't like to touch anything in my room and spent as much time as she could in her own little cubicle outside. She complained that there was never any room on my desk, which is true, but I think her real problem was that she really didn't like to be near all those symbols of death. I'm not sure what she was expecting when she accepted the assignment. As a pathologist I am fascinated by the changes brought about by death and disease. The shelves around the room are lined with bell jars and glass bottles filled with grim details of death bobbing around in formalin. Some of the smaller jars make great paperweights.

Her list was mercifully brief; the agenda for the staff meeting, confirmation of my hotel accommodation for the conference in Portland and a couple of phone messages, all neatly clipped together. There was a yellow Post-it note stuck on the computer screen. I recognized the flamboyant handwriting of Gina Fernandez.

"The perp's truck should be EASY to identify!"

I removed the note from the screen and stuck it onto the meeting agenda as a reminder to ask Gina what she meant.

There were about sixty new e-mails for me, which is fairly typical for a weekend off. I'm on lots of political and administrative group lists so could delete about half of those without opening them. Scanning the rest I opened one from the governor's office in Olympia. The CCIF report was due on his desk no later than Friday. I was to appear in person before his blue ribbon advisory panel two weeks after that. The message stopped short of calling it a pre-election-campaign-tactical-summit but that's what it was.

A footnote to the memo said that the composition of the advisory panel had changed due to the retirement of some CEO or other. The new roster was shown in the attached Word document. I skipped that part and moved on to another e-mail. In retrospect I wish I hadn't been so hasty. If I had looked at the list of board members it might have given me insights that would have saved a lot of misery. And lives.

An abrasive e-mail from the conference organizer in Portland confirmed the title, time and room location for my lecture, before reminding me that I still hadn't sent in my registration or faculty disclosure forms. That was enough for me. I logged off and turned my attention to the blinking light on my phone. I had three voice mails. The first two were administrative trivia. The last was from Linda Munro. Sent late last night, the stress in her voice was palpable.

"Donald, it's Linda. I'm sorry to call so late. I didn't want to call you at home and leave a message that your family might hear. The nursing home called to say mother has taken a turn for the worse. She's yelling, hallucinating, upsetting the other patients and they've had to sedate her. I'm sure something has upset her. I'm going to visit her tomorrow and I was wondering if you'd mind coming with me. You were a real doctor before you went into pathology, weren't you? I know I shouldn't ask but I thought maybe if you had to be back on the island for your investigation anyway maybe you wouldn't mind." There was a pause, as if she was trying to think up some more compelling arguments. "Sebastian says he won't come with me to the nursing home anymore, Donald. He's been quite cold and hostile, recently. He's no support at all, really. I don't know what's going on. I just want some company when I see mother."

There was something odd about this. I had severed almost all contact with her after The Hot Tub Incident and that was three years ago. We had exchanged perfunctory Christmas cards since then, nothing more. And yet here she was imposing on me as if we were best friends. I began to make a mental list of plausible excuses not to go to the nursing home when the temporary assistant popped her head inside the door to tell me that everyone else was in the conference room waiting for me.

The staff meeting went well. We all get along pretty well and avoid petty turf wars. I spotted Keith Jepson, the medical examiner who should have taken the Garfield case. He was looking healthy and fit as he chatted to the young man next to him. I could tell by the body language they were having guy-talk, recounting the play-by-play of a recent sporting event, sexual conquest, or juicy case they were involved in. I stifled my jealousy. It certainly wouldn't take me long to recount my recent sexual conquests. If you blinked you'd miss it.

We spent most of the meeting time discussing the Olympia summit. I asked for reports, graphs and tables to show not only our overall productivity at the Dell but to emphasize areas where "departmental overlap had been seamless." Jepson quipped that the Governor was sure to borrow that phrase for his upcoming election campaign. It had sound bite written all over it.

I cornered Gina as she was leaving the conference room. "I give up. What will make the truck ID so easy?"

Her warm open smile held a touch of mischief. "The marks on the grass were made by old tires. From a light truck. There is uneven wear and tear on the treads. Unique features. Real unusual fact is they are not both same brand. One tire is Michelin. The rear passenger side, I think. The rest are all Goodyear. Unless he is changing all the tires since the weekend it should be easy to find a match."

"Unless the guy lives a hundred miles away and has already gone home," I said. Gina looked disappointed. "But that's great, Gina. It'll make it easier for the police. Do you have a report I can give to Officer Pearson when she gets here?"

101

"Sure I do. I know just the way Katy likes it. One page summary with photos of the scene and the original plaster casts."

"You've worked with her before, then? Tell me about her, Gina. What's she like?"

"What you mean what's she like? Didn't you just spend all day with her yesterday?"

"Yes, but she seemed kind of distant. Unfriendly, even. I just wondered if she's always like that."

Gina Fernandez is probably less than ten years my senior but she cut through my smoke screen like I was just another of her clumsy teenage boys. "You wondering if she's single and available, Doctor McLure? Did she maybe just fall out with her boyfriend or something?" I blushed and tried to change the subject but I was too late. "You were wondering that, I think. I made you embarrassed. I can picture you and Katy together, though. Definitely. Katy Pearson is a very nice woman. Kind, thoughtful, very bright. Maybe you just got her on a bad day. She's not so happy right now. Under a lot of pressure. Doesn't have enough fun."

"Why's that?"

"Ha! Only a successful man could ask that. You think it's easy being a female homicide cop in a big city like this? She has to prove she's better than all the men."

"Everyone I talk to says she's great. Very competent."

"They all say nice things but when it comes to case assignment and promotion then we'll see."

"And you think she needs to get more fun, Gina? But you think everyone should have more fun in their life."

Her husky laugh echoed down the hall. "Sure they should. Everyone except my husband, that is. He has had way too much fun already. We got nine kids. But Katy she's having a hard time with her ex."

Gina might have said more but Rusty Bellagio rushed up, followed by Joe Wysocki, our senior microscopist.

"We got significant traces of alcohol and marijuana from the femoral blood sticks on the Garfield case, Donald. If you get me a good sample from the stomach contents I'll run that through the GCMS this afternoon. Ten bucks says those levels will be even higher. The GCMS never lies."

The Gas Chromatograph Mass Spectrometer is indeed a useful machine. It can break down unidentifiable pieces of dirt and powder into their chemical components and display them by quantity and molecular size. It can identify which flammable accelerant an arsonist used by examining the ashes of a fire. It can find traces of explosives or methylamphetamines from the dust on the walls of an abandoned meth lab. But Joseph Wysocki was less impressed than I was. He stood behind Rusty shaking his head with scorn.

"Listen to him, Donald. All that unfounded faith in machines. The only thing they seem to teach these youngsters how to do in science labs nowadays is to dilute and shoot. Grind up the evidence, dissolve it and inject it into a machine and then measure the size of the peaks it prints out. And if it's calibrated wrong you've not only got meaningless data, you've destroyed your evidence in the process. Come over here and let me show you something more interesting than Rusty's GCMS report."

Joe is from the old school. Tall and stooped with half-moon glasses perched on his thin curved nose he looks like someone who spends half his life staring down a microscope. His high forehead, thick white hair, bow tie and suspenders add to his professorial demeanor. He studied under Walter McCrone in Chicago, the guru of modern forensic microscopy. With the tails of his lab coat flowing behind him, Joe led us to a quiet corner of his lab where several microscopes were already set up for us.

"Tell me what you see in there boys. Go on, you can both look at once. I attached the dual eye-piece this morning."

"What is it I'm looking at, Joe?" I said, adjusting the focus. "It looks like the blighted scene after a volcanic eruption with tree trunks and boulders scattered around."

"Not a bad description, Donald, but what's odd about the boulders?"

"They're all the same size," I said.

"Good. What do they remind you of?"

Rusty chimed in. "Ball-bearings. Except that they can't be. No one uses microscopic ball bearings, do they?"

Joe beamed with self-satisfaction. "There's hope for you yet, Rusty. What you are looking at is the grit and fibers we removed from the hot tub filters. Those tree trunks are nylon carpet fibers, Donald. I've got a few more fibers set up under indirect illumination on this other microscope. And those little ball bearings are classic. They are made by the sparks from an oxyacetylene torch. Welding equipment. You've seen sparks flying when they are putting up new steel framework for buildings, I'm sure. Those sparks are molten metal. When they cool down they form perfect little metal spheres. Was the victim's body found on the ground near some new construction?"

"No, but she could have been moved and dumped into the hot tub," I said.

Joe continued his recitation. "We also found a few hairs with traces of pigment on them, some tiny flecks of zinc and a couple of strands of fiber glass. The pink kind that they use for these rolls of wall insulation. And the great thing is we don't destroy the evidence. I can keep these slides for years for future analysis if we need to." He punched Rusty playfully in the stomach and strode off down the hall. "I'll put my report on your desk along with photographs at a couple of different magnifications."

The office next to mine belongs to Keith Jepson. As I passed he had his feet up on his desk and was leaning back in his chair with the phone tucked under his chin. Something about the raunchy chuckles told me this was not a business call.

"You're a hell of a fast healer," I said loudly.

He mumbled a sheepish farewell and hung up. "What's that supposed to mean?"

"Less that twenty-four hours ago I was told you were sick as a dog, laid up with the 'flu, on your death bed."

He rubbed his throat and faked a little hoarseness. "It was pretty bad for a while there, actually. I've still got a sore throat and I ache everywhere but I thought I'd better come in to help out. I know how busy we're going to be with the extra reports to do as well as extra cases. I don't think I'm contagious anymore. Thanks for helping me out yesterday, Donald. I just lay around all day and pampered myself. Stephanie came over for a while, too, which was great."

That was it. Stephanie was the name of his latest conquest. A nurse at Harborview, I think.

"Yes, I'm sure she gave you some great physical therapy, Keith," I said, walking back to my own office.

"Come on, I thought you'd be thanking me. I hear you got Katy Pearson on the case. That ought to have put a smile on your face. It's pleasing having her around."

106

"It's pleasing because she's a sharp, conscientious investigator. I try not to mix work with my love life." I sounded like a prig.

Jepson always likes the last word. He yelled, "You're just jealous, McLure. At least I've got a love life!"

I was formulating a witty come back when a female cough got my attention. Katy Pearson stood in the door looking more amused than embarrassed.

"You did say the autopsy would be at eleven o'clock didn't you? Did I just miss something interesting?"

Another homicide detective stood beside her, a leering testosterone advert called Tucker. His bulging arms, chest and belly strained the buttons on his shirt. Prematurely balding with a ruddy, round face, he looked like a high school linebacker gone to seed. Judging by the smirk on his face he had enjoyed Jepson's parting shot.

I addressed myself to Katy. "I'm sure Officer Tucker might enjoy getting all the juicy details of Dr. Jepson's weekend, but I think it might be more enlightening for you to come and see what Myra Garfield has to tell us in the basement."

I know that was petty. I sounded like a humorless prude. A pompous workaholic. I should cut Jepson some slack. He is a good medical examiner. I was just jealous. At least he had a love life.

VIII

Dead Useful Information

George Dempsey, the senior mortuary attendant, was talking to a local funeral director when we all trooped through his office towards the changing rooms. A diminutive chain-smoking Irishman, he likes to thicken his brogue when newcomers are around.

"We're all set up at the center table today, Professor McLure. Should give you plenty of room for all your guests, I'm thinking."

The autopsy suite at The Dell is in the basement. White tile floors slope gently towards several large floor drains. Three stainless steel tables are set up in the center of the room. A large set of scales and an electrical outlet extension cord hangs above the foot of each. Sinks, shelves and metal cabinets line the walls. Trolleys of dissecting equipment and surgical tools stand ready in the corners, covered in green towels. It is all very practical. Very traditional. The only untraditional feature is that this is the first cutting room I've ever been in where there aren't exposed ceiling pipes clanking and shedding asbestos onto my head as I lean over the body.

We were all suited up and standing round the gleaming table when Dempsey wheeled in the body bag. With a dark sense of theater he bowed to me, deferential acolyte to sacrificial priest. I must admit that the set-up does lend itself to flights of imagination, a cross between a butcher's shop and a devil-worshipping church.

Dempsey broke the illusion. "Is there only the three extra people attending, then? I could have used the end table and saved myself the trouble."

There are often more people in attendance, especially on a Monday morning. Medical students or surgical interns from Harborview ER sometimes stand in. If they are close to an arrest the police often bring along a prosecutor from the district attorney's office. There was none today. Dempsey and I were in blue surgical scrubs with plastic aprons over the top. Katy Pearson, Machoman Tucker, and Rusty Bellagio wore green guest scrubs. All of us made a hooded, gloved and masked circle around the table onto which Myra Garfield's body bag was placed.

Rusty Bellagio and Jeff Tucker looked pale as Dempsey unzipped the body bag with a flourish and I helped him unwrap the white sheet leaving Myra Garfield lying on the slab. I was surprised at their squeamishness. This was one of the easiest corpses you were ever likely to get to look at. She was already naked and clean, freshly dead, almost unblemished. Peeling stinking clothes from a partially decomposed body is a lot less palatable.

Whistling "When Irish Eyes are Smiling" as he wheeled over the instrument trolley Dempsey jostled past the guests to bring the cart round to my side of the table. He threw off the towel like a matador. "Step right up, gents. The show is about to begin. Oh, pardon me, Officer Pearson, were you thinking I didn't recognize you? Even after the half a bottle of Jameson's I had last night there's not many men couldn't tell it was a woman under those scrubs."

Tucker guffawed loudly. Locker room etiquette suited him. At least Rusty made some attempt to stifle his laughter. With the lower half of her face covered by the mask I couldn't interpret the look in Katy's eyes. I gave her a long-suffering sigh. It would be a long morning if George Dempsey was in this kind of mood.

Inspecting the body for additional evidence is a painstaking business. Her hair had dried a bit, but the luster of youth still shone through, even in death. As I sifted through the silky strands I found another green carpet fiber and a long coarse pale brown hair that wasn't hers. Each item got dropped into a separate evidence bag, which Rusty held open. I was picking up grit and fibers stuck in the abrasions under her breast when it dawned on me what they might represent.

"Can you get Gina for me on the overhead intercom, George? Katy, who do we know in this case who owns a pickup truck? I wonder if she was dumped in a truck bed and acquired these abrasions when she was dragged out."

Although I spoke to Katy it was Tucker who pushed past her and leaned over the body for a closer look. He grunted, which I took to mean he wasn't convinced. Dempsey pointed to the ceiling to let me know that Gina was listening in.

"Gina, how different are the patterns of truck beds, in terms of how wide the ridges are and how far apart? Do you have a book that can compare Ford Rangers versus F-series, Chevies, Toyotas and so forth?"

Gina's voice crackled through the ceiling speaker. "I think they have that stuff on the Vehicle Identification Unit website. I'll check."

The weight and length of the body were noted. Dempsey handed me the portable ultraviolet light source and plugged it in to the dangling extension cord. We use this to scan the body surface for deposits of semen, which show up as fluorescent lilac blotches like starchy wallpaper paste. As I expected we found none today. Even if a dozen perverted gang-bangers had ejaculated all over her, several hours in the hot tub would have washed away all the evidence. The techs might find traces in the hot tub filters but there would be nothing left on the surface of the body. I pried open her mouth and commented to the onlookers as I squinted inside. Perfect teeth, no trauma, no semen.

She had several ring holes in both ears, her left eyebrow, and one above her navel but no jewelry had been found on the body. That struck me as a little odd if she had been going out on a date. Her pubic hair was perfectly trimmed and shaved leaving a neat central stripe. There was a small Playboy rabbit head tattoo that would be hidden below her panties. I wondered if her parents knew about that. It was all incredibly sad.

I found no semen in her anus but got a sizeable amount from the high vaginal swab.

"You'll want this to go to the DNA lab, won't you, Katy?" I said.

It was irritating Tucker that I addressed all my comments to Katy Pearson. He answered before her. "Course we do, Doc. I already checked to make sure they were setting up digests and gels on the sample we got from Klein."

Digests and gels, indeed. What Jeff Tucker knew about the lab procedures for DNA isolation could be written on a pinhead. He had obviously picked up a few random sciency-words from somewhere. I could tell that his comments were being said for Katy's benefit as much as mine. A few years her senior he was declaring his experience. Establishing his authority.

I untied the paper bag from Myra Garfield's right hand. Dempsey took it from me and silently handed me a blunt scalpel. He knew the routine. With her dying efforts she might have scratched or clawed at something or someone. There are often traces to be found under the nails. Unless someone has already scraped them clean.

"Has someone already done the nail scrapes?" I turned an accusing look at Dempsey, whose fiery temper is as legendary as my own.

112

He bristled with Celtic indignation. "Of course not. Do you think any of us would risk incurring your imperial wrath?" He inspected the two body tags on her ankle. "Mr. Bellagio here tagged her at the crime scene and I checked her into the locker room my own self. She's been in the drawer ever since."

"Well someone has. I can see some traces of blood and a few flecks of metal, as if someone already ran a sharp instrument under each nail to clean them out."

I found the same thing on her left hand. The toes and feet were untouched. It was unsettling and suggested a level of sophistication and knowledge that you don't see in your average rapist or murderer. I carefully scraped out what tissue I could get from her nail beds, placed it in sterile containers, and specified that I wanted DNA analysis on it.

I said, "It is a quarter past noon. Anyone want to stop for lunch before we open her up? I'd just as soon keep going."

Machoman Tucker slumped off, mumbling that he would find out how many of the victim's friends drove a truck. Everyone else stayed. I stood to stretch my back and walked to the dictating machine, which I have mounted on one of the columns using duct tape so that it's at my head height. It's a clumsy arrangement but means I can dictate as I go along. One of the secretaries picks it up as soon as I'm done. Some days the typed report is on my desk by the time I have showered and changed clothes. Coordination with Efficiency. Governor Eckhart would be pleased.

The others stood around quietly while I recounted the routine procedures - bagging, numbering, cataloguing the details. In some ways methodical routines make the whole procedure seem less important. They trivialize and dehumanize the process. But they are also important to follow to ensure that nothing gets screwed up.

Gutting the body is particularly crude and uncompromising. The initial cut is from shoulder to shoulder across the chest and then from neck to pubis cutting through the sternum. With the bone saw screaming like a dentist's drill the smell of burning flesh and bone is pretty hard to take. I asked Dempsey to turn up the air conditioner and started reminiscing to distract the onlookers.

"It's a funny word, 'dead,'" I said. "Growing up in Scotland kids used to use the word 'dead' as a synonym for very. They'd say, 'That spelling test was dead easy,' or 'You got a bike for Christmas? You're dead lucky, so you are!' I remember years later, listening to a pompous professor lecturing in the forensic class in Edinburgh on how useful the information was from a post mortem examination. Someone from the back of the class yelled, 'Aye, so it is, professor. It's dead useful!' He meant it as a joke but of course he was right. In skilled hands the information we gain from examining the dead can be incredibly useful."

In this case the cause of death was confirmed the moment I pried apart the sternum and looked into the chest cavity. Pale overinflated lungs began bulging out to greet me. They crackled under my hands like bubble-wrap packing and were grooved along their outer surface due to the impression left from the ribs against which they had pressed in her last few moments of life. Using blunt dissection with my hands and a few careful cuts I removed both lungs, connected by their main bronchi and trachea, and handed them to Dempsey. He received them as eagerly as an expectant new father being handed a newborn baby by the obstetrician. With a theatrical flourish he plopped the soggy mess onto the scales.

"Fourteen hundred eighty five grams," he announced proudly.

Katy's eyes met mine for explanation.

"In a girl of this size the total lung weight should be well under a kilogram," I said. "These have all the hallmarks of drowning; overinflation, crepitus, rib-notching."

I grabbed a knife and stepped to the side table where George Dempsey had laid the lungs on a dissection slab. I sliced carefully through one lung, exposing the inside of the bronchial tubes and trachea. The passages were filled with grayish white foam, flecked with blood. There were no foreign bodies in the airways, no soot or cancer in the spongy lung material. Just two young healthy lungs filled with the cold water of death instead of warm air and joy. Unutterably sad.

Her heart looked normal. I pierced the ventricle to get a large blood sample for toxicology. Her liver was perfect with no signs of cirrhosis or necrosis. Before I opened the stomach, I asked for the air conditioning to be turned off. I removed my mask and bent forward for a sniff. In the heat of summer this maneuver would produce complaints from Dempsey or others in the room, but on a cold February day it didn't make the atmosphere too much worse. It brought back memories of my Edinburgh University days and pub-crawls along Rose Street. Weaving your way home you had to be careful to avoid the numerous piles of vomit that you came across on the street corners. The smell of gastric contents laced with alcohol is very distinctive. I smelled it again today.

I said, "This looks like a sandwich and french fries. She doesn't chew her food very well. I'm not sure what the meat is. Chicken maybe."

"Impressive," Katy said. She seemed more relaxed now that Tucker was gone. I was glad to see the improvement in her mood.

"Impressive? Because I can correctly identify vomited food? That's the first thing I've done in two days that has impressed you, Officer Pearson."

The skin above the mask and around her big brown eyes flushed. She looked much softer. More human. She wasn't about to give up her position of superiority over me just yet, however.

She said, "I meant that it would fit. Pitman talked to some of Myra's friends this morning. They said they ate at Zoomies on Vashon with Myra on Friday night. They left her there at about five thirty, since she was going to be meeting Aaron Klein. Myra bought a grilled chicken breast sandwich and had eaten about half of it by the time her friends left."

I was still squinting into the soupy contents of Myra Garfield's half-dissected stomach. "There's some other stuff in here, too. I can't quite place the smell but it's got a medicinal tang to it. Get me some glass containers, please, Rusty. Let's send some of this to toxicology. I think I'll let Joseph look at it under the microscope, too."

I palpated her ovaries, fallopian tubes and uterus. A sharp scalpel opened them to show no signs of pregnancy and no IUD. I plunged a sixteen-gauge needle into her bladder to drain the contents and sent that off to the Tox lab, too. Certain drugs concentrate in the urine and so that might help.

The rest of the autopsy revealed nothing unexpected. Rusty took the various samples to the appropriate labs. I left George to stitch up the body and went to shower and change. Katy was waiting for me as I left the changing room. Joe Wysocki was with her.

I said, "Joe, could you tell if the girl's clothes had ever been worn, or had come straight out of her closet at home?"

"I might. They were in a neat pile, you said. Which item was on the bottom?"

"Why does that matter?" Katy asked.

Joe said, "If someone brought those clothes and laid them on the deck they had to transport them somehow. If they were lying on the front passenger seat of a car on in a car's trunk then the article of clothing that was on the bottom may have picked up something that could help identify where they've been. The green carpet fiber you found on the body matches the one stuck in the filter, by the way. Nylon carpet with identical refractory index. The grit is more welding debris. The pink fiber looks like another strand of fiber glass – the kind you get in those rolls of insulation."

Jeff Tucker joined us looking annoyed that he might have missed something. He announced that the Covingtons had an old truck they kept on the island in the garage but that it had a dead battery. The Kleins didn't have a truck. Tami Stillwell's stepdad, Frank, had an old beater. It hadn't been at the house when we were there yesterday but Sheriff Pitman said it would be there that afternoon. Tucker left shortly afterwards, taking Joe with him.

"Is he your sidekick on this case?" I said to Katy.

She winced. "Jeff Tucker is nobody's sidekick. He's got three years seniority on me so acts like he's in charge even though he only got involved this morning."

"You don't get along?"

"He woke me at six a.m. to say the chief wanted him to be my babysitter. To make sure I didn't break the departmental budget on one simple accidental drug death. It's hard to get along with someone who acts like that."

"What's with all the budgetary comments?" I asked.

"My guess is that Pitman called someone above me to complain that it was unnecessary to use the Olympia fingerprint lab and the

Total Station Crew for an accidental drug death."

"But you saw what we found this morning, Katy. There's a whole lot more going on here than that."

She smiled. "Even Jeff Tucker has figured that much out. That's why he's so pissed."

"What will you do now?"

"Mr. and Mrs. Garfield are back from Lake Tahoe. I'm going to interview them and also Mossandrian, Skunk Bucket's infamous base player. How about you?"

"I'm lecturing in Portland in the next couple of days so I need to clear things up around here. But I'd really like to check on a couple of details. I'd like to look at Frank Stillwell's truck for myself."

"You're going back to Vashon, too?" She looked surprised. And possibly even pleased.

I said, "Don't worry, I have my own transportation today. I can keep out of your way."

"No, that's fine. It's just that I thought you would send Rusty Bellagio or one of the other techs for that work."

"I like to stay involved and share the field work with them. It improves my credibility with them and builds rapport. Keeps us all close. Besides, I just remembered where I recently saw some welding equipment and green carpet. In the barn at the Stillwell's place. And didn't Sonya Stillwell mention that Frank was doing construction that involved putting in insulation and roofing. Correct me if I'm wrong but don't they use fiberglass for insulation and galvanized nails to tack down roofing felt?"

IX

Hostile Possibilities

There was hair growing from the roof of the Stillwell's trailer, the testosterone level in the air was so high. Two green and white King County Police Department cruisers and the sheriff's Jeep were parked in front of the barn, along with one of the forensics vans from the Dell. Two men from the van were examining a truck parked in front of the trailer. I drive a dented ten-year-old Ford Ranger but this one made mine look in pristine condition.

It was clear I had arrived in the middle of an argument. A young uniformed officer, Sheriff Gary Pitman and Detective Jeff Tucker surrounded a tall angry man who pointed at the truck.

"Come on you guys. Surely you don't need to impound my damned truck. How am I supposed to make a living? I'm a contractor, for God sakes. I need my truck."

He was a handsome stud, despite the sneer, and looked like he had just walked off the set of a cowboy movie. He would have played the hot-tempered ranch hand or the Mexican freedom-fighter, maybe. Six foot two or three, lean, muscular and fit, wearing tight blue jeans and well-worn cowboy boots, his eyes blazed at the police officers. Swarthy tanned skin, chiseled features, wavy black hair going gray at the temples and a thick jet-black moustache completed the image. Very photogenic.

I kept well clear of the argumentative quartet and moved towards the truck. The purple Cadillac was gone, I noticed, and the two llamas were huddled at the far end of their paddock. They too wanted to avoid the hostility.

One of the forensic scientists working on the truck recognized me. "This truck's tires match the tracks that Gina Fernandez got, Doctor McLure. Michelin on the right rear, Goodyear on the left. And we have two good latents on the side rail of the truck bed that match Aaron Klein's."

That last comment surprised me. I moved over to look inside the truck bed. Jeff Tucker peeled away from the other group and jogged over to intercept me.

"Careful you don't touch anything there, Scotty. We don't want to screw up the evidence."

I couldn't believe my ears. "Detective Tucker, I'm the guy who gives most of the lectures and workshops to gung-ho police officers like you on how to protect and treat a crime scene, remember?"

"Yeah, so I've heard. You're really long on theory. You write papers and give lectures. I wasn't sure if you knew the practical stuff, though. No offense." His grinning face told me he was delighted at the offense I had taken.

Don't rise to the bait, I told myself. "Who's that doing all the yelling over there?" I said.

"Frank Stillwell. He's the father of one of the kids who found the body. He's ticked off because we're going to impound the vehicle."

"Is he a suspect then?"

"No, he has a decent alibi for Friday night. He and his wife and their little kid took their other car, and were gone all evening. She and the kid were at a pottery class somewhere on Vashon. Big Franko, there, went bowling over in West Seattle, so this place was empty and the truck was left here. And get this. He leaves it in the driveway with the keys in the ignition. Says he does it all the time. "This is Vashon Island," he says. "Who's going to steal a goddamn beater of a truck?""

I said, "He's probably right. It's not very likely, though I suppose kids might steal it."

"Not only might, one of them did. Aaron Klein. Stillwell kind of knows the kid. Says he let's Klein borrow the truck to haul lawnmowers and stuff for his gardening jobs, so long as big Frank doesn't need it for himself. So guess what? We find Klein's prints on the side of the truck. We find tire tracks that put this truck at the crime scene. And it's Klein's sperm that's dribbling out the dead girl's crotch. Ta dah! We got the little bastard."

I am no prude, but I found Tucker disgusting. I said, "You've got a great way with words, Detective Tucker, but surely there are other possibilities. We still haven't explained the abrasions on the girl's chest, the discrepancy about what clothes she was wearing, the-"

"Are we moving a little too fast for you, Doc? Were you hoping to string this one out for a bit longer? Hoping to go into things with our Katy... in depth? Yeah? Can't blame you there. But we've got to move on. We don't need to use up precious resources on a simple case like this. You can go ahead and take your measurements from the truck now, if you're quick, or back at the Vehicle ID unit where it's going. I'll leave young Officer Sherbourg here for your protection in case Stillwell goes ballistic. Gary Pitman and me are going to arrest Klein."

There is no point in responding to a bully. I was seething from his insults and innuendo but tried to stay calm. "Everything you've got is circumstantial. Klein admits that he and the girl had sex. If Stillwell let him borrow the truck from time to time then it's not surprising his prints are on it and since we know he does gardening at the Covingtons it's maybe not such a surprise that there were tire marks on the grass."

"That's not how I see it, Doc." He began to walk away.

"Where's Officer Pearson?" I said.

"The lovely Ms. Pearson? I sent her off to break the news to Mr.

124

and Mrs. Garfield. You know, console them, hold their hands, get them a clean box of tissues. Girl's work. And it frees up the rest of the department to handle a bunch of other cases."

Tucker swaggered slowly back to his squad car. He had to swing each leg out so that his bulging thigh muscles could pass each other without chafing. He was in his element, here. Winning wasn't enough, it was the gloating and taunting he got off on. He had made his great Defensive play, rushing from the blind side, sacking the wimpy intellectual quarterback. Now he could rub my face in the dirt while he sauntered back to the huddle to design the next play. He waved over for Pitman to follow him.

I turned towards Frank Stillwell's truck so Tucker wouldn't see the anger on my face as he drove away. The technicians were done finger printing the outside and were working inside the cab. I slipped on my gloves and inspected the truck bed. An old plastic bed-liner was bolted to the floor. The distance between the ridges and the rough textured surface of the liner looked a perfect match for the abrasions on the dead girl's body. We would need to go over it carefully to pick up skin or blood traces but I was pretty sure we would find some. In the corners of the truck bed were some Styrofoam cups, a couple of bungee cords, loose nails, leaves and dirt. Three metal tubes about four feet in length had been welded onto each side of the truck to increase the depth. A longer piece was welded on the top of each vertical tube, running the length of each side. All the metal work looked a much more recent vintage than the rest of the truck.

I collected samples of grit from the truck bed and held the

plastic bag up to the light. There were tiny round balls of metal and a few pink fibers among it. I'm not a gambling man but I was willing to bet this grit would match the samples we had found on Myra Garfield's body and in the hot tub filters. It wasn't much of a stretch to conclude that this was indeed the truck in which Myra Garfield's body was carried. I handed the bag of grit to the senior tech and asked them to vacuum and scrape the passenger seat and floor to see if anything unique could be found that might match the clothing found at the crime scene.

Frank Stillwell was strutting around the yard like a rooster, talking into a cell phone while Officer Sherbourg stood nearby. Stillwell snapped the phone shut and strode towards me.

"You can tell your boss that I've been able to borrow a friend's truck for a couple of days so I'll manage to stay in business. I'm sure he'll be real happy and relieved to hear that. He seemed real concerned about the impact you're all having on my life. How long you gonna need to keep my truck, anyway?"

"Mr. Stillwell, the man you spoke to is Officer Jeff Tucker and he is not my boss. My name is Donald McLure and I'm the medical examiner and senior forensic scientist working on this case. I would guess we'll need to keep the truck for a few days. It will depend on what else we find."

"You Australian or something?" His eyes narrowed. "Are you the foreign dude that spoke to Sonya yesterday?"

"I did speak to your wife yesterday and I'm Scottish, not

Australian."

"Whatever," he said, turning away.

Sherbourg smirked. He looked like Tucker's protégé - twenty-two going on sixteen, a muscle-head who spent most of his spare time in the gym. He would enjoy sharing Stillwell's comments about me with Tucker in the staff canteen.

Just then the Stillwell Cadillac arrived in the clearing, announcing its presence with a series of bumps, shudders and a loud backfire that made me jump. Sonya Stillwell clambered out nervously and began apologizing to Frank for the noise the car had made.

He interrupted her. "Don't park there, for God sakes. Move it over under the tree so that these jokers can finish up and leave without bothering us again. And come inside when you're done. We need to talk."

Now there's an ominous phrase. Anyone who has read any self-help books of the Saving-Your-Relationship variety will tell you that when a person says, "We need to talk," they are really saying, "You need to listen." Did Frank Stillwell want to coach his wife on what she should say before anyone asked more questions, I wondered? I peeled off my gloves and moved over to greet Sonya as she finished trying to re-park the car to her husband's satisfaction.

"Hello, Mrs. Stillwell. Sorry to be back bothering you again. I'm Doctor McLure from the forensic team. I was here yesterday with Officer Pearson. It looks as though someone stole or borrowed

Frank's truck last Friday night while you were gone and used it to transport Myra Garfield's body to the hot tub."

You would have thought I had just doused her in a bucket of iced water. She froze, with only her eyes darting past mine towards the trailer. Frank's bulk filled the doorway.

"I thought I told you to come inside," he yelled.

"Sorry Frank, I was just coming. Shall I leave the groceries in the car or bring them in now?"

Frank Stillwell's cheeks colored. I couldn't tell if it was from anger or embarrassment at the fact that a complete stranger was observing him acting like an obnoxious boor to his simpering and downtrodden wife. I opened the passenger door and grabbed the two brown Thriftway bags.

"I can bring these in for you, Mrs. Stillwell. I'd like to ask you both a few more questions."

I nodded to Officer Sherbourg to join us inside, hoping that the sight of his police uniform and youthful muscles might temper Frank Stillwell's belligerence.

"I'm sorry for the inconvenience this is causing you both, but it is looking increasingly likely that Myra Garfield was murdered and that her body was transported in the back of your truck, sometime on Friday night. I understand you were both gone that evening and so the perpetrator must have taken the truck then. I'm just trying to narrow down the time of death. Could you tell me again when you left, Mrs. Stillwell, and when you returned?"

Sonya Stillwell sat hunched up in an armchair. Her husband stood to one side and behind her. He had a hand laid on her shoulder, which gave the impression of him as a benevolent protector. Except that I could see from the whiteness of his knuckles that his fingers were digging into her flesh to deliver a very different message with that grip. She opened her mouth to reply but he cut her off.

"I already told all this to Tucker. We left here about five thirty and got back here again a little before midnight."

Sonya turned her head towards him, seeking reassurance. Or further instructions.

I said, "And you drove the Cadillac, I understand. Was Starflame with you? I'm surprised you took only one car if you were going to different places. Did Tami need the truck?"

Frank Stillwell seemed to hesitate, then spoke with measured care. "We only needed one car. Sonya's pottery class was up at the north end of the island at a friend's house where Star could play or nap. I dropped them off on my way to the ferry."

"You went bowling in West Seattle?" I said.

"I already said so."

"I can't get the hang of American bowling. Ten pin bowling you call it, is that right? In Scotland we play lawn bowling. Actually it's mostly older men who play it. It's kind of like playing giant marbles on a perfectly manicured lawn." Stillwell kept his face blank, unsure where I was going with all this. "You play in teams don't you? In leagues? Is there a team from one of the pubs here on Vashon?"

Frank Stillwell spat out his reply. "There isn't a bowling center on the island anymore. I play on my own or with whoever is available. I like bowling. It helps get rid of the tension I get dealing with assholes all week."

I met his gaze steadily. "You know, Mr. Stillwell, I don't really care if you put me in that category or not. I intend to stay as long as I need to, come back as often as I have to, and take as much time looking over your truck as is necessary to get to the bottom of this murder. I would appreciate it if you could lighten up your grip on your wife and allow her to answer a few of my questions."

He removed his hand and folded his arms across his chest. "Go ahead, Sonya."

"Where exactly was the pottery class?" I asked. She gave me an address near SW Cedarhurst Road, which I wrote down. It was somewhere near the northwest part of the island. "And when did Frank pick you up again?"

"Just after eleven, I think." She glanced over her shoulder as Frank nodded his approval.

"Eleven? That's a long pottery class," I said.

"Oh, the class I teach goes from six till eight but I stayed on, waiting for Frank. I do the class at a friend of mine's. She has a big barn and a good kiln. After everyone left I went for a walk to rebalance my energy. The classes are pretty intense. Fun, but you give out a lot of energy. I didn't mind Frank coming back so late, really I didn't. I just went for a walk and did some meditation."

"Where was Starflame during all this?" I asked.

"He had fallen asleep at Elsa's while I was doing the class. I just let him sleep on until Frank picked us up."

I said, "You got back home a little before midnight. Was the truck here then?" They nodded in unison. "Parked in the same place as when you left?"

Frank Stillwell's response was heavy with sarcasm. "Sure. Even though it was pitch dark I remember noticing that the truck was in front of the barn in the exact same spot where it always is. Sorry, maybe I should have gone to get my tape measure to compare how close to the door it was."

Sherbourg was enjoying all this. I ignored them both. "And was Tami home?"

Sonya spoke up. "No, Tami got home around one a.m., I think."

"I didn't hear her." Her husband made it sound like an

accusation.

"You were asleep, Frank, but I was still awake."

"Does Tami have her own car?" I asked.

Sonya answered, "No, but she has university classes in Seattle on Fridays. There's a good bus connection that brings you all the way from downtown Seattle over on the ferry and down the main highway to near our house. That's what Tami uses on Fridays. Except last Friday there was a dance at the high school she wanted to go to. A concert, really but I think they dance in front of the stage. Anyway, she said somebody gave her a ride home."

"So your truck was left unattended from five-thirty till just before midnight with the keys in the ignition."

Stillwell's hand returned to his wife's shoulder. "Vashon's a safe place, mister. A real community. People try to help each other out. If somebody wants to borrow another guy's truck it's no big deal. Ask around. Other people do it, too. Maybe nobody behaves like that in Australia or Scotland or wherever the hell you're from."

I said, "Did you give the police a list of people who might know that you leave the keys in your truck?"

"No I didn't. You know why? Because they didn't ask me. They seemed to believe my goddamn story and didn't insinuate that I might be involved in the girl's death the way you are."

"Nothing I have said in any way suggests…"

"It's like deja-frigging-vu. This whole damned thing is like a nightmare that won't go away. It's like now everyone is looking at me as though I'm Tami's evil stepdad now. You're talking to the wrong damned stepdad, mister. It's Clayton van Allen you should be talking to."

Sonya burst into tears. "Don't say that, Frank. He's out of our life forever. You're just upset."

I gave them a minute or two to compose themselves. "Mr. and Mrs. Stillwell, my questions have been designed to narrow down the time when your truck could have been involved in the murder. Nothing else was implied. Frankly, I don't think that Officer Tucker got sufficient detail from you. Now would one of you like to explain the remarks about Tami's other stepdad?"

Sonya Stillwell inhaled slowly and patted her husband's hand as though it was a genuine comfort to her now.

"I think I told you and the lady officer, yesterday, that Tami's best friend in Houston drowned. This was about four years ago. Just before we moved up here. In fact that was the reason we moved. I didn't tell you all the details yesterday in case it upset Tami. I can't see that they're relevant, anyway. Just a coincidence, I'm sure."

"Even so, I'd like to hear about it. Tami's not here today."

It made me nervous just watching Sonya Stillwell twitching

on the edge of the chair. It was hard to imagine those trembling hands with their bitten fingernails creating any art from clay. She could barely keep the shaking out of her voice. "Tami's best friend in Houston was a girl called Magdalene Reilly. Well, I don't know if you'd call her a best friend, really but they seemed to get along. The Reillys were our neighbors. Magdalene was the only girl in the neighborhood who was Tami's age. Oh, I suppose I should have tried harder to find other friends for her-"

"He doesn't need to hear all that, Sonya, just tell him what happened." Frank Stillwell's impatience seemed to make her worse. She sat shivering and paralyzed.

He couldn't stand the silence. "Sonya's scumbag husband, Clayton van Allen, raped the girl then drowned her in their swimming pool and all because he was mad at Sonya."

"We don't know why he did it, Frank. You can't get inside another person's head like that. Clayton wasn't always like that. He was unhappy. He had anger issues and control problems. It wasn't entirely his fault."

"Sonya, he was a drunken scumbag. He used to beat you and hurt you. Wouldn't surprise me if he sometimes snuck into Tami's room during the night when you were out of it."

"He never ever touched Tami, Frank. I wouldn't have allowed that. She'd have told me if he'd tried."

Frank scoffed. "So you say, Sonya, but look what he did when you finally told him you were going to divorce him. Finds the nearest available young thing, rapes her and drowns her. You don't know what he might have tried on Tami. You're damned lucky to be rid of him."

"Where is van Allen, now?" I asked.

"In the State Penitentiary in Texas. He got life. Damned lucky he's not on death row."

Officer Sherbourg had his notebook out. "I'd like the exact location and date of that murder, ma'am. I need to make sure the information gets to Detective Tucker." I was surprised to find out that Sherbourg had been paying any attention to the conversation. He gave me a look of deep mistrust.

Sonya recited the date as though it was forever etched in her memory.

I said, "Tami would have been what, eighteen?" She nodded. "So this man, Clayton van Allen was your husband before Frank, but he wasn't Tami's biological father, either?"

"I only been married twice, Doctor McLure. I was real young when I met Clayton. He used to be a whole lot nicer. We had a lot of fun in the early days, him and me. He bought and sold jewelry all over the South. Native Indian stuff mostly. Some stuff that might have been real old. We lived out of a trailer better than this one and went to Fairs and Gun Shows all over the place. He was making good money for a while and then he lost a bunch gambling. Got

135

swindled, too. He started dealing in other stuff. You know, stuff people use that makes more money than jewelry."

"You mean drugs?" I said.

Frank looked uncomfortable again. "He doesn't need to hear all that, Sonya."

"We always wanted kids, Clayton and me, but we couldn't have any babies. I thought it was my fault. Clayton said so. But I guess it was him that was infertile. Frank and me had Starflame."

"Probably all the pot he smoked shrank his balls," Frank said savagely.

"Oh I don't know, Frank. I probably smoked more than him back then." She saw disapproval in the young uniformed officer's face, and smiled. "Not anymore, of course. So anyways, we couldn't have kids so Tami's adopted."

"Are you done asking questions?" Frank Stillwell said.

"Yes, but there is one other thing I'd like to take away for further examination. I noticed a roll of green carpet in your barn when I was here yesterday. I'd like the forensic scientists out there to examine it back at the lab. It's still out there, isn't it? You didn't get rid of it between yesterday and today? I think that whoever used the truck may have used the carpet to cover Myra's body. You both knew Myra pretty well, didn't you?"

136

The malice in Frank Stillwell's eyes made me glad that young Sherbourg was still in the room.

"I don't like your insinuation, mister. She babysat for Starflame because Tami always seems to be too busy. It's true, Sonya, you just make excuses for Tami. She doesn't give Star the time of day. So, yes, we knew Myra Garfield some and we're real sad that she's dead, so you go right ahead, Mr. Scottish know-it-all. Take away my truck and rip up my carpet for all I care. I got nothing to hide."

X

Not So Innocent Victim

It seemed to me that Frank Stillwell acted like someone with plenty to hide. I wrapped the green carpet in a couple of clean plastic bags and gave it to the forensic guys who were finishing up on Stillwell's truck. They could take it back to The Dell and let Joe Wysocki check it over. Back in my own truck I pulled out a map of Vashon Island. It was a FarWest Real Estate map of Vashon Island that Patricia Klein had insisted on giving me along with her card. It smelled of heavy perfume and hairspray. I marked the address of Sonya's pottery class then searched the coastline for Linda Munro's place. The two houses were less than half a mile apart.

I called Katy on her cell phone. She was still at the Garfields place. Her good-humored banter was gone. There was a steely determination in her voice. She had found some clothing that matched Aaron Klein's description of Myra's outfit on Friday night. Unfortunately Mrs. Garfield had been cleaning the house with a vengeance when Katy had arrived and so any evidence there might already be gone. Tucker refused to seal it off or treat Myra's bedroom as another crime scene.

I said, "The guy's a moron, Katy. A jerk, too but I'm more concerned about his stupidity. There's a lot going on with the Stillwells below the surface. Can I come over to where you are so we can compare notes?"

Katy met me in the driveway of Joan and David Garfield's sprawling ranch-style rambler. It was just north of Vashon town, half way between Burton and the north end, on the East side of the main highway, with a distant view of Mount Rainier on a cloudless day. Today wasn't one of them but at least we were between showers. The wind ruffled Katy's short brown hair as we talked, exposing some attractive blond highlights that I hadn't noticed before. There was warmth in her eyes, now, a tacit acknowledgement that we were on the same side.

"What have you got?" she said.

"It's a good bet that Stillwell's truck was used to transport Myra's body and the green carpet may have been used to cover her, but any number of people could have driven it. The alibis that Frank and Sonya Stillwell have for Friday evening are weak. Sonya's pottery class was a fifteen minute walk away from the Covington's place and there are over two hours of Sonya's time unaccounted for between eight and eleven p.m. She says she went for a walk but there's no one to confirm where she went or what she did.

"Frank claims he went bowling in West Seattle but can't give names of anyone who can vouch for that. Suppose he didn't go over to West Seattle at all. He acts nervous and guilty about something. Maybe he murdered the girl, drove home to change vehicles, carried her in the truck, dumped her in the hot tub, went home to switch vehicles again and then collected Sonya and Starflame. He had enough time to do all of that, I think."

Katy said, "Maybe Sonya helped him. Maybe Myra's body was moved later that weekend. On Saturday, even. No one saw her between Friday at nine o'clock and Sunday morning."

I shook my head. "I think she had to be in the truck bed on Friday evening. The condition of the abrasions on her chest suggests that she was alive at the time. The state of her stomach contents suggests she died before midnight on Friday, probably closer to ten p.m. She had eaten a chicken burger and fries around six p.m. according to what you found out. She was dead within four or five hours of that, I'd say. It all points to Friday evening."

Katy nodded. "That Cadillac's a distinctive car. I'll find out which ferry workers were on the Vashon to Fauntleroy run on Friday evening and ask if anyone remembers seeing Frank Stillwell or his car. I can also check at the bowling alley in West Seattle. I need to meet Frank Stillwell and interview him for myself. I just found out some very interesting facts about him."

I raised my eyebrows and cocked my head from side to side in a parody of inquisitiveness that would have made Taffy proud.

Katy smiled. "I've got a golden retriever who puts on that act when he wants a treat. Do you sit, beg, and shake with your paw, too?"

"It depends what treat is being offered. Tell me about Stillwell."

"First of all, Myra's father, David Garfield is the same Garfield who is a Vice President in Sebastian Covington's company. Garfield is in sales. Exercise equipment among other things. Frank Stillwell used to work as a sales rep under David Garfield but was laid off when they downsized last year. According to Mr. Garfield, Stillwell didn't take the news well and still bears a grudge. Against Sebastian Covington, mostly, but he blames David Garfield, too, accusing him of finding an excuse to get rid of him."

"Being laid off is hardly enough motive to murder your supervisor's daughter and dump her body in your boss's hot tub," I said.

"You wouldn't think so, although there may be more to it. I've been finding out more about our not so innocent victim from Mr. and Mrs. Garfield. Sounds like Myra has been a bit of a Lolita and had a thing for older men. I gather that, although they weren't totally enamored with Aaron Klein, Myra's parents were pleased that he was at least close to her age. She was almost nineteen and he's in his early twenties. She had a crush on her science teacher last year and he ended up leaving the school amid accusations of sexual harassment.

"You know Myra used to baby-sit for the Stillwells. Well, she recently told her parents that Frank sometimes came on to her when he got her alone. Mr. Garfield confronted Stillwell about it last

141

week but Stillwell denied it. He said that Myra was a flirt but that he didn't encourage her."

"Interesting, but that's one of those unresolvable "He said, she said," things," I said.

"There's more though. Apparently Stillwell came to their house to see Myra just last Tuesday. That was three days before she died. Joan Garfield arrived home just as Stillwell was leaving. She said he looked flushed and furious. Drove right past her on the driveway without stopping. Myra was in the den, looking very pleased with herself, according to her mom, but wouldn't elaborate for the parents about what had transpired between her and Stillwell."

"You should definitely talk to Frank Stillwell, then. Any other dirt on the girl?"

"Not too much. We can go look in her room. That's where I found the clothes. Her mother was about to put them in to wash. She had already cleaned and scrubbed the shower stall and sink in Myra's bathroom. She was also vacuuming the place when I arrived. Odd behavior, given that she had just been told her daughter had been murdered. I think she is just in shock right now and is filling her time with mundane household chores as a kind of therapy."

"Maybe she's in denial," I said.

"Could be. The father is sitting around pouring booze on his grief. He's already getting all maudlin and nostalgic. Myra had apparently expressed some interest in business. At least so her father says. I find

142

that hard to believe. She had done an internship with Covingtons last summer and went back again over the Christmas and New Year break. She actually worked with Sebastian Covington's personal secretary, doing filing and word-processing."

David and Joan Garfield were watching from the living room window as Katy and I spoke on their driveway. When we approached the house they moved into the deeper recesses of the house. The smell of grief and bourbon lingered in the hall as we entered. Myra's room was in a recently added wing with its own bathroom, utility room and small kitchenette. A wicker basket of dirty clothes stood in the middle of the bedroom floor with red silk panties right on top.

Katy said, "If I had been ten minutes later this would all have been in the wash. Mrs. Garfield had the basket in her hands when I came to the door."

The bedroom was uncluttered, the carpets spotless, and the bed newly made.

"Had Mrs. Garfield picked clothes up from the floor in Myra's room?" I said.

"No, she says Myra was always pretty tidy. These clothes were in the hamper which is kept beside the refrigerator in the little kitchenette."

"Could Mrs. Garfield identify the other clothes that we found at the crime scene?"

"Yes, they all belong to Myra, too."

I pulled on gloves and got out more evidence bags. The red panties were neither bloodied nor ripped. The hamper contained numerous pairs of socks, a couple of T-shirts and bras. There was also a white cotton tank top (that would be the "wifebeater"), a black and red checked flannel shirt and a pair of black jeans. I noticed a walk-in closet opposite her bed. On the floor I found a pair of green platform-soled sandals with traces of dark brown stain on the heels that could be blood. I bagged all the articles of clothing separately and browsed through the rest of her wardrobe. I was struck by the assortment of skimpy, low-cut cocktail dresses, black leather miniskirts and lacy lingerie on display. I remembered the sculpted pubic hair and provocative tattoo.

"This kid was still eighteen? This is the wardrobe of a seductress," I said.

Katy scoffed. "Oh that's overstating it a bit, Donald. A lot of high school kids dress like this, especially for parties and dances."

"My Jennifer's nineteen and she doesn't have any clothes like these. At least I don't think so."

I blushed slightly under Katy's skeptical gaze. Jennifer got the respect and privacy she deserved. I realized I hadn't had occasion to look in her closet or drawers for years. My frame of reference for typical teenage girl attire was limited, to say the least.

The machine-gun rattle and roar of a badly tuned car engine announced the arrival of an orange and white Volkswagen bus. It trundled down the driveway and pulled up in front of the house. By the time Katy and I got to the front door the driver, Jan Mossandrian, was getting into a screaming match with Joan Garfield. He was backing up against the side of his van with his arms raised in a gesture of submission. Mrs. Garfield's stream of insults was incoherent amidst her tears. Her corpulent husband tried to coax her back inside.

Mossandrian was almost a clone of Aaron Klein. Another stick puppet, he had the same rangy thin physique, poor posture, ripped jeans, dirty old sneakers and T-shirt. He differed by being considerably shorter than Klein was, and favoring a long ponytail of coarse brown hair rather than blond dreadlocks. He glanced anxiously towards us and addressed himself to Katy.

"Are you Officer Pearson?" His voice held a trace of Northern European accent, with prolonged emphasis on certain vowels, which reminded me that Patricia Klein had said he was Dutch. "I came to offer my condolences and this is what I get. I was trying to explain to Mrs. Garfield that Aaron really liked Myra and certainly didn't kill her if she died on Friday night. She was alive when I picked Aaron up and he was with me until the end of the concert."

Katy gave him a cool appraisal. His pale blue eyes and thin dry lips conveyed an indignation that seemed a little forced or rehearsed. He had pale, sweaty, post-acne skin and a weak chin. I found it hard to imagine hordes of teenage girls lusting after him but maybe I was missing something. Katy commanded him to stay put while she ushered Mr. and Mrs. Garfield back inside. When she returned Mossandrian had lit a cigarette and gathered his thoughts.

He confirmed Aaron Klein's story with emphasis on all of the same details that had troubled Klein during Katy's interrogation. It was clear that the two young men had talked it over since then. He had picked Klein up at the Covington place around eight-thirty. He had gone up onto the deck where Klein was getting dressed and a very lively and beautiful Myra had shown off her unblemished body from the hot tub. They had gone straight to the high school to set up their equipment and did their first set from ten till eleven p.m.

"How long was your break?" Katy said.

"About maybe forty-five minutes. That's longer than usual but we like to mingle with the fans and sell some CDs and T-shirts."

"Where was this?"

"In the lobby outside the auditorium. They sell juice and cookies there too but you have to go outside to smoke."

"I'm sure you took advantage of that opportunity. Was it raining at eleven?"

His answer was too hurried and impulsive. "I don't remember. Well, wait. Yes it was raining a little but there is a covered walkway outside where the kids can smoke if there are no teachers around."

"Did Aaron Klein leave during this intermission?"

Mossandrian shook his head vigorously. He had anticipated this question. "Only for five minutes. I was with him. We needed to get away from the fans for a few minutes. They were all over Aaron when we were inside. Listen officer, he didn't have time to drive anywhere. He stayed at the school. We started our second set at a quarter to twelve and played until around one a.m."

Katy said, "Was Tami Stillwell in the audience?"

He smiled fondly. "Tami? Sure. She likes to come right up front and talk to us between songs. Good dancer, too. There was probably a dozen or more girls dancing up front last Friday and Tami was one of then. She has great energy. I took her home after the concert."

"Did you have sex with her?" Katy asked flatly.

He looked indignant, as if Katy had insulted his code of conduct. "No I did not. She was hot for Aaron."

"So why didn't Aaron take her home?"

There was an embarrassed pause. "There was this other girl Aaron needed to see. It's not what you think, though. She was like an old girlfriend. Aaron wanted to break off cleanly from her so he could spend more time with Tami."

Katy said, "So let me get this right. After having had sex with Myra Garfield earlier in the evening he wanted you to take Tami home to keep her out of the way while he talked to yet another girl?"

Mossandrian turned sulky and shrugged his shoulders. "Something like that."

"And this other girl, did she drive Aaron home? I'd like her name please."

The rest of the interview added little. Mossandrian had hung out with Aaron Klein for much of Saturday working on new songs. He described Klein as being happy and relaxed and excited about seeing Tami.

"There is no way he killed Myra Garfield, Officer Pearson. I've known Aaron for nearly three years. He is not a violent person. He doesn't even play video games. And if something happened that he felt guilty about I would be able to tell. He was really scared when he found her body in the tub. He kept talking about how creepy that made him feel. That's what got him scared."

XI

Roadside Revelations

"What sequence of events would fit best with the evidence we have so far?" Katy asked me after Mossandrian had left. A light drizzle had started again but neither of us wanted to go back inside with the Garfields just yet.

I said, "I'd like someone other than Aaron Klein to verify what Myra wore the night she was murdered but if that is confirmed then the most plausible explanation to me is that she came home shortly after our two young rockstars left her at the Covington's place. She drove home in her mother's white Camry, took off her clothes, maybe to take a shower, and dumped them in the clothes hamper. The perpetrator must have seen her in the hot tub, followed her home and overpowered her there. I'm not sure how that was done. There was no sign of struggle or injury on her body except the possibility that she may have dug her nails into something or somebody. Perhaps ether or chloroform was used. The initial tox. report mentioned alcohol and marijuana but I thought I smelled something else in her stomach.

"When she was unconscious, the perpetrator - and let's assume for the moment that we are talking about a male perpetrator here. We don't know for sure but it is the most likely - he lifted her into the back of Frank Stillwell's truck bed, covered her with the green carpet. He wanted to take her back to dump her in the hot tub to implicate Aaron or Mosh. But he can't find the clothes she was wearing or maybe he didn't know what all she was wearing. That clothes hamper was kept in a nonstandard place, next to the refrigerator in the kitchen. It was dark. He had seen her wearing the fringed leather jacket. So he took that and then picked out some other appropriate items from her dresser and closet and put those in the truck as well. When he got to the Covington's place he drove onto the grass next to the deck, dragged her body towards the tailgate. She must have been lying on her front and side so got scrape marks on her chest and abdomen. He dumped her in the tub and held her head under until she drowned. Then he put the lid back on, drove back to the Stillwells to return the truck and the carpet then he left. Oh, and one last thing. If she did scratch the perpetrator he may have tried to scrape the evidence out from under her nails. Do we know if there were any scratches on Aaron Klein?"

Katy said, "No, but I'll have him examined. You are sure that she was transported in Stillwell's truck?"

"We don't know for sure. If we find traces of blood or skin in the truck bed that match Myra's then I'll be certain. Right now the evidence is strong but circumstantial only. That truck was on the grass by the deck. It had distinctive debris in it including welding grit, carpet and fiberglass particles that were also found on her body and in the hot tub filters. It's a good assumption that she was transported in it."

Katy nodded. "So I need to check up on anyone who might have used it. That includes the Stillwells, or people who knew them or their habits. The Stillwells all have alibis for Friday evening but Frank and Sonya's are weak."

I said, "I'll check on progress in the lab before I leave for Portland tomorrow. Are you going to be able to follow up on those leads? If Tucker is so sure it was Aaron Klein who did it he'll be wanting it all wrapped up quickly."

"Oh I'll find the time to investigate it all right. Your explanation about how the murder took place makes sense but it doesn't help me with the who or why yet. I need to enlarge the list of possible suspects with motive for killing Myra. I'm glad I've got at least one professional on my side who is using his brain. Thanks Donald."

Her smile kept me warm as I drove away. I made a mental list of possible flaws in my reconstruction of events and of things I needed to verify. The nail-scraping could have been self-inflicted or unrelated to the murder unless we found some human material from those scrapings that was definitely not Myra's. We needed to find some of Myra's blood or skin in the truck bed to be absolutely sure she had been there. A more detailed toxicology analysis might shed light on how she was overcome and rendered unconscious. Trace evidence linking the fresh folded clothes to Stillwell's truck would be nice. But the biggest problem was that we were totally lacking any evidence that pointed to a specific perpetrator. The stuff on Klein showed only that he had sex with her.

My cell phone went off. Callum's enthusiasm crackled in my ear. "Hey dad, are you going to be home soon?"

It was late afternoon, so I assumed that Callum was home from school. I said, "Not for a few hours yet, bud. Jennifer was going to cook dinner and check your homework tonight."

"Yeah, she's in the kitchen making some kind of bean goop. Can I have pizza instead? There's one in the freezer. And I already did my homework. Harley wasn't home after school so I took measurements on his old cold frame. Can you write them down and get the wood?"

I pulled over and jotted down the dimensions. I found myself parked right outside a lumberyard called LS Cedar. The planets must be in alignment. After I hung up I went inside and got enough wood for the project, including some extra pieces in case we screwed something up. On the way through Vashon I got a roll of thick, clear plastic, some nails, screws, tacks and a couple of brass hinges. I am no great carpenter but there is something very satisfying about building solid, practical things. I knew that Harley would appreciate it. Besides, projects like this do a lot to keep building a solid connection between Callum and me.

I fully intended to drive home at that point. The bland monotony of the drizzle spurred me on towards the ferry. I would have time to help Callum get started on the cold frame before I left for the conference in Portland. I could call Linda Munro from the ferry line and tell her I was too busy to visit her mother.

The turn off to Linda's house was just before the main highway turned to wind down the steep hill towards the dock. As I slowed to negotiate this I noticed two schoolgirls kneeling by the roadside laying flowers by a makeshift wooden cross. Another woman was talking to them. Linda's ample curves, covered in designer clothes were all too recognizable to me. It must have been guilt that made me stop the car and cross the road to join them.

The girls were an odd pairing. Both in their late teens, the one kneeling by the little cross was attractive and tearful. She kept wiping away tears and smudging her black mascara as she hung a chain of artificial daisies over the little cross. Someone had printed on it in felt-tip pen, "We miss you Myra." The other girl was bony, thin and much less upset. She saw me approaching and knelt down to warn her friend. By the time I arrived Linda was explaining to the girls who I was.

"This gentleman is trying to find out what caused Myra's death, girls. Thanks so much for coming back over, Donald. I knew you would."

The presumption of that remark irritated me into a gruff reply. "I had to come back to collect additional evidence. We're sure, now, that Myra was murdered."

The skinny girl giggled. "He has an accent. Myr-r-ra was mur-r-rdered."

The tearful one pushed her friend angrily and told her to shut up. She said, "I know. They've arrested Aaron Klein from Skunk Bucket."

I said, "So I understand. I'm surprised the news has got around so quickly. That doesn't necessarily mean that he did it, though, girls. It just means the police want to ask him some questions." The skinny kid started giggling again, then covered her mouth. "Are you both friends of Myra, then?"

Teary-eyes nodded.

I said, "Did you see her last Friday night?"

Linda answered for them. "Yes, Donald, they were just telling me they met Myra at Zoomies. They've already spoken to Sheriff Pitman."

I asked them if they remembered what Myra was wearing and got the confirmation I wanted, agreeing with Klein's description. And she had been wearing jewelry, they said. Rings for her nose and eyebrow and a couple of ear cuffs. It was another small piece of the puzzle, useful but hardly worth stopping for. But now that I had, I knew I hadn't the heart to tell Linda I couldn't go visit her mother. The best I could manage was to say I'd have to make it quick.

I followed her back to her house where the crime scene tape was still in place. While she went in to change I looked in the garage to check out the truck that Tucker said was there. One glance told me it was not involved with the murder. Rusted, with flat tires and a flat wooden truck bed, it hadn't moved from that spot for months.

I drove behind Linda back down the main highway to Burton. We passed the entrance to the nursing home and pulled in a few hundred yards farther on at a secluded house that looked out over the water from a high point of the Burton Peninsula. I parked beside her and waited while she primped. When she emerged, Linda had brushed her hair, applied more lipstick and perfume, and looked distinctly cheerful at the prospect of my company.

"Well, here we are. Mother's house is quite close to Goldentide, actually. I don't know if you noticed that we passed it back there up the road. This house is waterfront, of course, but high bank only, I'm afraid. The waterfront is not really useable though mother wouldn't use it even if it was."

It was exhausting to be around Linda Munro's endless efforts at impressing me with things I didn't care about. I stood silent and expressionless.

She said, "I'll just go inside for a minute, then. I want to collect some of her clothes and other favorite things. The doctor says if we increase her sense of comfort and familiarity her dementia may improve, or at least she might become less distressed.

I walked round to the front of the house onto the lawn that sloped towards the cliff edge. The ground fell away steeply to a rocky shore below. Half way down, with its roof poking out from the madronas and maples, was what looked like an old railway carriage. This was a great piece of property. Callum would love to go exploring down there. I took some deep breaths and let the wet salty breeze play over my face until I sensed that Linda had returned.

"Is that thing on your property?" I said.

"The caboose? Yes, I think the previous owners had it hoisted down there as a den or summerhouse for their kids. It doesn't have water or electricity or anything. Mother never used the place. We should probably get rid of it. It's just an eyesore."

"Callum wouldn't think so. He'd love to have a place like that for his secret base."

"I suppose kids would like it. I hadn't thought of that. I keep forgetting that you have children, Donald. How are they?"

The question was asked with the necessary politeness of social etiquette rather than any genuine enthusiasm. Under different circumstances my response would have been quite effusive. I usually purr with pride about how well Andy is doing in Medical School. I can get choked up in my praise for how well Jennifer copes with integrating her own complex schedule with mine and Callum's. I could have described Callum's energy and thoughtfulness with the cold frame project. But I didn't feel like doing any of those things, right then. Instead I made a few cursory comments and used the opportunity to remind her that I needed to get home soon to help Callum do some homework before I went to Portland.

"Portland? I used to live in Portland." She spoke as if waking from a daydream. "That's where I met Sebastian. Seems so long ago.

That was where he found me but lost his chance to have kids, though he didn't know it at the time."

The statement was left hanging enigmatically. I was supposed to ask for an explanation.

"What do you mean?' I said without much enthusiasm.

"God, it's ancient history. It's about twenty years ago. I can hardly believe it all now. It seems like another lifetime. You would still be back in Edinburgh at the time. I had only just come out to the States." She paused and gave me a meaningful look. I wasn't getting it. "I came over because you and Elspeth had got married and there was nothing left for me to hang around for, if you want to know the truth." Right then I really didn't want to hear about this particular truth but I could tell that she wasn't going to be denied. "I met Sebastian at a party two days after I got here. Slept with him the very first night I met him. I hadn't ever done that with someone before. Anyway, by the time we'd been seeing each other for about six weeks he asked me to move in with him. And then this other woman shows up to say she's pregnant and it's Sebastian's."

"And was it?"

"Probably. Definitely, he thought. He had been seeing her for over a year before he met me. He was pissed about it. Embarrassed, I guess. Annoyed at the complication. She was into drugs, didn't have much money, but she wouldn't get an abortion. Sebastian said he'd pay for it and that just made her worse. It got ugly."

"So what happened?"

"He gave her some money. Quite a lot, I think. He told her she could use it for an abortion or anything else she wanted but he was going to be out of it. He wasn't ready for kids. We never saw her again. Actually we moved to San Diego about a month later."

"You told me the other day that you and Sebastian decided not to have kids."

"We talked about it in the early days. We would do it later. When the time was right. But of course it never was. I started putting pressure on him about five years ago, just before I turned forty. I came off the pill and told him I couldn't wait any longer."

"But you didn't conceive?"

She laughed. "That's right, but I don't think it's my biological clock that's the problem. I still get my periods right on time. I can even tell when I'm ovulating. It's just that we hardly ever have sex anymore. A tragic waste wouldn't you say?"

She ran her hands over her curves and gave me an exaggerated "come hither" look that she held a little longer than the joke demanded. It was an excruciating moment. I should have said something to bolster her fragile ego and cover her embarrassment but I wasn't up to it. I didn't want to revisit the connection that she and I had once had. I was too angry at the embarrassment she was causing me. The implication was that I was somehow responsible for her choosing Sebastian Covington on the rebound. And now we were both unhappy in our marriages. I can't figure out women. Was I supposed to tell her that I wished that I had chosen Linda instead of Elspeth all those years ago? I don't know. I'm not very good at this stuff.

I looked pointedly at my watch. "Come on. Let's go and visit your mom."

XII

Locked in Hell

Like most people, I don't relish senility. I hope that I will live a long healthy life and that I will die in my sleep at a ripe old age after having had an invigorating day hiking in the hills followed by a fabulous meal and great sex. I pray that God spares me a nursing home fate.

With its circular driveway, pillared porch and tall arched entryway, the architect of Goldentide Residential Nursing Home was probably trying to convey a sense of elegant sophistication and opulent comfort. But approaching the place in the watery afternoon light, Goldentide was about as warm and inviting as a funeral home. I imagined that a lot more people went in through those doors than ever came back out again. Several guests lay in wait for us under the porch. I suppose they were called "guests" rather than "inmates" or "the condemned." In wheelchairs, with blankets draped over spindly knees, they stared balefully out at the world passing them by. Linda hurried me through the gauntlet with her eyes downcast but I felt obliged to offer some of them a smile of warmth and condolence as

I passed. There was a loneliness in their eyes. Loneliness, confusion, and a kind of desperation. A longing for recognition, a hope that some kind stranger would snap them out of the nightmare and give them back their memory, their vigor and their youth.

The Goldentide foyer was designed to be light and airy, which is hard to pull off on a day overcast with gloom. The ceilings were tall, there was plenty of glass but the cold slate floors echoed the way they do in half-empty churches. One carpeted alcove held a gas fire and a few armchairs where a social worker or chaplain was consoling some weeping relatives. Beside the reception desk and administrative offices was the donor wall, a huge slab of marble on which were printed the names of local benefactors in varying sizes of print to match their contribution. At the top were the Platinum Sustainers, mostly local corporations. Their large lettering could be seen from the other side of the room. The Gold Sponsors featured a few well-to-do families, prominently displayed at head height, and easily read as you walked past. The bottom portion of the wall contained a long list of Silver Supporters whose generosity needed a magnifying glass to achieve recognition. The whole thing seemed inappropriate. Somehow, the use of marble seemed in poor taste. It looked like a headstone in a cemetery.

While Linda made some inquiries at the reception desk I checked out the gift shop. There must be a single franchise for hospital gift shops in the USA. They all contain the same depressing items. There are the ever-present furry teddy-bears (in sizes to fit every budget), silk flowers, porcelain figurines, sappy cards, calendars of puppies and kittens, and books filled with inspirational sayings or quotations from children. You're supposed to find their precocious remarks to be cute and endearing. I settled for a box of expensive chocolates with soft centers and no nuts. That's the kind my own granny used to like. She could enjoy them even with her dentures out.

Linda smiled her approval and squeezed my arm with something between gratitude and longing. "Mrs. Burley, the matron, is with another family right now but apparently mother is feeling a bit better today. Her room's down this way."

On the wall above the entrance to the corridor was a large mural of surf crashing on a beach at sunset so that the foam was tinged a deep golden red. A banner beneath the painting said, "Welcome to Goldentide." An old man shuffled off down the hall ahead of me with his pajama bottoms hanging off and his wrinkled old butt crack showing. There was a piece of paper pinned to his back that said, "My name is Gilbert. Please return me to room 43." We met some other lost souls in the hallways, scraping along on their walking frames or dragging a paralyzed right or left leg and arm. Some were accompanied by excessively cheerful nurses or physiotherapists offering advice and encouragement. Others, like Gilbert, wandered alone in the wilderness, shuffling off into the sunset. Welcome to Goldentide.

We found Agnes Munro sitting alone in room 16. It was over ten years since I had last seen her. She seemed smaller today, in every way, sitting with a tartan traveling rug across her lap, clutching her purse and staring out the window at the rain. The room itself was the best one in the place, Linda had assured me. It was a single room with a view out over the water, and everything she needed close at hand. A television hung down from the ceiling, showing an afternoon soap with the volume turned down low. A handsome young couple shouted quietly at each other before she slapped his face and walked out the room slamming the door. The credits rolled. Tune in at the same time tomorrow for the exciting continuation of The Young and The Restless. Stay tuned now for Days of Our Lives, after these important messages.

Bland prints of generic scenery hung on the walls. Around her bed were some framed family photographs. A younger, smiling Agnes with her now deceased husband were captured in their heyday, dressed for the opera or some other formal function. The light of wealth, power and success shone in their eyes. In another frame Linda and her older brother, David, posed proudly in their university graduation gowns. David, who had lost his battle with lymphoma about five years ago, had at least provided Mrs. Munro with two grandchildren before he died so there were various pictures of them in school uniforms and rugby shirts. Pictures of Sebastian Covington were conspicuously absent.

Linda bustled around the room trying to get her mother's attention. An untouched food tray lay on the bed – limp salad, cold meat loaf and a plastic tub of red rubbery Jello.

"Oh Mother, have you not eaten your lunch? Look, here's the menu for tomorrow. Let's go through it and pick out something you'd like."

The old lady turned from the window and gazed at us with blank astonishment. She squinted first at Linda then fixed me with an unfathomable stare of bafflement and suspicion.

"That's not David. Who's this you're bringing to see me?" Her voice was strong and imperious, the refined Edinburgh brogue still pronounced.

"This is Donald McLure, mother. You remember Donald. He and I were at the university together. He's a doctor now."

"Why does David never come to visit me? Is he too busy to come and see his own mother these days?"

Linda knelt in front of the chair, held her mother's trembling hand and looked up at her, trying to penetrate the fog. "I've told you, mother, David can't visit anymore. David's dead."

The old woman's face became wracked with the abject shock and grief of someone hearing horrifying news for the very first time. "Dead? David's dead? Oh God, no."

She began to wail and howl with inconsolable sorrow as Linda put her arms round the trembling woman and rocked her gently. Her cries set off some answering wails and moans from neighboring rooms and brought a nurse rushing through the door pushing a cart.

"Is she having a seizure?" she said.

Linda shook her head. "No, she'll be fine. She's just upset at hearing some bad news again. I have to go through this four or five times every visit."

The nurse looked at her watch and began unlocking the cart. "It's nearly time for her evening meds. She might as well have them a bit early." She dished out an assortment of multicolored pills and capsules and handed them to Mrs. Munro in a plastic medicine cup. "Come on now, Agnes, here's your medicine. Did you not like your lunch, then?"

The old lady stopped crying at the nurse and accepted the cup of pills obediently. "The men will never get the hay baled, now, you know. They should have done it yesterday when they had the chance. I'll need to bring in the washing, of course. It'll be getting soaked in this rain."

The nurse handed her a glass of water. "That's right, Agnes, just you swallow your pills and I'll see to the washing for you." She winked at me. The old woman watched the exchange between us with a momentary flicker of insight, enough to know she was being patronized. She scowled.

"How's she been today, nurse?" Linda asked.

"Much better than yesterday, that's for sure. Doctor increased her Haldol. That helped. Had a good bowel movement this morning, too, didn't you, dear? And you're getting your hair done tomorrow, Agnes, aren't you? That'll be nice, won't it?"

Agnes Munro's scowl deepened. Please, God, spare me a nursing home fate.

The nurse left to continue her medication rounds. Mrs. Munro stared down at my feet for several seconds and began shaking her head.

"My, my, these are fancy shoes, son. Where did you get these fancy shoes?"

I was wearing a pair of walking shoes, a cross between sneakers and hiking boots. Practical and comfortable and totally commonplace around here. But not something you would see in Scotland in the 1950's where she seemed to spend most of her inner life.

She looked up at me with renewed suspicion. "You're not David."

Linda braced herself for the repeat performance but I was spared the agony of responding by the entrance of Mrs. Burley, the nursing director for Goldentide.

"Sorry I'm late, Mrs. Covington, I was with another family. I wanted to speak to you about yesterday. Agnes got quite agitated. She got into a fight with one of the visitors and took a tumble. She's all right though, nothing broken. The other woman has some scratches on her arm but isn't going to complain."

"A fight?" Linda said in horror.

"She was a bit more confused than usual, yesterday, I think. She got a bit muddled. Actually I wasn't on duty at the time. One of our volunteers came and broke it up. Let me see if I can find the girl so she can explain what happened. She should be here again today."

Mrs. Burley left and the atmosphere of awkward silence returned. The four walls of the room seemed to be closing in. Linda looked over at me, her eyes full of sadness and concern.

"Thanks for coming today, Donald. It helps just to have someone else understand what it's like."

The old lady continued looking at my shoes in apparent wonder. A pile of Readers Digest Condensed Books, Large Print editions, was next to me on the bedside table. There was a FarWest Real Estate business card lying on top. The name on the card was Patricia Klein. I held it up for Linda to see.

"Are you trying to sell the house?"

"Is that a card from Aaron Klein's mother?" Linda sounded exasperated and tired. "God, that woman is pushy."

"You've met her then?"

"No, but she has called me every other month since mother has been in Goldentide. I've told her we don't want to sell. This is just temporary, until mother is feeling better. Isn't that right, mum?"

The old lady was staring out the window again, humming to herself.

"Excuse me." Tami Stillwell hovered in the doorway, reluctant to enter the room. "I think what has happened is that Mrs. Klein may have given up on you and is harassing your mom instead."

Tami looked rested and happier today, in tight leggings, thick socks and boots, an oversized fleecy sweatshirt and long scarf. The bag of books she carried suggested that she had come here straight from her classes. She approached Linda apprehensively and held out her hand.

"I owe you an apology Ms. Munro. I had no idea it was your house that Aaron was taking me to on Sunday. I feel so ashamed."

Linda jumped to her feet and hugged the girl, who seemed stiff and awkward in the face of this show of affection and forgiveness.

Linda said, "You poor thing. It's me that feels terrible for you. That was an awful thing to witness."

Tami shook free. "No, it's me that should apologize. I shouldn't have been there. I think I'll drop that psychology class. You won't want me in the audience. It'll be too embarrassing."

"Of course it won't. Please don't drop the course. You would have been welcome to use the tub if I'd known. I sometimes invite my tutorial group to a retreat out here. I've had eight people in that tub all at once. Sometimes we go to one of the natural Hot Springs in the mountains, instead. In fact I'm planning to do that this weekend. Why don't you come with us? It's a Women's Studies group so it's all girls. I'm sure you'll know some of them. Please come."

Tami seemed unprepared for these offers of friendship. She was determined to deliver her lines. Lines she had rehearsed and steeled herself to recite. "When Doctor McLure told me it was your house I just about died. And then he said your mom was in Goldentide. I came to introduce myself to her yesterday, to try to kind of make up for it somehow. But Mrs. Klein was already here."

"Talking to mother?"

Tami's laugh was scornful. "Of course. She talks to all the clients who have been in for a few months, anyone she thinks might be in here permanently but who owns property on Vashon. Her little business cards are scattered everywhere."

"That's a bit callous of her," I said.

"She makes money at it, though. She preys on the relatives, too. Plays one off against another. I don't know how Aaron can stand living with her."

"You know they've arrested Aaron, Tami," I said quietly.

A tear started to form. "His mother called to tell me this morning, as if it was my fault. It's ridiculous. I just know Aaron didn't do it. I trust him more than I'd ever trust her, I'll tell you that. She's ruthless."

I said, "What makes you say that?"

"When Aaron's dad left her she found out he was bankrupt. She had to sell stuff to pay off his debts and now she's bitter. She's like a vulture around this place. I don't know why they allow it except that she seems to know Mrs. Burley pretty well. And her husband, Mr. Burley. Patricia Klein is great at kissing up to men to get what she wants."

"What happened yesterday?" Linda asked.

"I came by to say hello and maybe ask your mom if she'd like me to read to her. Most of the old ladies like that. But she was really agitated. She was trying to tug a real estate brochure away from Mrs. Klein. Agnes scratched her arm. Tried to bite her, too." Tami smiled at this.

Linda looked appalled. "Tried to bite her?"

"Yeah, and so I went over to break it up and try to calm your mom down but then she scratched me, too." Tami pulled up her sweatshirt sleeve, revealing some loose white bandages wrapped round her forearm. "It's no big deal. She didn't know what she was doing. It served Mrs. Klein right, anyway. The doctor came and gave your mom a sedative after that. She would be fine if they just left her alone and stopped bugging her."

Tami bent to touch Agnes on the shoulder but the old woman shrugged her off and began to wail.

"I'll come back another time, if you'd like," Tami said.

Linda smiled warmly. "I'm sure she'd like that, Tami. I really appreciate it. I'll have a word with Mrs. Burley about keeping any realtors away from her."

Tami left and Agnes returned to her vacant humming.

"I need to go, Linda," I said.

I knelt and put the chocolates on Agnes Munro's lap. She picked up the box and turned it over and over in her hands as if it were an alien moon rock. There was a lifetime of stories in those hands. Those frail, knobbly old hands had done their fair share of work in their day, I was sure. They had put bandages on scraped knees, and written insightful letters in a strong firm hand. They had caressed lovers, kneaded bread, or held a violin with grace and poise. These were hands of strength and character. Yet, as I patted them and prepared to leave there was something odd about them that I couldn't quite place. Something that didn't quite fit.

She watched me rise to go, and frowned. "You're not David. Where's David? Why doesn't he ever come to visit me anymore?"

A chorus of banshee wails followed me back down the hall and echoed off the slate and marble of the foyer as I hurried out into the darkening sky.

XIII

Late Night Feelers

The ferry gods were smiling on me for once, and I drove straight onto the Issaquah with no wait. I'll say one thing about traveling by ferry; it gives you some enforced downtime. Time to breathe deeply and reflect. The problem was that my reflections kept returning to broken relationships and dementing twilight years. Punching in the pre-set buttons for my favorite radio stations wasn't enough of a distraction either. NPR reminded me that there were terrible problems all over the world and that we weren't doing enough to alleviate them. The chat on the Sportstalk stations was tedious. February has to be the dullest month in the US sporting calendar. KBSG, the oldies station, brought back a flood of youthful nostalgia that I didn't want to deal with right then. There was nothing else for it. I pulled out a pad and began to doodle on it, making lists of what I knew already about the case and what things still needed to be done.

The sequence of events on Friday night was becoming clear but no evidence pointed conclusively to any particular culprit.

Sometimes evidence is easier to find if you know who you're looking for. More to the point it is easy to overlook something if you have wrongly ruled somebody or something out as irrelevant. It pays to keep an open mind.

From what we had learned of Myra Garfield, she had left a lot of jealous or jilted men in her wake for someone so young. Aaron Klein seemed an unlikely candidate for her murderer. He appeared to get enough sex and adulation to satisfy his ego. He had a solid alibi for the evening unless Mossandrian was lying, and Katy would look into that. The fired schoolteacher was another possibility. As a science teacher he would have access and knowledge of various chemicals and poisons. Katy hadn't mentioned if he still lived locally or not. Perhaps the high school gossip circuit would throw out a few more spurned lovers.

But what if Myra Garfield wasn't the real target? Suppose someone was trying to terrorize the Kleins? Had someone followed Aaron and Myra on Friday night then murdered the girl to frame Aaron and get back at his mother? Her ex-husband perhaps, or maybe the relative of some geriatric resident at Goldentide whom she had scammed. There were too many possibilities. The police would have to look into it if they felt so inclined.

Frank Stillwell required more serious investigation. Had he had an affair with the flirtatious babysitter? He had a grievance against Sebastian Covington and David Garfield. Was Myra's murder a clumsy attempt to get back at all of them? His alibi for Friday night was weak. If it didn't hold up then the circumstantial evidence against him was strong.

But what if someone was terrorizing the Stillwells? Maybe Frank was being framed. Maybe Tami was the target. That seemed unlikely. Nothing I had seen or heard about Tami suggested that she had enemies. Except that there was the Texas connection. She had been traumatized by seeing a drowned victim, once before. I fished out my notes, called the switchboard at The Dell and got the number for the appropriate medical examiner's office in Houston.

Long distance business calls can really test your patience. I heard enough Country music clichés to last me a lifetime as I was repeatedly put on hold or was transferred to someone else who made me repeat my enquiry all over again. The Magdalene Reilly case, did I say? What was the date again? Could I please hold? The lazy singsong drawl of Southern politeness gave me no reason to expect results anytime this decade. The medical examiner no longer worked in that jurisdiction but she thought he still worked in Texas. He'd be gone for the day, most likely. Did I realize they were two hours ahead of Seattle? Could I leave my number and she would try to have him call me?

• • •

The Paperboys were blasting from the CD player in the kitchen when I got home. Jennifer was standing at the sink, dancing while she cleaned up dinner dishes. Callum sat at the table with his legs swinging in time to the music, intent on some writing project.

"Can you concentrate on your homework with that amount of noise and distraction?" I said after kisses and hugs of hello.

174

"I've done all my homework and Jen's corrected it. I'm just drawing. Did you get the wood?"

"Yes, and some nails and hinges and plastic sheeting. We could get started cutting out the pieces tonight, if you're not too tired?" Now there's a stupid question to ask a ten-year-old. He put his pencil down and struck his best not-at-all-sleepy pose. I said, "Any food left, Jen? I seem to have missed dinner somewhere along the way."

Callum said, "There's a choice of two, Gaylene Jarvis's toxic waste or Jennifer McLure's bean glop." He clutched his throat as though being poisoned, and began to slide off his chair.

Jennifer threw a dishtowel at him. "You said the bean casserole was great, you little monkey. You cleared your plate anyway."

"I was just being nice. Trying to make you hap-hap hap-hap-happy."

Jennifer said, "Gaylene came by, dad, to ask if you got her card. She was pleased to see half the casserole was gone. We hadn't the heart to tell her you had given it to Harley and Taffy."

Callum looked horrified. "But we haven't seen them all day, Jen. Maybe they keeled over in the basement after eating just one toxic mouthful. Now they could be frozen in suspended animation and agony. And only Gaylene knows the antidote."

I said, "Callum, why don't you unload the wood out the truck while I zap some bean casserole. I'll meet you in the basement. Any messages, Jen?"

She hesitated, waited until Callum was out of the room then spoke with false nonchalance. "Just two. Somebody called you asking about a golf game this weekend, and there was a cryptic message from mom."

I paused with my hand on the fridge door and tried to read her face.

"She's not coming back, Dad. I'm sure of it. Things are apparently better ... no, make that somewhat better ... between her and Jack What's-his-name. You'll be fascinated to know that they are going off somewhere together this weekend to see if they can ... work things out. Why the hell is she telling us that, Dad? Does she think we are hanging on her every word, hoping and praying that things work our for ... her?"

I hugged Jennifer close and let her sob into my shoulder. Her body throbbed with anger, love, energy and confusion, the words almost lost in the wool of my sweater. "I wish she'd just stay away and stop stringing us all along. Things will never be like they were, like they could have been. We need to build our own new ... reality."

"Aw, Jen, you should have called me. Have you been bottling this up all day?"

"I didn't want to bother you with it while you were working. It's not like there's anything any of us can do to change things."

"You're right love. All we can ever control is our own actions, and even there it's hard enough trying to figure out the right thing to do, sometimes. Do you want to talk by the fire once Callum's in bed?"

She wiped away some tears. "That'd be great. I've got a paper I need to read for tomorrow. You go pound in some nails with Callum. He's been wanting to do that all evening."

"Pound in some nails? This is precision craftsmanship, here. We're talking power drills and saws."

She managed a smile. "He'll like that even better. I'll put in my ear plugs."

An hour of project work with Callum is one of the best forms of psychotherapy I know. He shows no signs of affecting the cool or cynical demeanor favored by some of his classmates, and he continues to take delight in learning new things. I heard all about why frogs have wet skin but toads have dry skin and what the major produce was in Nepal. Apparently it is rice and textiles. I had always thought it was Sherpas, Yetis, and "I climbed Everest" T-shirts. So much for my education. By the time I had tucked him into bed with a hot water bottle, the cold frame was taking shape and my heart was feeling sturdier too.

Jennifer and I didn't actually talk all that much by the fire. At least not about Elspeth. She curled up beside me on the couch cradling her hot chocolate, and talked about some of her friends and their plans for vacations or careers or boyfriends.

I said, "I worry that I'm holding you back, Jen. You shouldn't be having to do as much for Callum and me. You could be living in an apartment with your friends."

"I like it here, Dad. You and Callum are not the problem."

"What about boyfriends? You haven't mentioned Todd much recently."

The phone rang and we waited to see whose voice came on after the answering machine message had finished. It was a male Texan voice asking for me. Jennifer seized the opportunity to escape. She pecked me on the cheek and disappeared to her room, saying, "I'll give you a Todd update in the morning."

"Professor McLure? Is this the same Donald McLure who'll be lecturing in Portland tomorrow? Why what an honor it is to talk to you, Sir? My name is Newton, Lyle Newton, and I am speaking to you tonight from San Antonio, in the great state of Texas. I have read all of your articles and am eager to meet you in person. Well, when I say all of your articles I may not be speaking entirely accurately. I am sure a man of your stature has written more than I have been able to find or assimilate."

I tend to be put off by people who are gushy and flattering towards me. The Presbyterian in me is suspicious and uncomfortable with such overt demonstrations of emotion. It seems so insincere. I assume the person is either selling something or concealing something. Besides which, Lyle Newton sounded more than just garrulous. He sounded a little drunk.

"The Magdalene Reilly case? Why I remember it well, and even though I am currently residing in San Antonio I did, in fact, bring with me some personal notes and photographs pertaining to the case. I would be glad to call the Houston office first thing in the morning and have them fax you some of the reports and transcripts. In addition it would be my pleasure to bring with me on the plane to Portland the additional notes and photographs which are currently in my possession. Perhaps we could meet up tomorrow after your lecture and discuss the case at the hotel over a drink? I would sure enjoy your company, Professor McLure."

I had already had more than enough of Lyle Newton's company but I was too intrigued to pass up the opportunity to look over the official and unofficial documents relating to Magdalene Reilly's death. We were both staying at the hotel where the conference was being held so I arranged to meet him in the lobby.

I hung up and began throwing a few random clothes into my overnight bag. When the phone rang again I assumed it was Newton calling back with more details but it wasn't. It was Katy Pearson.

"Hi, sorry to call so late but you're going out of town tomorrow for a couple of days, aren't you? I've made some progress since we were at the Garfields and I wanted to catch you up. Did you get your personal stuff taken care of?"

"I've had a mixed day," I said. "On a positive note I got the wood

179

and hardware I needed to help my son with a school-related project that will also help my neighbor. I spent the evening getting splinters in my fingers and learning a few new Knock-knock jokes from Callum. That stuff was fun."

"And on a negative note?"

"Och, I won't bore you with those details. I didn't learn anything much of relevance to the Garfield case except maybe indirectly. Remember when you and I talked to Sonya Stillwell yesterday she mentioned that Tami's best friend had drowned in Texas? Well, today, when I talked to Frank and Sonya together, when Tami wasn't there, they gave me more details. It seems that the best friend didn't just drown, she was raped and murdered by drowning. Tami found the body and it was her previous stepfather, Clayton van Allen who was convicted of the murder."

"Do you think that might have relevance to this murder on Vashon? You think we have a serial killer here?" She sounded skeptical.

"Hard to say but I was intrigued at the similarities. Turns out that the guy who did the post-mortem in the Houston case is coming to the conference in Portland. He is going to send me details of the case and bring me some photos."

"But you said they had caught, tried and convicted the perpetrator in that case. He'll be locked up in Texas if he hasn't already been executed. They don't hang around in Texas when it's a capital case. Why don't you give me the name and date of the case and I'll follow up tomorrow?"

"Okay. You said you had made some progress yourself?" I said.

"I interviewed the Covington's closest neighbor on Vashon. She's a retired teacher. She heard noises at the Covington's house on Friday evening, but earlier, maybe around five o'clock or so. She went over to check and guess who she found prowling around the place? Patricia Klein. Klein asked the neighbor if she knew when the Covingtons would be around this weekend and left her card and a real estate brochure on the step."

"Did the neighbor hear any noises later?" I asked.

"No, I'm afraid not. She goes to bed about eight thirty and takes a sleeping pill, so that's a dead end. I had more success checking up on Frank Stillwell, though." There was excitement in her voice.

I said, "I'm glad you got to meet him. How did he strike you?"

"Frank Stillwell is one raw, ragged, angry dude. He is covering up something, I'm sure, but he gave me the same story he told you. Everyone's against him. He never laid a finger on Myra Garfield. The whole bit. He was pretty evasive when I asked him who all regularly used the truck, apart from himself. Aaron Klein was the only person, recently, and him only since he had been seeing Tami. Stillwell has maybe two or three other friends who have used it once in the past year, but not for months. He has an electrician friend called Brogan, I remember, and a couple of others whose names I wrote down. I'll ask Tucker to have someone interview those guys tomorrow. I'm more interested in what Stillwell did last Friday night. Or rather, what he didn't do."

"What do you mean?"

"I talked to some of the ferry crew who were working the Fauntleroy-Southworth-Vashon run last Friday night. One of them says he's sure he saw the lilac Cadillac on the 6:35 ferry to West Seattle. He didn't see Frank but he noticed the car. The ferry guy said he does vintage car restoration as a hobby and was disturbed to see how beat up and neglected Stillwell's car was. I could have told him it wasn't half as beat up and neglected as Stillwell's wife but I didn't. Anyway, it's a pretty fair bet that Stillwell's car went over to West Seattle the night Myra was murdered. We don't know if Frank Stillwell was driving it though, or when he came back onto Vashon if he was the driver. But I'm sure of one thing. He didn't go bowling."

"How do you know that?" I said.

"When I talked to Stillwell he was very specific. He said he got to the Bowling Center about 7:15 which would fit if he was on the 6:35 ferry off Vashon. He said he played three complete games, all by himself and left again about ten thirty and caught the 10:50 boat back to Vashon."

I said, "That would fit. Sonya said he picked her up a little after eleven. The ferry trip takes about fifteen minutes and the pottery class was at the north end of the island."

"Yes, but I also talked to the manager of the West Seattle bowling place. He thinks he can recall seeing a guy around the place recently who fits Stillwell's description – a surly character who is a loner and has been coming there for the past few months. The manager wasn't on duty Friday night so can't verify whether Frank Stillwell was there that night or not. But the manager was called in at eight o'clock because of an emergency. They were having "Space Wars" night, a special promotional thing to encourage a younger clientele back to bowling. They flood the lanes with carbon dioxide smoke and get strobe lights going. Like at rock concerts."

"Sounds wild," I said.

"And certainly memorable, right? Well the manager said they had a power outage just before eight o'clock last Friday. The fire alarm went off. They had to evacuate the building. They didn't get it fixed until almost ten o'clock. So for two hours the customers were standing around in the parking lot getting pissed off. Most of them got their money back. But you know what? Our friend Frank made no mention of any of this. He is lying through his teeth, Donald. I can't say where he was or what he was doing, just yet, but I know one thing. Frank Stillwell was not at the West Seattle bowling alley on the night that Myra Garfield was murdered."

TUESDAY/ WEDNESDAY

186

XIV

Imperfect Symmetry

The error light on the fax machine winked at me as I crossed the laboratory floor in the early hours of Tuesday morning. The LCD screen said, "Error 29. Consult manual or contact service center." Predictably, the manual was nowhere to be seen. I couldn't even find the 1-800-GET-LOST number of the service center so I was spared the ignominy of having some arrogant young pipsqueak on the other end of the line giving me incomprehensible instructions on how to distinguish between paper jams, memory overloads or toner cartridge replacements, none of which I have a clue how to fix. This was the disadvantage of coming to work two hours before anyone else. Luckily, the incoming fax tray held a large stack of paper, most of it from Houston, so that was something. The advantage of coming in early was that I would get uninterrupted peace and quiet to go through it.

The February rains had paused for breath and the sky wore a black sequined dress sparkling over the West Seattle rooftops outside my office window. I scanned my desk for signs of any potential crises.

Nothing was piled on my chair, but a biochemistry report dangled from the computer screen, taped there to get my attention. The yellow sticky note on it said, "Good call Donald. Barbs ++, Rusty." Barbiturates had been found in Myra Garfield's blood, stomach and bladder. How much and what specific drug were still unclear. The screening test uses a two-step reaction involving cobalt acetate and isopropylamine in methanol, which turns a pleasing violet-blue color in the presence of any barbiturate. The femoral vein blood sample that I had taken from Myra Garfield at the crime scene contained clear evidence of barbiturates. The urine levels from the post mortem bladder sample were even clearer, which is typical. Barbiturates get concentrated and excreted via the kidneys. Traces of barbiturate had also been found in the stomach contents, which completed the picture. Whether or not she had ingested enough of the drug to render her unconscious remained to be seen. The quantitative assay would be done later in the week.

Twenty-five years ago those results would not have surprised me. Barbiturate and alcohol was one of the most popular cocktails for suicide attempts. Capsules of secobarbital could be found in the medicine cabinets and bedside tables of almost any elderly household. But finding them nowadays was definitely unusual. The place of barbiturates as the ubiquitous sleeping pill has been usurped by the benzodiazepines in recent years. Benzodiazepines have a wider therapeutic index. In other words the gap between the dose which gives a beneficial effect and the dose which can kill you is wider, so benzodiazepines are somewhat safer. This means that they can be prescribed with even more reckless abandon than barbiturates. Consequently, barbiturates have fallen out of favor for most clinical purposes nowadays, and since they had never gained much popularity for recreational use it was a surprise to find them used for poisoning. I placed the report in my In-tray to remind myself to think about it more when I got back from Portland.

I sorted and stapled the faxed papers from Texas into a sensible chronological order. There were seven reports in all, which was more than I had expected. They all related to the murder of Magdalene Reilly in Houston four years before. I began with the incident report of the uniformed officer who had first arrived on the scene. His clumsy turgid prose catalogued the relevant details without emotion. I skimmed the pages for the salient points and filled in the gaps from my imagination to complete the picture of a suburban tragedy on a balmy summer night in Texas.

```
Time: June 12th, 10:34 p.m.
Location: 22513 Rochester Heights Grove

No signs of forced entry to house or
premises. No one at home. One car (a
Chevrolet Suburban) in the driveway.
On arrival I was approached by three
persons:

Tami van Allen of 22511 Rochester Heights
Grove. White female, 18 years old, in
tearful and emotional state.

Mrs. April Horst (age 45) and Mr. Graham
Horst (age 52) of 22515 Rochester Heights
Grove. Caucasians. Married couple.
```

Neighbors of deceased family.

Mrs. Horst remained on sidewalk with Miss van Allen. Mr. Horst directed me to the rear of the Reilly premises.

There was a hand-drawn diagram inserted here showing a sheltered paved patio surrounded by hedges and fencing at the rear of the house. A kidney-shaped swimming pool, about twenty yards long, formed the center of the sketch. Poolside furniture was drawn with care; circular table, four plastic chairs and two reclining tanning beds, all labeled precisely. Various other items were indicated with arrows and letters. A small stick figure was drawn in the center of the swimming pool.

The deceased, Magdalene Reilly, aged 16, of 22513 Rochester Heights Grove, was found floating face down and naked in the center of the pool (see arrow in diagram). There were no signs of blood or injury to the body. Poolside furniture was not overturned or broken. There were no signs of violence and no blood on the patio surrounding the pool. One swimsuit (female), two towels and one sweatshirt were folded neatly on one of the poolside chairs (marked 'a'). One partially full pitcher of fruit punch and two plastic glasses, one empty and the other half-full, were sitting on the table (marked 'b'). Some of the punch was spilled on the table and paving stones below (area approx. ten inches in diameter, marked 'c').

Miss van Allen states that she came home from the airport at 10:00 p.m. and found her mother drunk and injured. Miss van Allen then came over to visit her friend, Magdalene, at approx. 10:15 p.m., found the deceased, in the swimming pool, and immediately ran to Mr. and Mrs. Horst's house from where the 911 call had originated.

According to Mrs. Horst, the deceased is the only daughter of Mr. and Mrs. James and Roberta Reilly. They were out at the theater and were expected back a little before midnight. Mr. and Mrs. Horst had spent the evening at home watching television. They did not see any unusual persons or activity in the house next door or in the neighboring vicinity. However, at 6:30 p.m., when Mrs. Horst went to the kitchen to make coffee before Seinfeld started, she noticed Mr. Clayton van Allen driving away "fast and angry."

Crime scene secured: 10:47 p.m.

Homicide contacted: 10:48 p.m.

The second incident report was from a female homicide detective, Michelle Chaisson, who had gone to the van Allen household to interview Tami and her parents in more detail. The information from Tami added little to the first report. Tami had just returned from a long weekend visiting friends in Eugene, Oregon. It was the rest of detective Chaisson's account that particularly got my attention.

Mrs. Sonya van Allen was found in the bedroom in no fit condition to be interviewed. She was barely conscious, and smelled strongly of alcohol. A nearly empty bottle of Smirnoff vodka (taken as evidence, tagged MR0613-B160) was found on the counter of the en-suite bathroom off the master bedroom. Mrs. Van Allen was wearing only a dressing gown. Numerous bruises, contusions and abrasions were noted on her face, neck and upper arms (photographs taken). There was dried blood on her lips, tongue, chin and also on the inner parts of her upper thighs.

Medical examiner and Sex Crimes Unit contacted at 1:05 a.m. on June 13th.

On the bathroom floor next to the bedroom

was a discarded vaginal diaphragm.
Material on the diaphragm and surrounding
floor resembled semen and small amounts
of blood (photographed and taken as
evidence, tagged MR0613-B162).

Tami van Allen supplied the make, color
and license plate of her father's car.
An APB went out for Clayton van Allen at
1:12 a.m. on June 13th.

There was a second report from this homicide detective, the
transcript of an interview she had with a now sober Sonya van Allen
from a hospital bed at 2:30 p.m. on the following day.

CHAISSON: Do you remember what happened
yesterday evening, Sonya? How did you get
these injuries?

VAN ALLEN: You said you picked up
Clayton, right? You got him in custody
and all?

CHAISSON: He's in the downtown precinct
jail, Sonya, being interrogated right now.
We're not going to let him go, so he can't
hurt you anymore. You're perfectly safe.

VAN ALLEN: Sure don't feel safe. Clayton's
got some kind of temper, you know? Don't

reckon he meant to hurt me bad. Not really. He was mad, though. Thought I was cheating on him. Got madder than hell and then got horny, like he always does when he gets mad. I didn't feel like doing it. He wasn't being nice so I told him I had a stomachache and then he got real mad.

CHAISSON: What happened then, Sonya? Please don't just shrug. We're recording this. Tell me in your own words what happened next.

VAN ALLEN: What you think happened? He did me over on the bed.

CHAISSON: You mean he had sexual intercourse with you?

VAN ALLEN: Yes.

CHAISSON: And beat you up?

VAN ALLEN: Got a little rough is all. He likes it rough sometimes. Well, most times, if you want to know the truth, but not usually that bad. Like I say, he was mad at me cause I didn't want to do it.

CHAISSON: What time was this, do you

194

think?

VAN ALLEN: About five or six o'clock, I guess.

CHAISSON: And when did he leave?

VAN ALLEN: Dunno. When he was done, I guess. I was a little drunk.

CHAISSON: You were more than a little drunk when I found you at around midnight. What did you do after he left? We found a vaginal diaphragm on the bedroom floor. Was that yours?

VAN ALLEN: Yeah, I pulled that sucker out soon as he was gone. Couldn't stand the thought of him inside me. It felt kind of humiliating, though I guess I deserved it in a way.

CHAISSON: No woman deserves to be treated like that, Sonya.

VAN ALLEN: I suppose. Anyways I was feeling pretty sick and my jaw hurt real bad so I had me a little more vodka.

This passive acceptance of brutality was hard for me to take,

even if I can understand why it occurs. I walked to the lunchroom to clear my head and zap my coffee before picking up the next section of the faxed material. This was another transcript, an interrogation of Clayton van Allen taken at almost the same time that his wife was recuperating in a hospital bed. A pair of detectives, Jason Donetti and Charles Price, were putting Clayton van Allen through the good-cop/ bad-cop routine.

DONETTI: So tell us again, Mr. van Allen, what were you doing at 3:30 a.m. out on Dry Creek Road when State Trooper Brian Scardale pulled you over?

VAN ALLEN: What was I doing? About twenty-six in a thirty-five zone. I sure as hell wasn't speeding, I know that.

PRICE: He didn't ask you what you weren't doing, wise ass. So what were you doing? Picking up some flowers to give to your wife in hospital or to take to little Magdalene's funeral?

VAN ALLEN: I don't know what you're talking about.

PRICE: No? So how come you yelled, "The bitch deserved it" when Trooper Scardale pulled you over. Sounds like a confession to me.

196

VAN ALLEN: I was referring to my wife. I had nothing to do with the girl. I didn't even know she was dead.

PRICE: You lying piece of-

DONETTI: Cool it, Chuck. Let me take over, okay? But you do admit, Mr. van Allen, that the first thing you said when you rolled down your window was, quote the bitch deserved it, close quote? Is that correct? You need to do more than nod your head Mr. van Allen. We need to get an oral record of all this.

VAN ALLEN: Yes.

DONETTI: And what did you mean by that remark?

VAN ALLEN: Sonya wouldn't put out for me. Said her stomach hurt or something. But she was getting ready to screw somebody else. I knew that. If her stomach hurt so goddamned bad how come she'd put her diaphragm in?

DONETTI: How do you know she had her diaphragm in?

197

VAN ALLEN: I'm not stupid. I seen the empty case in the bathroom and asked her about it. She said it was burst and she needed a new one. Lying bitch. I put my finger up and felt it, didn't I? It was sitting there all nice and cozy waiting for someone else, wasn't it?

PRICE: So you raped her to teach her a lesson, did you?

VAN ALLEN: Screw you. She's my goddamned wife. I'm entitled.

DONETTI: And you left the house around six thirty, you say? Where did you go then? Next door, maybe to Magdalene Reilly's house?

VAN ALLEN: The hell I did. I already told you. I went to an art auction out towards Alvin.

DONETTI: That's a long way to go for an art auction.

VAN ALLEN: It's my job, buddy. It's how I make a living. It was a special auction, anyway. There was some real good stuff on

198

offer.

DONETTI: And yet we can't find any mention of it in the newspapers. Wasn't it well advertised, Mr. van Allen? If it was such a good auction-

VAN ALLEN: It was for people in the trade, only.

PRICE: And what trade is that, van Allen? The smuggling trade? The black market trade in Native American artifacts trade? The drug trade?

DONETTI: You said you bought a couple of pieces of pottery but there was nothing in the trunk of your car when you were picked up.

VAN ALLEN: I was to pick them up today. Right about now, in fact.

PRICE: But you conveniently lost the address and you can't remember the woman's name who sold you the stuff or her phone number either. You think we are stupid or something? You know what I think? I think you left the house after beating the snot out of your wife and then you drove off to cool your jets and think it all over. You came back a little later and you saw little Magdalene lying out on a sun bed by the pool looking all perfect and inviting. You were still mad so you took it out on her. You raped her and drowned her in the pool and took off again. You'd have been headed for Galveston or some place if the State Patrol hadn't got you when they did.

VAN ALLEN: That's bullshit. I left the house a little after six and spent the whole damned evening at the auction. I was headed home when they picked me up. I had no idea something had happened to the girl.

DONETTI: But you did know Magdalene Reilly, Mr. van Allen, didn't you?

VAN ALLEN: Course I knew her. She was the kid next door. Nice kid. Kind of quiet. Didn't see much of her.

PRICE: Yeah, but I'll bet you always wanted to see more of her, scumbag, didn't you? You saw plenty of her last night, didn't you? Every last perfect square inch of her poor naked little body. Was that the turn on, van Allen, a nice innocent young thing with perfect skin? Nice change from the wrinkled old drunk that you usually sleep with, eh? Did you ever try getting it on with your own daughter, with young Tami?

[Suspect overturned the table and attempted to assault Officer Price. Officers Garrison and Mondallio entered the interrogation room to help restrain suspect.]

DONETTI: That's enough, Chuck. Let's take a break.

The next two reports were in the way of character witness testimonials. I was curious why Newton had chosen to send me these particular excerpts from the case file. It made me wonder what he hadn't sent me. There was a statement from Sonya's sister saying that she had filed for divorce a few days before Magdalene's murder. The sister also mentioned that Sonya had been physically abused by her alcoholic father, growing up, and had sustained a major skull fracture and concussion at the age of fifteen. The sister didn't know if Sonya had been sexually abused by her father but said she had never approved of her hooking up with Clayton van Allen. It made depressing reading - the sad and all too familiar tale of an abused girl apparently seeking out an abusive man to live with when she leaves the parental home.

Mr. and Mrs. Reilly's devastation came through in their statement. Magdalene was a nice girl, a quiet girl, an exemplary student who went to church and had no boyfriends. It was not the picture of a flirtatious tease but then this was the perspective of her grieving parents. They were hardly likely to be totally objective, or to be privy to all of their daughter's activities. Still she sounded like a very different personality than Myra Garfield.

The laboratory was waking up behind me. I could hear sounds of activity building up in the adjacent rooms and the floor below. I had one more document to review - the autopsy report from Lyle Newton. With my flight leaving in less than two hours I didn't have time to slake my professional curiosity very thoroughly but I wanted to give it a quick look for similarities to what was found on Myra Garfield. In the event it was disappointingly brief and sloppily written. Lyle Newton was a lot less thorough than I was or than he should have been. The cause of death was recorded as drowning. He had found semen in the vagina and no signs of injury or struggle. There was nothing else remarkable mentioned. No comments about finding anything under her nails, or whether he ever checked to see if she was pregnant. Not even any mention of the state of her heart or liver. It was a hurried and superficial examination. And yet Lyle Newton had been eager to return my phone call last night, remembered the case vividly, had brought his personal records with him to San Antonio, had arranged to fax me more documents than I had requested and was apparently bringing photographs to Portland with him. It was odd behavior.

I leaned back in my chair and made some mental comparisons between the two murders. Both were young women who had died of drowning after some sexual activity in secluded suburban settings but without signs of violence or struggle. Both were found naked and with their clothes piled neatly nearby. But Myra was promiscuous where Magdalene was apparently a saint. Magdalene's body had been found within hours, not two days later. With Magdalene everything had happened at the scene whereas Myra had been drugged at a different location and transported several miles in the back of a truck before being dumped in the pool to be drowned. There were certainly a few similarities between the cases but it was an imperfect symmetry.

I was halfway down the hall on my way to the airport when Ms. Efficiency, the temporary secretary, caught up with me.

"Professor McLure, I didn't know you were in the office already. There was a paper jam in the fax machine when I got in this morning so some of the overnight faxes didn't come through. After I fixed it the machine printed out page twenty-seven of a fax from Texas but I can't find the rest of it anywhere."

"I have the rest of it already, I think. I picked most of it up when I got in this morning. Thanks."

She sounded peeved. "I wish I had known. I've been asking all over the lab for the rest of the fax. Well you'll probably want this last page for completeness."

She thrust the page at me and stormed back to the orderly safety of her cubicle. I watched her firm young rump wriggling irritably inside her too-tight black skirt. I am sure those curves had caught the attention of several of the male members of staff but they did nothing for me. I don't even think they would have if I had been twenty years younger. Petty sniping and pouting body language is not a "turn on" for me. I like to think I gravitate towards women who seem happy with themselves and can roll with the unpredictabilities of life. But that is probably a fantasy on my part. I did end up with Elspeth Paterson after all.

I glanced at the missing page with little interest. I expected it to be another page from Newton's sloppy autopsy on Magdalene Reilly. Instead it was the toxicology report from the same case. Samples from the fruit punch found at the scene along with blood and urine samples from the girl's body all contained high levels of metabolites of the same drug. Barbiturates.

XV

An Elegant Discussion Of Death

The historic Multnomah Hotel in downtown Portland is a very elegant and sophisticated setting for an academic conference to discuss violent death. Although currently part of the Embassy Suites chain, it belongs to a very different era. It was built at a time when, rather than flying airplanes into large public buildings, it was considered a newsworthy publicity stunt to fly an airplane off the roof of a building, as Silas Christofferson did here in 1912. The hotel covers an entire city block adjacent to Burnside Street. Crystal chandeliers hang from the ornate gilt ceiling held up by twenty-four marble and terra cotta columns. Across from the reception desk a cheerful fire burns in the stately fireplace around which guests linger and recline in high-backed mahogany chairs or soft fabric couches. A wide staircase sweeps up to the graceful balcony of the mezzanine level, which overlooks the lobby. Banquet halls and meeting rooms open off the mezzanine. Discreet signs and helpful managers in smart gray livery guided me to the location for my workshop in much the same way that they have been escorting Presidents, Kings, and celebrities for the past hundred years.

I like to make my workshops as lively and practical as possible. With the help of the conference organizers I had six booths set up around the room. Each booth represented a different crime scene, with photographs, diagrams, 3-D models and evidence bags laid out on tables or pinned to boards. Once each display was set up it was covered with curtains and screens. Conference attendees were locked out until everything was in place. The hundred and fifty pathologists and forensic scientists who filed in at one p.m. entered with the eager anticipation of children descending the stairs on Christmas morning.

After some introductory remarks I invited the audience to divide into groups and to spend forty-five minutes moving around the room looking at the material in the displays. They were to evaluate each murder scene, look for mistakes and give a critique on how each crime scene should have been handled. For the next two hours we worked together to deconstruct and revisit those investigations with new insights and ideas.

The organization of criminal investigation in this country is surprisingly variable and loosely regulated. As an optimist I can argue that this allows for great diversity, experimentation, and comparison, which stimulates innovation and progress. As a pessimist this lack of standardization gets me down. It increases the rate of mistakes and miscommunication, and decreases the number of convictions. Most criminals escape justice not because they are especially smart but because of inequities in the system. If they have enough money the defense can mount a coordinated attack on the law enforcement and criminal investigators who support the prosecution. They can point out errors of omission and commission, inconsistencies and breeches of protocol.

Too many of the counties in the USA still use coroners, elected officials with little or no forensic training. The autopsies are carried out by doctors who may only do pathology as a part-time activity, don't visit the crime scene and remain unconnected to the forensic scientists or police investigators. The body is picked up by disinterested technicians who transport it to a location where it is given a cursory examination without attention to the crime scene or other clues to the circumstances surrounding the death. Inexperienced law-enforcement officers walk all over crime scenes and ruin much of the evidence. Only crimes that are obviously major get the attention of finger print experts or the precise documentation of the crime scene using the techniques of the Total Station Crew. Too often a crime is thought to be minor or routine, is treated as such, and by the time its true significance is understood the evidence is tainted or lost.

There were murmurs of admiration and jealousy when I finished my talk with a description of our set-up at The Dell. A long line of attendees stayed around to ask questions at the end, which is always the best indication of a successful workshop.

As the crowd thinned I became aware of a plump unattractive man hovering at the rear, trying to ensure that he was the last person to speak to me. No matter how much I wished it to be otherwise I knew this had to be Lyle Newton. The Western-style checked shirt and leather bolo tie said, "Texas." The egg stain on the sleeve and uneven tie-ends said, "Slob." It should be against the law to make tight fitting blue jeans for a butt that big but this is The Land Of The Free. His cowboy boots were unpolished. His flabby jowls dripped sweat onto dandruff-covered shoulders, which was surprising given how little hair he had left. His floppy wet lips might have looked better on a bigger person. Like a horse, maybe. Restless eyes looked out from doughy mounds of flesh. His vigorous handshake was like holding onto the frantic death throes of a wet fish.

He glanced around the now-empty room. "You got the stuff I sent you, then? I've got the photographs right here."

I said, "That's great Mr. Newton. I'm really looking forward to seeing them, but could I just take an hour to unwind in my room, unpack and take a shower first? Perhaps I could meet you by the fireplace in the lobby?"

He seemed flustered and disappointed as he stuffed the photographs back into the envelope. "Sure. Of course. You must be exhausted. It must be intense doing a long workshop like that. Great job, by the way. Want a drink in the bar? No? Okay, I'll see you at five, then. By the fireplace in the lobby."

The message light was on in my room. A cryptic message from Linda Munro said she had some good news to share and left me a Seattle number. She picked up on the first ring.

"How's your mom doing?" I asked.

"It's sweet of you to ask, Donald. She's better. Definitely better. She had a good night's sleep last night so I'm sure her neighbors did, too. And guess what? I had another talk to Tami after you left. I think I've persuaded her to come join us at Kamagutsz this Saturday."

"You've lost me, Linda. Which "us" are you referring to and what is Kamagutsz?"

"The Kamagutsz Hot Springs out on the Olympic Peninsula. I thought I told you I was taking some of my Women's Studies students for a retreat at the Hot Springs this weekend. There will be nine of us altogether, ten if Tami comes, so I booked the whole place for the day. Do you not wish you could be a fly on the wall, Donald? Ten naked women in a secluded cave beside a waterfall on a tree-covered mountain – I'd have thought that would be a nice fantasy for you."

"I'll pass. The idea of naked women in Hot Tubs has lost some of its appeal for me recently." I was thinking of Myra Garfield's murder when I said it but the sharp intake of breath on the other end of the phone made me realize that Linda had taken this as an indirect slight on her behavior during "The Hot Tub Incident" of three years ago. I blundered on. "Did your other students not mind having a stranger join them for the retreat?"

"Not at all. One of them kind of knows Tami and they could all empathize with what she's been through. They can do some bonding, and practice group facilitation techniques. Should be a lot of fun."

I was glad to get out of my stiff sports jacket, shirt and necktie and take a long hot shower after Linda hung up. In a pair of comfy corduroy pants, open-necked shirt and crew-neck sweater I felt more like myself as I descended to the lobby a few minutes before five. Lyle Newton was already well ensconced round the fire. He had placed his briefcase and jacket on adjoining chairs to warn off other guests, and was nursing a large drink. Rum and Coke would be my guess. The alcoholic's friend. To an untutored eye it could pass for a soft drink and for anyone else there was no way to know what proportion of the glass contained Coke and how much was alcohol.

"Suitably rested and refreshed, Professor McLure? Let me buy you a drink."

A waitress materialized at his side. Cocktail waitresses have an instinct for which customers merit frequent attention. I ordered a glass of Bridgeport Blue Heron Ale, one of Oregon's many excellent microbrews. Newton gulped down his nearly full glass and ordered the same again. His anxious trembling seemed less noticeable than it had when he had approached me after the workshop. He slid a large brown envelope across the glass coffee table towards me and leaned back with anticipation.

"What do you make of these?"

"What am I looking at?" I said.

"Photographs taken by me and my assistant during the autopsy on the Reilly girl."

My first sinking thought was that Lyle Newton must be a pedophile. All the photographs were close-ups of a young girl's perineum. In some, her legs were placed together demurely, showing a healthy growth of unshaved pubic hair and the soft curves of her early womanhood. In others her thighs were spread wide apart to emphasize the absence of bruising, scratches or injury. Several close-ups showed the gloved fingers of Newton or his assistant spreading her labia widely to reveal the most intimate details of her vagina. In another setting it would have been certifiable as child pornography but the emphasis here was on anatomical detail, not titillation.

Newton leaned over and poked a stubby finger. "That one shows it best."

In the small vaginal opening behind the labia a pale flimsy membrane could be seen extending across the upper third of the hole. It had a ragged edge and crossed the gap at an oblique angle. Below this the pink moistness of the vaginal lining was revealed along with some tenacious gray liquid. The wooden stick from a medical sampling swab protruded from the sticky goo.

"Are you saying that she was a virgin?" I said.

"The presence of the remnants of her hymen is incontrovertible, Professor McLure. Not only was Magdalene Reilly a virgin at the start of the evening of June 12th, she remained one to her death. No man could have penetrated that tight young hole without tearing her maidenhead."

Maybe he really was a pedophile. He seemed to linger over his sentences. Spittle formed on his loose wet lips as he savored the luscious sound of the words he selected. I quickly covered the photographs as our waitress returned. She looked to be many years and many men beyond her own virginity but I still didn't want her seeing those graphic photographs. Newton sucked down his Rum and Coke like he was the first man at the oasis, and ordered another.

"I take it that is semen you are sampling?" I said when she had gone.

"Absolutely, and it is Clayton van Allen's semen at that. The genetic match was perfect."

"What's your explanation?"

"My interpretation is that Clayton van Allen was a psychopath. A pervert. He got his sexual pleasure from violence and death. I think he killed her first and then masturbated over her."

"But your autopsy report makes no mention of violence. She appears to have died quietly, drugged with barbiturates and then drowned. Was there any alcohol in her system?"

"None."

"Any blood or skin under her nails? Any needle marks? Your report is remarkably detail-free. You don't even mention her virginity and yet you took those photographs."

Newton looked truly uncomfortable for the first time. He drained the rest of his glass. The waitress whisked it away before his hand had time to replace it on the table. I was beginning to lose count of how many he had consumed, but I bet she hadn't.

"I was not exactly free to write the report I wanted, Professor McLure. I was what you'd call "on probation" at the time."

"For what?"

"A trifling matter. Unsubstantiated allegations. The details don't matter. However, my superior in Houston insisted that I submit a draft report to him, which then got edited. Only what he considered to be the relevant details were to be included. There were no lies, you understand, just the omission of any details that might confuse a jury." He must have noticed my look of disgust. "I can see that you disapprove, Professor McLure, but consider this. Clayton van Allen was a marked man. A known felon. Detectives Price and Mondallio had been tracking him for months. He was suspected of selling artifacts robbed from sacred Native American burial sites. And he dealt in drugs, too. This conviction was too good to pass up. I mean there was no doubt that he did it. They just wanted a nice clean case for the jury."

The more I listened to Lyle Newton the less I liked him. Medical examiners should not work for either the prosecution or the defense. It is our professional obligation to seek the truth and present all the details that might shed light on how our clients, the deceased, have died.

"What's your estimate of the time of death?" I said.

"Between seven thirty and ten fifteen," he said with confidence.

"Based on what evidence?"

He gave me a slimy grin. "Magdalene called a friend at seven thirty and sounded quite coherent. Tami van Allen found her body at ten fifteen."

"Was there any spermicide found along with van Allen's semen?"

His look of admiration was as obsequious as his grin. "You are a man who likes his details, I see. The answer is "yes," a fact that the prosecution used to further implicate van Allen."

"How so?"

"They argued that he had already had intercourse with his wife a few hours before he murdered the Reilly girl. Mrs. Van Allen had a diaphragm and used a liberal application of spermicidal cream with that. Traces of spermicide would be all over his penile skin unless he had washed himself between the events, which seems highly unlikely. The presence of spermicide made the possibility of the act being committed by another suspect less likely. At least the jury agreed with the prosecution on that point."

"That's pretty weak conjecture. Was van Allen's defense lawyer asleep?" I said.

"More or less. Van Allen couldn't afford a good attorney. Turns out van Allen was in serious financial debt. His wife said she had no idea. After the trial his house was repossessed. The wife and daughter were left with practically nothing. Van Allen had to use a court appointed public defender, a guy close to retirement, chosen with care by the judge and prosecution, I'm sure. He lives in Florida, now, I believe."

Sometimes the unfairness of or judicial system depresses me. Van Allen's lawyer hadn't even made rudimentary challenges to the case. I said, "Had Clayton van Allen ever been circumcised?"

Newton was taken aback by that question. "I have no idea. Why ever do you ask?"

"I have a very hard time buying the argument that a guy would retain enough spermicide on his skin so that it would contaminate an ejaculate occurring several hours later. Especially if you postulate no direct bodily contact between van Allen and the girl, which is what your photographs suggest. It would be an outside possibility if the guy was uncircumcised. The extra fold of skin might catch and hold more of the ejaculate and protect it from being rubbed off by his underpants. But in the absence of a foreskin I'd say it is highly unlikely that enough spermicide would be retained. It is a testable hypothesis, though. I should ask for a few volunteers from our lab to do some experiments with me."

He gave me a distasteful look. "Your passion for scientific

study far surpasses mine, Professor McLure. I believe the man was guilty."

"So why have you kept the photographs? What bothers you about this case four years on?"

"I modified my reports in order to keep my job. My circle of friends is all in the Houston area. But two months after van Allen's conviction I was transferred to San Antonio. It was presented as a restructuring within the department but it was a demotion. I believe I have been treated unjustly. I want to appeal to be transferred back to Houston. I was hoping that you would act as a reference to vouch for the true thoroughness of my work. Your name would help a lot."

I couldn't bear to look at the man one minute longer. When he became preoccupied with re-ordering his umpteenth drink I tossed a few dollars onto the table to cover the cost of my beer and departed to my room.

The rest of my stay in Portland was pleasant enough. Wednesday was taken up with committee meetings for the Western Section of the American Society of Forensic Pathologists. I checked in with Callum, who reassured me that Harvey and Taffy had not in fact been poisoned by the toxic casserole. Instead the three of them had gone to Golden Gardens Park so that Harvey and Callum could satisfy their stone-throwing urges by hurling rocks into Puget Sound while Taffy rampaged over the beach looking for dead seagulls to roll in.

On Wednesday evening I had a great meal, on my own, at Mother's Bistro, a few blocks from the hotel. Mother's is my favorite restaurant in all of Portland, combining great food with a homely atmosphere and very reasonable prices. And I approve of their culinary approach. They don't drown perfectly good meat or fish in half a pint of caramelized-fennel-mint-marionberry-demi-glaze. I ended the evening by previewing a PG-13 action-adventure film in my room to see if it would be suitable for Callum to watch sometime. I know that some parents let ten-year-olds watch all the R-rated movies they want. Call me overprotective, if you like, but I'm in no hurry to expose Callum to the sordid side of adult life.

On Thursday morning I ran along the Willamette River for a few miles and then had a swim amid the marbled columns in the basement swimming pool at the hotel. I participated in a Meet-the-Professor breakfast where conference delegates presented puzzling cases and asked a panel of experts to comment. I saw Lyle Newton taking copious notes in the back of the room but he asked no questions and made no further attempt to contact me again.

I was stuffing wet shorts and dirty T-shirts into my case before checking out when Katy Pearson called my room. She seemed friendly and even a little playful, connecting on a level that hovered between well-respected colleague and interesting potential new friend. Or maybe that was wistful thinking on my part.

"Hi, how is the academic world treating you? Must be great to cast out pearls of wisdom to the adoring masses while reclining on your bed ordering room service in a fancy hotel."

"Actually, I don't do those activities at the same time. I dispense the pearls in a lecture hall, but only invite a few of the prettier and more devoted attendees back to my room to peel me some grapes and help me relieve the tension in my taught, muscular body. That gurgling sound you hear in the background is two of my concubines filling up the tub with asses' milk for my bath. Or maybe it is wise-ass's milk."

I liked her laugh. It was full, throaty and self-confident. "I asked for that, I guess. Good comeback. Anyway, I didn't just call to tease you. Remember the Texas case you mentioned to me Monday night? The one I said couldn't be related to the Garfield case since the perpetrator has already been caught and locked up?"

"I certainly do. I've been pouring over the details of that case for the past two days. There are things about it that trouble me, even if it is not connected to Myra Garfield's death."

"But what if it is related, Donald?"

"What do you mean?"

"Clayton van Allen was released from prison five weeks ago."

Katy made me summarize what I had learned before she gave me the details to back up this bombshell. She was interested but not totally surprised in what I had to say.

"Sounds like the statement van Allen gave to the police was accurate," she said. "He's been pleading his innocence and filing the same story to an unbelieving and unyielding Appeals Panel for the past three years."

"What do you think made them change their mind?" I said.

"He got a lucky break. An altruistic young woman, straight out of Law School, was defending a female client on a charge of selling stolen artifacts. She cross-checked and found her client's name also showed up in van Allen's appeals. Turns out the woman had sold van Allen two legal and legitimate pieces the night of the Reilly girl's murder. The woman was surprised when he never showed up to collect them the next day. She had held on to them and was eager to showcase how honest she had been, so she testified to meeting van Allen on the night Magdalene Reilly was murdered."

"And her alibi stood up in court?"

"Two other dealers corroborated it. And the time of their meetings was from eight to ten p.m. The auction was close to a hundred miles from his home. He would have needed to drive fast to get to the auction site by eight if he left at six thirty. There was no way he was anywhere near the house during the time when Magdalene Reilly was murdered."

"And he was released five weeks ago?"

"There's more, Donald. His parents are dead and he doesn't keep up with his siblings. The only person he kept up any correspondence with from prison, apart from his lawyer, was a cousin who lives … guess where? In Burien, a couple of miles south of the Fauntleroy ferry terminal and just across the water from Vashon Island."

220

THURSDAY

XVI

Fight Or Flight

It is a short shuttle flight from Portland back to Seattle but it still gave me plenty of time to rethink the possibilities linking these two murders. To my mind they had to be connected. There were just too many similarities for it to be a coincidence. Three days before Magdalene's murder Sonya Stillwell had filed for divorce from a man who regularly beat her up and was on the brink of leaving her penniless. Yet she had inserted her contraceptive diaphragm that evening in anticipation of sex with someone. The name that kept popping into my head was Frank Stillwell. Had he shown up for a clandestine meeting that evening? Maybe Sonya had told him that Clayton would be far away at an art auction and that Tami wasn't expected back till late. But when he showed up Sonya was battered and semi-conscious. Frank would have been enraged beyond reason. But then I had to postulate that he ran next door and murdered an innocent girl. Cleverly, too. Without signs of violence. He then inserted semen, tinged with spermicide into her vagina from Sonya's discarded diaphragm in order to frame the hated Clayton van Allen. It was an unlikely sequence of events, to say the least. A man who

223

was apparently fond of Sonya and expecting an evening of romance would not behave like that.

The plane had touched down and I was picking up my truck from the airport Park'n'Ride when another possibility struck me. What if Frank showed up, found Sonya seriously injured and ran next door for help? There, to his horror and surprise, he found poor Magdalene floating dead in the swimming pool, a tragic victim of teen suicide. Maybe she had been repressed and friendless in her stuffy religious suburban shackles. So she had washed down her mother's barbiturate sleeping pills with half a jug of fruit punch, then staggered to the swimming pool to give her parents a shock she felt they deserved. I pictured the events in my mind to make them seem more real and believable.

Maybe big Frank stumbled in on the scene at the swimming pool and panicked. It wouldn't look good if he called the police. Or maybe Tami came home and found him there with Tami's mother beaten up and her best friend drowned. Frank's evening would go south in a hurry if either of those things happened. He would have to think fast. Maybe he decided to take advantage of one person's tragedy to prevent his own. Hell, he could convince himself that he would even be doing the Reilly family a favor. It would be much easier for Mr. and Mrs. Reilly to accept that their little saint was raped and murdered than that their own insensitivity and poor parenting caused Magdalene to take her own life. So maybe Frank lifted her out of the pool. Would he have been able to do that without scraping her on the sides? Sure, he's a big strong guy. He could manage that. So he laid her on her back, snuck back to Sonya's bathroom and got a teaspoonful of Clayton's slimy ejaculate. Then he tiptoed back to the side of the pool without spilling any. After carefully inserting the incriminating mess inside the girl's vagina he could have pushed her quietly back into the water. Finally, he would leave the scene and slip away, dripping wet, into the muggy Texas evening.

It was a stretch, I realized, but it was theoretically possible. By the time I drove away from Sea-Tac I had convinced myself that is was not only possible, it was a perfect explanation and I was nothing short of brilliant. So much more that a mere forensic pathologist, I was the all-purpose investigative and deductive genius. I would run it past Katy and soak up her amazement and adulation when I got back to The Dell.

The route I take back to Delridge Way from the airport actually takes me through Burien. As I stopped at every traffic light I found myself looking at strangers suspiciously, wondering if one of them was Clayton van Allen bent on revenge. Daydreaming, I strayed from my usual route and found myself winding down past the Fauntleroy YMCA towards the ferry terminal just as the three-thirty-five from Vashon was unloading. I ground to a halt behind a Metro bus as a uniformed policeman held us up and directed a stream of cars off the boat. I was cursing my stupidity when I spotted Frank Stillwell. I almost had to pinch myself. It must be a cosmic sign.

He was on his own behind the wheel of the Cadillac, turned right off the dock and drove past me heading south. That would take him towards White Center, and beyond that was Burien. I was sure he hadn't spotted me in my nondescript gray truck, tucked in behind a bus. I found a gap after three more cars, did a quick U-turn and caught up with him again going east on Roxbury.

I find it hard enough following another car in convoy even when I know roughly where I'm going and the guy in front is being cooperative and drives slowly. Frank Stillwell must have been an inner-city cab driver in a previous life. He weaved from lane to lane without any signals or concern for his fellow drivers. His interpretation of traffic signals was that red means "stop," green means "go," and orange means "go fast." I nearly lost him twice as we wound our way deeper into the no-man's land to the southwest of the airport.

The scene was gradually changing. The shop fronts were shabbier. There were pawn shops and check-cashing outfits, and a variety of Vietnamese and other low-income Asian markets. To say we were on a major flight path is a major understatement. The street he turned into felt like it was about a hundred feet from the black rubber skid marks on the runway.

They say if you live near the freeway you can learn to convince yourself that the constant noise of traffic is like the ocean surf breaking gently onto the beach. I wondered what mind games a person would need to use in this situation – that there's a tidal wave or a tornado blowing through your neighborhood every three minutes? The street that Stillwell stopped on contained a dismal row of squat, unloved houses. Hunkering close to the ground, their roofs were curling up at the edges, ready to come off like scabs that had festered there just long enough to be picked at. Not a living soul ventured out of doors, not even a stray cat. The only vegetation in the tiny yards was some sickly crab grass clinging for dear life to the ground. Presumably everything else had long since been uprooted and blown half way to Tacoma by airplane backdrafts.

Stillwell pulled in between two partly dismantled junk-cars. He was taking his chances in that neighborhood. The Cadillac fit right in. He was likely to find the car sitting on four piles of bricks with the wheels missing by the time he returned. I cruised past him with my head turned away and did a slow turn out of sight at the far end of the street. On the way back I parked about fifty yards beyond the Cadillac, on the opposite side of the street so that I could see Stillwell and his car in my rear view mirror.

He stalked up and down the street consulting a scrap of paper in his hand before selecting a particular house and marching up to the door. I took a note of the number. The house shuddered under his fist, although it could have been from the Boeing 747 that happened to be thundering above the roof at the time with its wheels almost scraping the tiles. It was a long time before a woman answered. At least I think it was a woman. I had to turn around for a better look, which was very unprofessional of me, I'm sure. A wiser man might think I was getting cocky, but not me. I was warming to my new role as Ace Investigator. Stillwell towered over the woman in the doorway waving his arms and occasionally pounding a fist on the door jam. After several minutes she must have let him in. The door closed. I waited patiently, the way I imagined Ace Investigators might need to in these circumstances.

I almost missed it in the gloom. A crouching figure suddenly ran round the side of the house from the back. It was a man, but a good six inches shorter than Stillwell. He crossed to my side of the street, hopped into a car and was pulling away from the kerb when

Frank Stillwell exploded out of the front door again in pursuit. I caught sight of the driver as his car passed mine. He had a stubbled chin, crewcut, and sunken eyes set into waxy gray skin over taught cheekbones. He looked thin, unhealthy and had the steering wheel in a death-grip. I think I glimpsed an earring in his right ear but couldn't be sure.

The car itself was a generic dark blue mid-size sedan, a rental car most likely. I couldn't see the make or license plate so I pulled out and began to follow him. I think my plan was to get close enough to get those pieces of information about the car and then call Katy. It wasn't a great plan. By the time we got to the first traffic lights there were two cars between me and the stranger. When I paused to review the situation I had precious little reason to think the stranger was Clayton van Allen. I had just decided that it was. I did, however, recognize the belligerent bully in the large lilac car sitting right on my tail as Frank Stillwell. Well done, Donald. This was a great plan, right enough. Now I was caught in rush-hour traffic, on wet streets in the fading light careening around aimlessly into an unfamiliar industrial wasteland. To spice it up a little more I was sandwiched between two potential murderers. Maybe I should stick to cutting up dead bodies, after all, and leave the heroics to others.

I had figured out that the stranger's car was a Japanese import of some sort and was closing in to read the license plate when he made an unexpected sharp left turn. We were in some derelict area where huge disused earth-moving vehicles and broken down semi-trucks were stored among piles of gravel behind high metal fencing with razor wire on top. Ahead of us the red and white barrier of a railroad crossing was descending and the flashing lights and clanking bells told me that a train was approaching. The stranger pulled up a few yards short of the barrier and looked anxiously behind him. He ignored me as I skidded to a stop right on his tail. His eyes were fixed on Stillwell, who came within an inch of rear-ending me. Before his car had even come to a halt Stillwell threw open the door and began rushing towards the blue sedan.

The Burlington Northern freight train was less than fifty yards from the crossing when the stranger's car lurched forward, swerved round the barrier and bounced across the railway line in front of the train, spraying gravel as it went. A chorus of angry car horns and screeching train brakes on metal rails provided the sound track to the drama. By the time Stillwell reached the barrier the first of about a hundred clanking container trucks began trundling past. In the gaps between them I could see the blue sedan disappearing into the darkness of the winter afternoon. Frank Stillwell flung back his head and roared impotently against the sides of the railway cars. Then he turned round and recognized me.

His eyes registered complete amazement and utter menace in equal measure. Under different circumstances I might have been willing to have a philosophical conversation with him about wild coincidences, missed opportunities, and how they are all delicate threads woven into the rich tapestry of Life. But this was not the time. I cranked the engine and made an attempt to swerve past him and turn around to make my escape. Unfortunately, I am no stunt driver. He grabbed the passenger door handle and tried to yank it open. The door wasn't locked but luckily for me it doesn't open easily either. A major dent from the horn of an angry Highland bull in a moonlit field in Okanogan last year saw to that. But that's a different story.

I had to stop and back up or I would have wiped Stillwell along the side of the freight train. Before I could get the truck back into first gear he had flung himself onto the hood and was pressing his face against the glass, daring me to drive away.

I rolled down the window and yelled. "I've already called the police, Stillwell. They'll be here in no time." It was a total fabrication on my part, but I managed to deliver it with some semblance of authority.

A large hand reached in through the open window and grabbed my wrist. He shouted, "What the hell do you want with me? He's the guy you ought to be following."

"Was that van Allen?" I said.

He screamed in disbelief. "You don't even know? What the hell are you doing here? I thought you were a goddamned doctor. Get out the truck right now and tell me what you're doing here."

I had serious doubts that it was conversation he wanted to inflict on me right then but I was running out of options. My father always taught me two rules about facing bullies. The first is to go on the offensive without showing fear. The second is to be ready to run like hell if rule one doesn't work out. I flung open the door assertively and jumped out into the open with my knees bent and my feet slightly apart in the stance for a good running start.

"What did you want with van Allen, Frank? Did you find out that he'd been released, that plan A hadn't worked in Houston? Was it time for a more direct approach, eh?"

He stared at me as though I were a particularly irritating mosquito that just won't take the hint and leave him alone. He measured his words with heavy emphasis. "I came to ask his cousin to tell him to stay the hell away from Sonya or I'd break every bone in his thieving little body. I don't give a damn whether he's in prison or out of it so long as he stays away from Sonya and me. Do you have any more stupid, off-base questions?"

That response seemed to be giving him the moral upper hand. I didn't like the way he was clenching and unclenching his fists. I needed to make another wild stab at pre-emptive offense or I'd be implementing rule number two in a hurry. I said, "It depends. Is there any reason for me to think I'll get honest answers, Frank. Do you want to try telling me again where you were last Friday night? You told Detective Pearson you played three games at the West Seattle Bowling Alley. I'm wondering how you managed that. Everyone else was standing in the parking lot for two hours waiting for the Fire Department to turn the lights back on."

That stopped him cold. There might even have been a melodramatic silence after that, except for one thing. The train had finally passed, the barrier was lifting and a dozen car horns were encouraging the two lunatics at the front of the line to move. Stillwell caught me off guard and shoved me against my truck.

"Pull over to the side and I'll tell you," he said.

I felt distinctly more vulnerable after the train had clanked off into the distance and the angry column of motorists had shouted the last of their insults at us and trundled off to the warmth of their homes. The civilized lights from downtown Seattle seemed a very long way away to the north. The chill evening air enveloped me like a shroud. My teeth began to chatter even though I wore a thick sweater and jacket. Stillwell was only in shirtsleeves and yet he steamed with fury. He sensed my discomfort and laced his words with sarcasm.

"The police are taking a while to get here, Doc. Sure you called the right number?"

"When they get here they'll ask you the same question I just did," I said. "What were you really doing the night Myra Garfield was murdered?"

"I went to see Covington."

"Sebastian Covington? At the bowling alley?"

"At Salty's. It's a restaurant over by Alki."

"I know where it is, Mr. Stillwell. I've eaten there more than once. Why didn't you tell me that on Monday?"

The hostility was beginning to leave him. "I didn't want Sonya to know that was what I was doing. Covington laid me off last year and gave me a lousy severance package. I was going to negotiate a better deal."

"Do you blame Covington more than David Garfield for your termination? You look surprised. I know more than you think, Mr. Stillwell. I know that David Garfield was your immediate boss. I also know that his daughter, Myra accused you of molesting her, or harassing her sexually, at least, and that you came round to her house to confront her about it three days before she died."

His head fell forward like a discarded string puppet. The rain had started again, too, which added to the picture of his dejection. He looked almost vulnerable. For the first time he seemed cold enough to start shivering.

There was quiet irony in his voice. "Ah, Myra. Sweet innocent Myra. Scheming, manipulative, ruthless, conniving, self-centered, power-hungry little Myra. I never laid a finger on her, Doc. Some poisons I can recognize. Besides, I've got principles. She flirted with me plenty but I expect it was done to irritate her parents or to make someone else jealous. She actually seemed to have a soft spot for me. It was Covington she wanted to hurt. She wanted my help doing it."

"Why? I thought she had interned with him last summer," I said.

"She did more than intern with him. She slept with him. You don't believe me? Ask him. He admitted it to me. No, that's too mild. He bragged about it is what he did. A brief fling for four weeks last summer. At least that's all he wanted. A few platefuls of Spring

Lamb while his wife was on vacation. But Myra wanted more. She doesn't take rejection well. She enjoyed being in the limelight, being the rich suave CEO's special personal assistant. Have you ever met Covington? He's a smooth operator. I don't know how his wife puts up with it."

I wasn't in the mood to hear any more about Linda Munro's tragic life, right then. I felt guilty enough about her already. Besides, I was having a hard time keeping up with Frank Stillwell's story. Or believing it. A thought occurred to me.

"Had Covington ever been to Myra Garfield's house? Did he know where she lived?"

He shrugged. "More than likely. I'm sure David Garfield had him over to schmooze with the boss. I don't know if he was ever there with Myra on her own, though."

"You said that Myra wanted to enlist your help."

"She knew I was sore about being laid off. She wanted me to tell Covington that I knew about their affair together and that I would make it public knowledge, go to the press and all that, unless he took her back on as an intern and started seeing her again."

"Why didn't she just confront him herself?"

"She thought that would push him away. She wanted me to come across as the bad guy and portray Myra as the love-struck innocent who wanted to be back in his royal favor again. I guess part of that

234

might even have been true. I don't know. She had a devious little mind. She must have called Covington on the Friday morning to warn him that I wanted to talk to him, but she wouldn't tell him what it was about."

That was interesting. If true, it meant that Covington had been forewarned about Stillwell's visit. From what I had heard, Sebastian Covington was a man who could think and plan fast and might just manage to make use of that piece of intelligence to arrange things to improve his own position.

"What was supposed to be in it for you?" I said.

"I could use the information for my own advantage, too, she said."

"You mean to blackmail him for your own benefit as well as for hers"

"It's easy getting on your moral high horse when your life's going great, Buddy. It's a hell of a lot harder when you're trying to scrape by. All I wanted was what was rightfully mine. Other employees who had been laid off after four years of good service and sales to the company were getting termination bonuses of ten, twenty or even thirty thousand dollars. I got five. That extra money would come in real handy right about now, before I start framing in the new house."

Flashing lights and sirens descended on us out of the darkness to the north. A spotlight pinned us against the cyclone fencing and a gruff voice on the police bullhorn told us to freeze. After thirty minutes of sweating in the soaking wet February air it was an easy command to obey.

XVII

Stir-Fry Emotions

"I thought you and I were supposed to be on the same team!" Katy Pearson's phone voice sounded a lot less cuddly and warm than it had earlier in the day. I stood dripping onto the bathroom floor with one towel round my waist, rubbing my hair dry with another while she vented. "Jeff Tucker is having a field day with this. Squad cars from Burien and Tukwila converge on the industrial district in response to nine-one-one calls from several motorists who are stuck in a back-up because of a violent altercation at a railroad crossing. And what do they find? The chief medical examiner from Delridge Way going toe-to-toe with a prime suspect in a murder investigation."

"Prime suspect? Since when has Tucker considered Frank Stillwell to be a prime suspect? That's the problem. No-one except you and me has been considering anyone else but Aaron Klein."

"I've been working on Tucker all week, Donald, trying to convince him to consider Frank Stillwell. Now it looks to him like

I've been working behind his back, getting you involved in things that are way beyond reasonable for your job description. So why didn't you call me? I could have called in some back up. You know, people who actually know how to tail and confront a potentially violent suspect."

That was a low blow. Totally justified, but a low blow nonetheless. I said, "I planned to call you, Katy. Events kind of overtook me." There was an angry silence on the other end of the phone. So much for basking in her adulation. "Look, I'm sorry. I'm feeling duly humbled and embarrassed by all of this. I'm also standing here dripping wet and shivering. If you want to shout at me some more then come round and do it in person. I need to get dressed and grab something to eat."

"I can't. I'm at the downtown office. I haven't had dinner yet either."

She hesitated just enough to embolden me. I said, "How much longer do you plan to be at the office?"

"I don't know. An hour at least, maybe a little more."

"Swing by on your way home and let me feed you, then. I was going to do a Stir-Fry. There's plenty for two. Callum and Jen have eaten already." I could tell she was swithering. "Go on, Katy. I make a really good Stir-Fry Peace Offering. I can have it ready in about an hour. Besides, if you come over I can tell you more details. I didn't actually tell the police who it was that Stillwell and I were chasing through Burien, but I'll tell you. It was Clayton van Allen."

I hung up before she could respond, dashed to the bedroom to fling on some clothes, and then surveyed the contents of the refrigerator. Jennifer usually has it well stocked with produce but I had been gone for three days. She might have reverted to her freshman college student diet of Cheerios or Ramen noodles three times a day. As it turned out there were a few celery sticks that were still crisp, one red onion that was going soft on one end and a bowl of leftover boiled potatoes that might fry up nicely, but the mushrooms were wrinkled and dry. It was lean pickings.

I made a quick dash to Market Time on Fremont Avenue and got some fresh prawns, a red bell pepper, another onion and a handful of mushrooms. I went back and forth about which variety to buy. I prefer Shitakes but didn't want it to look like I had gone to a lot of bother. Plain brown button mushrooms would do. But what about wine? Would that make it seem too presumptuous of potential romance? And would she disapprove of someone who drinks alcohol during the middle of the workweek? Or was she one of those Native Washingtonian zealots who disapprove of anything except Washington State wine and frown on Californian or European imports? Whenever I catch myself acting like an insecure adolescent I break out in a cold sweat and curse my repressed Scottish upbringing. "Live dangerously, Donald," I told myself. "A drink sounds good, right now." I grabbed a bottle of decent Australian Chardonnay and headed home.

By the time the doorbell rang I had the rice on and everything cut up ready to go. I assumed that the thundering feet down the stairs was Callum but when I went to check I found Jennifer and

Katy introducing themselves to each other in the living room. They were both smiling in that way women have when they are sharing a joke about inept men.

Jennifer was in breezy mood. "Hi Dad. I was just thanking Katy for driving you around last Sunday."

I could see Callum's big brown eyes peeking through the banisters, taking in everything. Jennifer scooped him up on her way back upstairs.

"Don't burn the rice, Dad," she said.

While I busied myself with the Wok, I outlined my theory of Magdalene Reilly's suicide and how it just coincidentally happened on the night Clayton van Allen beat up Sonya and so gave Frank Stillwell a golden opportunity to frame van Allen for murder. It sounded a lot less convincing than it had on the airplane earlier in the day.

Katy listened politely but I could tell she wasn't impressed. She was wearing a burgundy sweater and a dark brown waistcoat and dark red earrings to match her sweater. She kept pushing imaginary strands of hair behind her ears. It was a cute gesture, and made me wonder if she used to have long hair and couldn't break the habit of messing with it. It also made me think she was getting tired of my wandering and ill-founded theory. She waited until I faltered, then pointed out that there was no specific evidence suggesting that the girl had committed suicide or that Frank Stillwell was involved in any way.

I quickly moved on to a description of my early evening adventures in Burien and down by the Sea-Tac industrial area. As I described the meeting of Frank Stillwell and Sebastian Covington on the evening of the Garfield murder Katy hung her head in frustration.

"Damn it, Donald, after spending all week trying to convince my superiors that Stillwell could be the murderer you're telling me that he may have a cast-iron alibi. I've even got a meeting set up with Tucker and Duane Walton, our captain. I've been telling them that his alibi is weak and that all we need is some specific physical evidence tying him to the girl. I really need to track down Covington and see if his story matches. If it does then neither Stillwell nor Covington was responsible for Myra's death," she said.

"Maybe not directly, but one of them could have had an accomplice," I suggested.

"You could equally well argue that Clayton van Allen had an accomplice in the Texas murder. You're convinced that the two murders are connected. Does that have to mean they were done by the same person?"

I said, "That's the most likely explanation, but not the only one. I'd say that whoever killed Myra at least had detailed knowledge of the Texas case. Suppose Clayton van Allen had an accomplice in Texas who was involved with his other shady dealings. Maybe that person murdered Magdalene Reilly so as to frame van Allen to get him out of the picture. Maybe van Allen figured that out while he was in prison and came back for revenge."

"So you are postulating that his accomplice is someone around here? Like Frank Stillwell, or Sonya, his ex-wife? It's possible, Donald, but there are a lot of what-ifs and maybes."

"Who else would know that van Allen had been released from prison, Katy? And when did they know?"

She sighed. "I guess I could make some more inquiries with the contacts I made in Texas. But for now we need to focus on the facts. The physical evidence in each case links the dead girls to two different men, Aaron Klein and Clayton van Allen. Those men appear to have no connection with each other and nothing in common except that neither you nor I think they did the murders. We are not in a very strong position to charge anyone else, right now."

I poured some wine, served the meal and we both ate in silence for a while. It felt strange to be sharing a meal with an attractive woman again. Strange, but really nice. She was right, of course. Although the number of interconnecting players seemed to be growing in the two murder cases, we had little concrete evidence tying them together.

I could tell that we were being watched even before I saw Katy look up and smile at someone standing behind me. It was Callum.

"Are you guys on a date?" he said.

"No," I said, a little too firmly. I knew the wine had been a bad

242

idea.

Katy laughed. "Hardly. This is not the stuff I talk about when I'm out on a date."

"What were you talking about?" Callum is quick to pick up on when he has a kinder-and-gentler audience.

"We were talking about murderers," I said. "And how to catch the bad guys."

Katy said, "What made you think we were out on a date? Is this what your dad always cooks when he's trying to impress a new woman?"

"No way! I don't think he ever goes out on dates, even though he and mom are split up. Jen thinks he needs to."

I almost choked on my food. Jennifer stormed into the room with color in her cheeks and gave Callum the evil eye.

"Callum, that's quite enough," she said.

Katy seemed totally comfortable and addressed herself to Callum. "Well, if I was on a date with your dad I might ask him what his kids were like, but I'm finding that out for myself. I just met your big sister when I came to the door and she seemed really nice."

"I'm really nice, too," Callum said.

"Oh are you, indeed?" I said. "We can discuss what constitutes being really nice tomorrow, Callum, or maybe at our next family meeting. Right before we discuss your allowance."

Katy came to his rescue. "I hear you play the fiddle. Can I hear you play, or is it too close to bedtime?"

Callum beamed at me. He has great instincts for when I'm going to cave in. He grabbed Jennifer's hand and pulled her from the room, returning within moments with his fiddle, my guitar and Jen's flute.

Impromptu concerts are a common occurrence in our household. Learning at least one musical instrument was a mandatory part of my middle-class Scottish upbringing. It is something I insisted on with my own kids, despite Elspeth's eye-rolling disapproval. I'm glad that I persisted. Music pulls people together in ways that nothing else can. If Andy had been home from the hospital that night he would have joined us on his mandolin.

We played a few jigs and reels right there in the kitchen. Katy seemed genuinely delighted, if her tapping feet were anything to go by. At one point Jennifer whispered into Callum's ear, and the two of them switched into a slow waltz-time rendition of "Ye Banks And Braes Of Bonnie Doon," a romantic Burns standard that we all like. Jennifer kicked me and mouthed over that I should sing, so I belted out a few of the well-known verses. I don't think I had sung it since Elspeth left us six months before. The beautiful imagery of betrayal in the last verse caught me unawares. I had to cover a tremble in my voice on the last line:

> "Wi' lightsome heart I pu'd a rose,
> Fu' sweet upon its thorny tree!
> And my fause lover stole my rose,
> But ah! She left the thorn wi' me."

We finished with a hornpipe to bring the tempo back up before Jennifer took Callum away to help him get ready for bed. Katy and I were left with an awkward silence in the room after they were gone. I don't think either of us were all that eager to get back to talking about the case, but it felt more comfortable to appear business-like and cover up any acknowledgement of the chemistry that had begun to develop.

Katy said, "Let's forget the Texas murder and get back to the Garfield case for a minute or two, since that is the only case that is in our jurisdiction. Here's a few details that I verified while you were gone in Portland."

She got out her notebook and flipped to a page labeled, "Share with Donald." I liked seeing my name written in her book in that bold, confident scrawl.

"You mentioned that Myra may have scratched her assailant," she said. "I checked with the doctor and intake nurse who booked Aaron Klein in at the King County Jail. He has no scratches on him anywhere. His mother, on the other hand, has several scratches on her right forearm. She showed them to me very briefly and claimed they were from one of her cats. I'm not expert enough to tell the difference between human and feline scratches but they looked recent."

"And she was seen at Covington's Vashon house a few hours before Myra was murdered," I said.

Katy ignored my implication and moved her finger down the page. "Then there's Frank Stillwell. Did you notice his forearms down in Burien?"

"I wasn't looking for scratches, Katy. I was too busy waiting to see if he was going to throw a punch at me. He had on a long-sleeved denim shirt, I think."

"Well both of his arms are covered in scratches. He took great pleasure in giving me a close up look. He said that he and Sonya have been clearing a patch of blackberries near the foundation of their new house. He took me to look at Sonya's arms also. They were scratched, too. Freshly scratched. He made a point of showing me their forearm veins, saying, "See, no needle tracks, either. Sorry to disappoint you." He really is an angry son of a bitch."

"We are not narrowing things down much, are we?" I said.

"No. I did track down the science teacher who lost his job because of a relationship with Myra last year."

"And does he still live locally?"

She shook her head. "On the evening Myra was murdered he

was doing parent-teacher conferences in Bismarck, North Dakota. I also had the pleasure of watching Skunk Bucket rehearse at Jan Mossandrian's house in West Seattle, yesterday."

"That must have set your heart racing," I said.

"Actually, they bickered more than they rehearsed. They seem to miss Aaron Klein's charisma and leadership, if you can believe that. They are all on the skinny side and wore cut-off tank tops. No scratches on their arms either. I talked to each of them separately. Two others were able to confirm seeing Tami dancing up front and hanging around with Mosh after the concert was over."

"Are you ruling all those people out then?" I said.

"Not at all. I guess those without scratches are less likely, although it is possible that Myra's scraped nail beds are unrelated to the murder and might even be self-inflicted. But even if she did scratch her attacker, the person could cover it up by scratching themself with something else afterwards."

"Like blackberries," I said. "So who is your likeliest suspect, Katy? My money is still on Frank and Sonya Stillwell, maybe acting together as a husband and wife team. Covering for each other."

Katy nodded slowly, as if reluctant to share her thoughts. "There's another husband and wife team that deserves more attention, Donald."

"Not the Garfields?"

She looked at me steadily. "Do we know what Linda Covington was doing on Friday night?"

"Linda! Och don't be ridiculous, Katy. She wouldn't have had anything to do with the girl's death. I've known Linda all my life."

"You told me last Sunday that you had seen her on an occasional basis for thirty years but that you don't really know her. Which is it?" I blushed but kept my mouth shut. "Look, Donald, who knows what exactly goes on between her and her husband? We know that he's been a philanderer and that he was screwing a teenager, Myra Garfield, behind his wife's back last summer. Maybe Linda is okay with that, or at least accepts it and uses it to secure her position with him. If Sebastian Covington knew that Myra had told Stillwell about their affair and that Stillwell was going to confront him about it on Friday evening, Covington might have confided in his wife that he was about to be blackmailed."

"But how would she know that Aaron Klein was going to take Myra to their hot tub that evening?" As soon as I said it I knew it sounded weak.

"He was her gardener, remember? She made it clear to Gary Pitman that she doesn't mind the idea of schoolkids using her tub. She might even have suggested it to Aaron Klein."

"Have you interviewed her yet?"

"No. The idea only really occurred to me this evening after you told me what Frank Stillwell said about Myra and Covington's affair. Maybe Linda has got a solid alibi for last Friday night but you've got to admit she is worth considering."

I stayed silent. I knew I wasn't being objective but the thought of Linda in that kind of role was too alien for me to consider.

Katy continued in a quiet, reasonable tone. "Do you think Linda's interest in Tami is truly altruistic or could it be out of guilt and sorrow for how her actions have affected the girl? Or worse, Donald, maybe she wants to keep a close eye on the girl in case Tami knows something incriminating and becomes a threat."

I gave a grudging nod. She closed her book and stood up. "I'd better go. I've got several more leads to follow up on tomorrow. I really appreciate your help, Donald."

I helped her on with her jacket. It gave me an excuse to catch a whiff of perfume from her warm neck.

I said, "I've got a lot of evidence to sift through tomorrow that might help you narrow things down. What we really need is some hard physical evidence tying Myra Garfield to a specific perpetrator. The lab may have got something specific from Stillwell's truck. There are also the hairs and fibers found on the green carpet. And the folded clothes might show something. I promise I'll stick to the areas where I've got real expertise. Sorry I messed up in Burien."

"I'm not. If you hadn't then you might not have got that information from Frank Stillwell about Covington's connection to

Myra Garfield. Besides, if you hadn't messed up then you probably wouldn't have invited me round. This was a lot more fun than I expected. That was an excellent meal you whipped up. Thanks. And you've got great kids."

I mumbled, "Thanks," and stood there awkwardly as she opened the door and let the cold night air intrude.

She looked back and smiled before closing the door. "And you've got a great singing voice, too."

FRIDAY

252

XVIII

Pressure From On High

Pounding five miles on a treadmill, like a caged hamster on a wheel, is supposed to be good for me. All the Men's magazines tell me the same thing every month. "Great Abs and Better Sex in just TWO weeks – Let us show you how!" As an added bonus it is supposed to strengthen my heart, reduce my waistline and prolong my vigorous and active life. What a deal! It's just hard to believe all of that at five a.m., while staring at a blank wall in the basement, when your muscles ache, your left knee swells and your throat feels like you are rubbing it with sandpaper. Sometimes I think that an extra hour of sleep in a warm cozy bed would do me a whole lot more good.

But this morning the Calvinist in me felt the need for self-deprivation and penance as punishment for my idiocy the day before. If I was going to go chasing dangerous criminals into uncharted industrial wastelands I needed to stay in shape. Besides, if I wanted women like Katy Pearson to show anything more than professional interest in me I had better melt away the flab from around my gut and reveal those "Washboard Abs." You can laugh if you like but apparently millions of women are out there, lying in their beds unable to sleep, lusting after men with rippling hard abdominal muscles. It must be true. The editors of Men's magazines wouldn't lie to me.

I made use of the mindless running to focus on the unanswered questions in the Garfield case. As I wheezed and groaned and willed the electronic display to move faster I thought of the charismatic nineteenth century Frenchman who had distilled forensic investigation down to a single principle. Edmond Locard's Exchange Principle simply states that whenever two objects come in contact with each other there is always an exchange of material. Always. You just have to find it. When the rubber belt finally stopped after an interminable thirty-nine minutes I had a clear plan of action for the day. I would sit down with some of Locard's modern-day disciples and piece together the trace evidence into a complete picture. Urgency and decisiveness would be my watchwords. I would avoid all distractions.

I limped and coughed my way to the bathroom to hurry through the rest of the ritual ablutions which society deems appropriate for middle-aged men. My nose and eyebrows were duly inspected for rogue hairs that had decided to put on an unwanted growth spurt. Trimming those hairs was the charming prelude to scraping the gray stubble off my chin and removing sweat and grime under a scalding shower. After a quick scrub dry I slapped stinging alcohol onto my raw facial skin and rubbed perfumed sticks of moisture-retardant under each armpit. Human beings are a strange species.

A quick sprint to the kitchen was rewarded with a bowl of dry, gravelly cereal chased down with tasteless blue milk. It's supposed to be good for my cholesterol. As I ran for the car I crammed my mouth full of unnecessary vitamins and a handful of "joint support" supplements of marginal benefit and unknown side effects. At traffic light stops on my way to work I completed my tasks by dragging long pieces of mint-flavored waxed nylon thread between my teeth to remove bacterial debris and stale food. By the time I pulled into my parking space at The Dell I was certifiably presentable to re-enter civilized society for another day.

Unavoidable distractions ambushed me the moment I got to the laboratory. I placed my hand on the doorknob to my office and had a momentary vision of myself opening a familiar and seemingly innocent closet door only to become deluged and submerged under an avalanche of unexpected junk. Notes were taped to the door as bait. While I stood looking at those the temporary secretary thrust a thick stack of phone messages under my nose before sulking back to her cubicle where she was clearing out her desk. This was her last day and I still couldn't remember her name.

I divided the phone messages into three categories. There were several from the governor's office in Olympia, a few miscellaneous ones from people I knew and three that puzzled me from the offices of The Jaratto Group. Around Seattle Kenneth Jaratto was practically a household name these days, maybe not in the same league as the founders of Microsoft, Amazon.com or Starbucks but almost. With the Jaratto Opera House, the Julia Jaratto Children's Museum and the new Jaratto wing at Children's Hospital devoted to childhood cancers, Kenneth Jaratto was certainly putting his benevolent mark on the community. I had read a recent editorial by some cynical columnist in the Seattle Times suggesting that Jaratto was trying to deflect attention from the fact that his company was systematically tearing down affordable housing near downtown and replacing it with corporate office buildings. The latest rumors about a proposed Jaratto Panda House to be built at the Woodland Park Zoo were receiving mixed reviews. I was curious to know what his company wanted with me.

The folder, which dominated the center of my desk, was stuffed with summaries from every department at The Dell for the Combined Criminal Investigation Facility report that was due in the governor's offices by the end of the day. I placed it next to the piles of phone messages and opened my e-mail. Scrolling down the screen gave me a visual crescendo of urgency. The daily volume of messages, the rank of the senders, and the number of envelope-icons that were red, all increased as the week progressed. I saw one from Jack Detmer and opened that first. As overall director of the Washington State Crime Labs, Detmer is my immediate boss. He had been instrumental in recruiting me and was an enthusiastic supporter of The Dell. I was surprised, therefore, to read the stiff and rather formal tone of his message. He reminded me that the original concept for the Delridge Way facility was to use integration between different forensic disciplines in order to promote speedy resolution of major crimes. Due to recent and unspecified complaints the grand plan to build other regional CCIFs in Spokane, Bellingham, Tacoma and Yakima was now on hold pending a re-evaluation of The Dell. He finished with a vague threat that my report had better be impressive, since he had just been summoned to attend the board meeting next week.

I went back to open the sequence of e-mails from the governor's office. These began with simple reminders about the report and the meeting, but the last one, sent yesterday afternoon, sounded like a subpoena. It informed me that I was to present my report at the beginning of the three-hour meeting and then leave. Two new agenda items would occupy the rest of the board's time. The first was a discussion of proposed re-structuring of the Delridge Way facility, in which the heads of individual departments would now report to an overall administrator, a career bureaucrat appointed by the governor. The administrator would in turn report to three separate house and senate committees in Olympia. I was flabbergasted. Not only would this represent a demotion for me, it would be a major step backwards to the politics of Divide-and-Conquer where investigations would stagnate and stall because the left hand didn't know what the right was doing. The second agenda item was to be a re-evaluation of the proposal to build four more CCIFs around the state. Jack Detmer was listed as an invited guest.

You need to have a devious mind and endless patience to thrive in politics, and I'm afraid I have neither. I couldn't begin to figure out what was behind all this but I had one ally on the CCIF board who might know. Bruce Hendale was a public defender when I first met him ten years ago. Since then he had switched to prosecution and had risen to Assistant Attorney General. He had the governor's ear, political aspirations of his own, and seemed to revel in political intrigue. I called his office and asked my secretary to put his call through to my phone as soon as he called back.

The next e-mail I opened shed a little light on the situation.

257

The chairman of the Washington State Association of Sheriffs and Police Chiefs, the good old boys' club for senior law enforcement officers, wanted to know if I was aware of the embarrassment and unpleasant publicity which had landed at the feet of one of their most generous contributors. Was I aware that Mr. Sebastian Covington had donated substantial amounts of money to the Police Activities League and had supplied numerous police departments with exercise equipment at no cost?

My hackles were rising when the phone rang. "Bruce? This is Donald McLure. Thanks for calling back-"

The lengthy pause on the other end of the line told me this wasn't Bruce Hendale.

"What a wonderful brogue you have, Mr. McLure. You sound just like the caddy I had on the links at Gleneagles last month. Pleasant memories indeed."

"Who is this?" I said with irritation.

"I'm sorry, I thought your personal assistant would have told you. This is Kenneth Jaratto. I just had breakfast with John Safford and Gerald Piknoski and they said you were the man to talk to."

Kenneth Jaratto certainly knew how to command attention. If the cultured, confident timbre of his voice wasn't sufficient, name-dropping the mayor and police chief for the city of Seattle added to the effect. He waited for all of that to sink in before continuing.

"As I was telling John, one of my business partners is being harassed by the press because some young woman got herself murdered on his property. I understand that the police have already made an arrest but the media are clamoring for salacious details. You know the press, I'm sure. If they don't get the facts in a timely manner they engage in wild speculation, so the sooner the case is resolved the sooner they will move on to other stories. Piknoski said this was a King County investigation and didn't involve the Seattle Police Department. He said that you were coordinating the analysis of evidence and were a true man of action."

It annoys me that rich people expect to get preferential treatment for everything in their lives. It annoys me even more that they usually get their way. I said, "That particular murder is one of our top priorities, Mr. Jaratto. I have several people working on it right now."

"Splendid, splendid. Setting appropriate priorities is the mark of good leadership, but it can also be a curse. As I said to Mayor Safford this morning, leadership is such a fragile and evanescent burden. Not everyone is able to carry it for long."

He hung up so as to deny me the opportunity to fire back. I stormed out to take out my frustration on the temporary secretary but she remained unruffled. She had only five more hours of this assignment to suffer, and was filing her nails patiently while she waited.

She said, "Mr. Jaratto said that you were expecting his call and that I should put it through right away. I have a Mr. Hendale on the line now. What would you like me to say to him?"

Bruce Hendale was as puzzled as I was about the changed agenda for the upcoming meeting of the CCIF advisory board. Until I mentioned my conversation with Kenneth Jaratto.

"He's obviously flexing his muscles, Donald. Jaratto is one of the two new board members. Didn't you get the e-mail last week?"

I scrolled back up and found the memo I had glanced at before leaving for Portland. The memo whose attachment I hadn't bothered opening. When I did so, now, I already knew who the other new board member would be. Sebastian Covington.

I spent the rest of the morning reviewing the material for the CCIF report, adding some sections of my own, then preparing a one-page executive summary with the highlights. I was proud of our accomplishments. I wrote an impassioned cover-letter to Governor Eckhart, faxed this to his private secretary, then called to have a courier swing by to take the full report to Olympia that afternoon. It was lunchtime by the time I had cleared my desk and went looking for Locard's disciples.

Joe Wysocki was not at his desk, if you can call the random pile of papers spilling off one end of a laboratory bench a desk. Modern crime labs spend vast financial resources on getting the most up to date scientific equipment. They don't waste money on the personal space for the scientists. Benches jutted out from all the walls in the laboratory forming a series of U-shaped working areas. Joe, Rusty and Gina shared one of these alcoves. Each of them had

260

their own computer, shelves, pencil drawer and stool, from which to create their personal desk area. Gina's was homey, with stuffed beanbag toys draped over her computer monitor, family photos, kids' drawings and a few motivational religious mottoes. Rusty's desk reflected his military mindset; pencils were lined up and sharpened, paper clips sorted by size. On his bulletin board were tables of normal laboratory values, nomograms and formulae. The only personal touch was an action snapshot of an attractive young woman playing soccer at Greenlake.

It looked like Joe was somewhere in the building. His wet hat and scarf were lying on his stool. The pencil drawer was pulled open revealing slide trays, bits of loose carpet, a tobacco tin full of exploded bullets, a can of WD-40, and a rusty penknife that looked like it might have been used in the Civil War.

Gina Fernandez bustled past me and placed her huge handbag on the floor by her desk. "If you're looking for Joe, he's with a whole crowd outside the lunchroom. They having a party, I think." I thanked her and made my way to the door. "Any improvement in your love life since we last talked, Doctor McLure?" her mischievous tone suggested she had inside knowledge, and made me blush.

I found Joe and Rusty, surrounded by a group of colleagues, pinning a homemade poster on the wall of the corridor leading off the reception desk on the fourth floor. It showed a chronological series of photographic headshots of an unsavory drug dealer who had recently been put away again thanks to the work of several people at The Dell. The photographs covered a twenty-year period and comprised unflattering mug shots from arrests in various States, fake drivers licenses and passports. He had recycled various names, and favored several renditions of straggly mustaches and goatees but the rapid and unhealthy aging was dramatic and relentless. The arrogant twenty-year old cocaine dealer with a full head of hair and a challenging thrust to his chin metamorphosed into a haggard, balding, floppy-joweled cynic who looked closer to seventy than forty in his last shot. Picked up in an abandoned meth-lab in Spanaway, he was a chilling reminder of the effects of two decades of illegal drug life.

Rusty waved me over. "Hey Donald, get a load of these. This guys's a great advert for the glamorous life of crime, isn't he?"

I said, "That's a great poster, lads. Well done. Teamwork nailed him in the end. Speaking of which could you and Joe meet me in the small conference room in a few minutes to review where things stand in the Garfield case?"

They had made impressive progress during my three days in Portland. Material retrieved from the hot tub filters included metal spheres like those in Frank Stillwell's truck. The green carpet fiber in Myra's hair was identical to the carpet found in Stillwell's barn. There were traces of blood and skin found in the truck bed, presumably scraped off Myra's body as she was dragged out. The DNA analysis, which could confirm that, was underway.

Joe was eager to share a new finding. "Remember the neatly folded clothes found behind the deck? Gina is pretty sure that the mohair sweater was on the bottom of the pile so I taped it and vacuumed it for unlikely contaminants. There were pine needles and other organic material from where it was lying under the bushes but I also found specks of paint. Lead-based marine undercoat to be precise. Didn't you say you'd seen an old boat being repaired at the Stillwell's place?"

"Yes I did. He had obviously been sanding the hull before repainting it. There was paint dust all over the barn."

Joe said, "It's everywhere, Donald. We vacuumed the passenger seat of his truck and found the same paint there. The GC-pyrogram gave us a definitive match. It is an old lead-based undercoat made by OrcaMarine. They don't make it anymore but it is in the database."

Rusty said, "So apparently there is some value in dilute-and-shoot chemical analysis from gas chromatography after all, Donald, even if it sticks in Joe's throat to admit it."

Joe gave a wry smile. "I've also got three fibers of mohair from the seat, which match the girl's sweater. It's a certainty that the pile of clothes was transported in the front seat of the truck."

Rusty said, "It gets better, Donald. We may have material from the assailant, himself. One of the long brown hairs we found on the girl's body definitely isn't hers. I looked at it under the microscope just to please Joe. It's weird looking. Nothing like the girl's hair. I gave it to Joe to be sure but since the hair contains an intact root I think we should send it to DNA analysis so we can compare it to Klein's or whoever else they think might be the killer."

Joe had been waiting for this moment. "I don't want to cramp your enthusiasm, Rusty, but I wouldn't waste too much time and money with a DNA analysis of that hair. At least not unless you want to get control samples from the Woodland Park Zoo. It's animal hair. I compared it to our hair library. It's probably from a llama. Now I've heard that llamas are smart and ornery, but I doubt one of them is responsible for the girl's death."

I covered Rusty's embarrassment. "It adds more weight to the association with Frank Stillwell's truck, though. He has two llamas on his property. However, it still doesn't tie the death to any specific perpetrator. Do we have any preliminary analysis from the nail scrapings?"

Rusty's excitement returned. "We sure do. We ran a quick RFLP and got three haplotypes on chromosome six."

"Can you explain that in plain English?" Joe said. "My knowledge of genetics hasn't been updated for thirty years."

Sometimes Joe Wysocki lays the "old school" image on a bit too thick. Although most forensic scientists specialize in their own particular field these days Joe knew more about basic molecular biology than he wanted to admit.

I gave Joe a scowl of admonishment. "Go on then, Rusty, indulge Joe's pretence at ignorance."

Rusty said, "It's pretty straightforward, really, Joe. You know that humans have twenty-three pairs of chromosomes, right? Each chromosome has thousands of genes along its length. There are two copies of each gene, one on each chromosome. Those are called haplotypes. The haplotypes can be the same or they might be different, but one person can't have more than two haplotypes at any position. If they find more than two different haplotypes this proves that we have genetic material from more than one individual. They'll need to do PCR amplification to get more material before they can do more extensive typing but my guess is that we have material from the victim and the assailant all mixed together. It will take time to sort out but I think we'll be able to find some epitopes that are specific to the perpetrator and then we can compare them to samples from Aaron Klein or Frank Stillwell or anyone else the homicide cops have in mind."

I said, "That's terrific, Rusty. This is the first lead we've got that may identify a specific person as the killer. Why don't you both get me copies of your reports and I'll pass them on to Detective Pearson to show what progress we're making."

Joe said, "Better get copies to Jeff Tucker as well. He has been calling or stopping by at least twice a day since you left."

I spent the rest of the afternoon going through my In-tray. Near the bottom of the pile I came across Myra Garfield's preliminary toxicology report again. Barbiturates had been found in her blood, stomach and bladder. The screening test couldn't say what specific drug or how much was present. The definitive analysis would have been done later in the week so I searched towards the top of my In-tray until I found a typed report stapled to a roll of graph paper.

I'm still too much of a bench scientist to accept reports without seeing the raw data as well. It also gives me a chance to check the quality of the work in other departments. I unfurled the thin roll of paper and weighed down each corner with some of the formalin-filled specimen jars that had grossed-out the temporary secretary.

In gas chromatography the test substance is forced down a long narrow column of liquid-coated beads by a carrier gas. The components of the test substance vary in how fast they can pass through the column. Those with little affinity for the beads pass though quickly. Others are retained in the column for longer. As each component exits the column a heat-sensitive stylus records it as a peak on a moving roll of graph paper. In the example I was looking at the position of each peak distinguished a specific barbiturate while the area under the peak told me how much of the drug was present.

The two commonest barbiturates we see in forensic work are Pentothal, the short-acting anesthetic, and Seconal, an old-fashioned "sleeping pill." Under the standard conditions of gas chromatography these two drugs have retention times of between two and five minutes. But there were no peaks to be seen corresponding to those. Instead, at the far right-hand side of the graph was a huge broad-based peak, representing a substance that had taken over eleven minutes to pass through the column. Myra Garfield had consumed a massive amount of Phenobarbital before she died.

I called Katy Pearson. It gave me a chance to thank her again for coming over for dinner the night before. The very sound of her voice was a pleasant interlude in my day. I gave her a brief account of the political pressure that was building around the Garfield case.

"Can you find out if any of our suspects or their families or friends have access to Phenobarbitone?"

She hesitated. "Sure, but how likely is that? I'm not familiar with Phenobarb. as a street drug. Who would be likely to use it?"

I said, "It has been used for decades to treat major epileptic seizures. It is not a first-line treatment, because of its side effects, but sometimes it works better that the alternatives."

"What side effects?"

"It is addictive, interferes with other drugs and makes you drowsy. It is a powerful sedative, especially when mixed with alcohol."

"I can ask at the pharmacy on Vashon and at the Health Center."

"The Nursing Home may have some patients on it," I suggested.

Katy said, "It's a controlled substance. I could check the DEA database but that will take a while." She sounded discouraged.

"Are you okay?" I said.

"I'm sick of Jeff Tucker breathing down my neck all the time. He's pissed because it is looking less and less like Aaron Klein is guilty. The Kleins have a sharp lawyer, who put enough heat on the DA's office that we had to release Klein today. I've been asking

Tucker to reconsider Frank Stillwell all week but now that I told him that Stillwell might have met with Sebastian Covington the night of the murder Tucker is mocking me for changing my mind again. Since the evidence is only circumstantial, Captain Walton wants something definite before we arrest Stillwell. So far I can't even prove or disprove his story for Friday night."

"For what it's worth I didn't think Stillwell was lying?"

"I would like independent corroboration of his story, Donald. I haven't been able to get hold of Linda or Sebastian Covington today. I still don't know what either one of them was doing the night Myra was murdered. Aren't you going to a party at their Seattle house tonight? Could you ask them what they were doing last Friday?"

I groaned. "I had forgotten all about the party. I can think of a few hundred things I would rather be doing tonight. Covington's sphere of influence is beginning to interfere with my work."

I told Katy what I had learned from my e-mails and phone conversations.

She said, "Maybe Covington is jealous that his wife still has romantic interest in you?"

I said, "He certainly doesn't seem to have much interest in her. Everything I hear about the guy makes me dislike him more, and I've never even met him."

"I don't want to fan the flames, Donald, but there is something else you might want to know about him. I called his office today to try to set up an interview. His secretary said he was unavailable but passed me on to one of the company vice presidents. The guy had a southern accent, which intrigued me, so I asked him how he liked our cold, wet, Northwest winters. He said he really missed Texas but had to move here because of his job. The corporate headquarters for Covingtons has only been in Seattle for four years, Donald. Before that they were located in Houston, Texas. According to the VP, Linda and Sebastian Covington used to live down there too. They relocated to Seattle in the July of the year that their corporate headquarters moved. I checked the dates. They left the Houston area about a month after Magdalene Reilly's murder.

XIX

Scouting Party

By the time I was driving to the Covingtons' house in Seattle I was well and truly pissed off. I hate stuffy high cocktail parties at the best of times. Being shy and having a low tolerance for pretentiousness and bullshit makes me picky about who I spend time with. I meet plenty of strangers in my professional life. If any of them seem particularly fascinating I enjoy getting below the surface in substantial one-on-one conversations. Dancing minuets around neutral topics of conversation is excruciatingly dull. Since politics, religion and philosophy are disallowed you are left with discussions of the weather, the traffic, how delightful the food and décor is, where you have been on vacation or what you do for a living. With my job and my accent I am an easy mark for predatory partygoers. People assume that I'll be fascinated by their skin rash, or their mother-in-law's horrendous cancer story. And I'm just bound to collapse with laughter at their Beam-me-up-Scotty-Star-Trek impersonation. I'm sure you know the one.

"The war-rrp dr-rrive's leaking, Captain. She'll not take much mor-rre of this. Ah cannae wor-r-rk mir-rrrracles, you know!"

No, standing around in uncomfortable clothes being embarrassed by complete strangers is not my idea of a good time. Even on a good day. And so far this day had been anything but good. Struggling to stay afloat in a bureaucratic and political quagmire is a part of my job that I have to accept. But having bullies prodding me and threatening to wreck my career had disturbed some smoldering cinders inside me today. By now I was looking to have someone pour on a little gasoline.

When I had accepted Linda's invitation five days before I felt sorry for her and neutral about her husband. But now I had a nagging worry that one or both of them might be involved in Myra Garfield's death. They might even be using me as an opportune shield, a convenient sap whose insignificant career might get erased in the process. I was about ready to buy the gasoline, and apply it myself.

The maze of residential streets that wind their way towards Lake Washington in the Madrona and Mount Baker neighborhood is unfamiliar to me. The drizzle of the day had thickened to a steady downpour with a touch of sleet among it, which my ancient wiper blades smeared across the windshield. By the time I found the address, cars lined the streets surrounding the Covingtons' house for three hundred yards in all directions. Actually, "cars" is an inadequate word to describe the convoy of personal armored tanks I encountered. The standard vehicle for the well-to-do American family is about the size of your average Scottish farmhouse. Jacked up high enough to ensure its occupants could look down on the plebs through tinted glass windows, each vehicle took up about half a city block. A mile from the house I finally squeezed in behind a Lincoln Navigator. Raindrops bounced off its gleaming wax finish. Interior alarm lights blinked at me and gave off warning chirps defying anyone to so much as smudge its paintwork.

As I plodded back towards the house an icy wind off the lake spat stinging rain onto my face, whipped slush up my pant legs, made a tossed salad of my hair and drove a damp foreboding under my skin. My frozen knuckles flinched in agony as they pounded on the huge slab of mahogany that barred entry to Covington's house. A warm cloak of cigar smoke, brandy fumes and complacent power was thrown around me as the door opened and a nervous young man ushered me inside.

He seemed unable to categorize me. Steam rose from my shoulders. Ice melted off the sleeves of my jacket and formed puddles around my feet, spoiling the lustrous sheen on the beautiful slate floor.

"Excuse me, Sir, can I take your, er..?" he began.

There was nothing about me he wanted to touch. I had no camelhair overcoat, no white silk scarf, no wide-brimmed hat and no stylish wrap. I have no style at all, really, if truth be told. By the time I have picked up on a particular fashion statement it is already passé. In recent years the male wardrobes for Seattle's rich and famous have included some baffling items. Pale, crinkly suits, that are purposefully oversized and ill fitting, were everywhere for a while. Silk shirts with tight round collars, worn without neckties but with impossibly intricate buttons, also had their day. Yesterday. Let's just say that my battered Harris Tweed jacket, with its dogtooth pattern and damp smell to match, was not being featured in Nordstrom's spring collection. Nor was the plain white shirt and narrow tartan tie I wore underneath. And no other guests were stepping out in wrinkled brown trousers with a decorative mud splatter up one side. The doorman gave me a pitying smile and waved me towards a curved archway beyond which the party sounds emanated.

White-aproned caterers weaved among the guests with silver trays sparkling above their heads. I passed on any alcohol but tried some of the hors d'oevres. The little triangles of dry toast covered with pink paste and cucumber wedges were pretty good. Except that the black globules of caviar kept rolling off onto the carpet before I could catch them, so I still can't tell you why someone thinks the salty half-fermented eggs from a big ugly fish are worth a hundred dollars an ounce.

Linda was hovering on the periphery of a group of men in black tuxedoes at the other side of the room. She wore a tight red cocktail dress, one size too small, with a low scooped neck and a slit up the side. A string of large pearls bounced on her ample cleavage as she tottered across the floor towards me on backless low-heeled shoes.

"You're here, finally. I thought you'd maybe..." She trailed off, perhaps deciding from my glowering look that a different opening gambit might work better. "Thanks for coming, Donald. It'll be nice to have some real conversation at last. How was Portland? Have they got you a drink, yet? You should try the appetizers. They're from Pagliacci's in the market."

The group of tuxedoes split open. My proletarian father always referred to formal eveningwear as bourgeois "penguin suits" but the term didn't apply to this gathering. Penguins don't have that snobbish, patronizing look in their eyes. Besides, the diminutive man who strutted from their midst was more like a wee banty rooster patrolling his barnyard for unwanted competition. As broad as he was tall, his hair looked dyed as well as slicked up with gel in an attempt to counteract the fright of his battered face. It didn't work. He looked like a pugnacious ex-boxer who should have retired before his failing reflexes gave the advantage to his opponents. He was barely the same height as Linda but she shrank in his presence. His smile pulled the skin tight over high cheekbones. His handshake dared me to flinch. I had seen his kind stalking outside the school gates of my high school in Ayr, looking for a fight. I didn't flinch then or now.

He spoke with a suave sneer. "So this is Linda's knight in shining armor. I didn't think that Scotland had knights. Thought that was a particularly English pretension."

"Scotland had a few," I said. "Sir William Wallace for one."

"Scotland had a fyooo. I just love the accent. Much stronger than Linda's. It's Donald, isn't it? Well, make yourself comfortable, Donald. Linda and I need to circulate." He clamped a hand on Linda's arm and prepared to leave. Fifteen seconds of platitudes was all the time that I merited.

I said, "I don't think Linda ever told me you were a boxer, Mr.

Covington. Did you fight at featherweight or lightweight?"

He spoke with quiet menace. "I'm no lightweight, Donald, I can tell you that. I boxed in the army. Special Forces. I won plenty of fights above my weight division, too. Try me sometime."

He ran his eyes up and down me with deliberate scorn. Linda tugged at his sleeve and mumbled about neglecting other guests. Competitive malice throbbed from Sebastian Covington's core. He seemed to despise Linda's self-deprecating demeanor towards him yet expected no less. I felt more sorry for her than ever. He steered her towards another group of obsequious company underlings who stared at Linda's chest anytime their boss wasn't looking.

I scooped up a couple of puff pastry things, filled with crab and shrimp mush, and let the scene wash over me for a while. There is something about the human ear that can pick up on the intonation and significance of sounds beyond the spoken words. I remember being at a conference in Nagasaki and passing three young Japanese women admiring each other's newborn infants. Even the babies were babbling and gurgling with Japanese accents, tuning in to the sounds around them. Tonight, as I moved among the party groupings I detected several descants, counterpoints and minor variations on the main theme of smug opulence.

There was plenty of original artwork on display. A collection of ceremonial African masks was featured prominently on one wall. Whether they were there to ward off evil spirits or to intimidate houseguests I couldn't tell. Callum is fascinated by African art so he and I have spent many hours at the permanent display at the Seattle

Art Museum. I'm no expert but I can certainly recognize some of the symbolism. There was no particular theme to the masks in Covington's collection. They were just expensive trinkets to impress house guests. I did notice that none of the masks honored women or represented fertility.

On a table below the masks was a modern sculpture. A pristine, white marble torso was surrounded by a tangle of rusty barbed wire. The marble had been carved beautifully to represent the ambiguous folds and curves of female sexuality. One strand of wire ran cruelly right through the middle of the marble, disturbing the softness of the lines. I was leaning down for a closer inspection when I felt a presence behind me.

Sebastian Covington had returned, accompanied by an older and taller man whose face I recognized even before he spoke.

"Kenneth Jaratto, Mr. McLure. We spoke earlier today. When Sebastian said you were here this evening I thought I should come over and introduce myself."

My good humor had all but evaporated. I said, "Honored, I'm sure. Did you want to give me another instructive dissertation on the importance of leadership and priority-setting, Mr. Jaratto? I didn't have time to take notes or ask questions this morning. You hung up on me too quickly."

Jaratto laughed lightly. "I didn't want to waste your precious time, Mr. McLure. I'm sure there are thousands of little details to attend to when you are hot on the trail of a killer. I'm surprised you found time for a pleasant social gathering such as this."

Covington was enjoying every second of the great man's droll wit, as he toyed with the Scottish buffoon.

I said, "There's nothing very pleasant or sociable about this evening, as far as I'm concerned. I came out of a sense of duty and obligation to an old friend who seems to have a pretty miserable existence despite the outwards trappings of wealth and success." I turned to Covington. "I've been looking around. I don't see Mr. and Mrs. Garfield anywhere. I expect there are thousands of little details to attend to when you are arranging for your daughter's funeral. A pity they couldn't have come here tonight to draw strength and support from this warm social gathering."

Covington's smile disappeared. He spoke through tight trembling lips. "Myra's death was a tragic loss."

Jaratto placed a paternal hand on Covington's shoulder and addressed me with distaste. "I would imagine that Mr. and Mrs. Garfield would draw comfort and strength from knowing that their daughter's murderer was apprehended. You would do well to focus on your job, Mr. McLure, and refrain from making offensive remarks. Myra was a much-loved intern with Sebastian just a few months ago. Her death has affected him deeply."

I said, "I'm sure it has. It's a funny word, "intern." It has taken on a whole new meaning since the Clinton presidency. It means "inside," of course but I've never been sure if that means it gives the intern an opportunity to be inside the inner workings of the

277

company or if it gives the CEO an opportunity to get inside the intern's pants."

"Really!" Jaratto was appalled.

Linda materialized at her husband's side, trembling and scared. Sebastian Covington stood his ground and glared at me.

I said, "Where were you last Friday night, Mr. Covington? The night Myra Garfield was murdered in your hot tub. I know the King County Police Department will want to ask you in person but they have been having trouble finding a gap in your busy schedule."

His response was clipped and deliberate. Almost rehearsed. "I was at the theater last Friday night. As I recall Linda had a touch of the flu and stayed home, so I went to the theater on my own."

"Really? And was that before or after you met with Frank Stillwell at Salty's on Alki?"

I saw the first crack of vulnerability and fear show on Covington's face. Linda shot him a look of accusation, which he ignored. He seemed more interested in retaining the support of Kenneth Jaratto.

I said, "I'm sure you and Frank had plenty to talk about. Were you discussing his severance package, comparing notes on Myra's curvaceous young figure or were you reminiscing about old times in Texas?"

Covington's neck veins bulged above his starched white collar. "Whatever Stillwell told you, he's lying. I'm not going to stand here and take any more of your sarcasm and innuendo, McLure. Kenneth, I'm sorry you were witness to this."

Jaratto said, stiffly. "On the contrary, Sebastian, I have found it most instructive to get some insights about the character of the current director at Delridge Way."

He placed heavy emphasis on the word "current."

280

SATURDAY

282

XX

Frosty Atmosphere

At nine fifteen a.m., exactly twelve hours after I had left the Covington's party, Clayton van Allen was found dead. I heard the news from Katy Pearson a little after ten. I had just dropped Callum off at his fiddle lesson. After that he was being whisked away to a birthday party that involved ice-skating and a sleepover, so I was looking forward to some time for personal reflection. Katy's phone call changed my agenda in a hurry.

"Van Allen has been shot in Frank Stillwell's barn. Point blank. Looks like he was set up. Stillwell and the gun are missing. Get here as quick as you can, Donald. Captain Walton, our section chief, is on his way. Tucker's about to blow a fuse." She slammed the phone down sounding angry and hurt.

• • •

The Friday evening sleet had turned to a hard frost overnight. The muddy rutted lane leading to the Stillwell's property was covered with a hard white crust, which was already churned up by the dozen or so cars that lined the edges of the yard. Ragged clouds hung over the place like dirty underwear shedding foul karma on all those below.

Katy was in her Jeep, talking on the phone. She didn't acknowledge my arrival, and seemed irritated and intense. Officer Sherbourg, Tuckers' muscle-bound protégé, stood off to one side interviewing a bear of a man who towered over the uniformed officer and kept pointing at the barn. Near the doorway of the trailer Sonya Stillwell and a bawling Starflame were being comforted by a female uniformed officer. In the middle of the yard, blowing clouds of steam into the frosty air like rutting bulls, were Jeff Tucker, Sheriff Gary Pitman, and Captain Duane Walton, head of King County Homicide Division. A handsome black man around my own age, Walton had worked with me on several cases since the inception of The Dell. He recognized me and waved me over.

"Where is the body?" I said. They seemed in no mood for pleasantries.

Walton said, "In the boat in the barn. Shot in the head. Once, at point blank range. Probably a handgun."

"Do we have an ID?"

"Two people identified him as someone called Clayton van Allen." Walton sounded vaguely bemused by this.

I said, "You know about van Allen?"

"First time I ever saw the name was over a cup of coffee this morning. As a matter of fact I was reading about him in one of Officer Pearson's reports when I got the call that he'd been shot."

Tucker scoffed. "Yeah, she spends plenty of time on reports. Reports about everything. She suspects a different person every day."

Walton bristled. "Whereas you picked Aaron Klein on day one and have been building a case around him despite mounting evidence that didn't fit."

If there is one thing I hate about my job more than the politics and the paperwork it is listening to the swaggering machismo from policemen trying to make each other look stupid. I already felt stupid enough all by myself. Not only had Frank Stillwell duped me, I had had the arrogance to stray into areas of investigation and speculation where I had no business. And why? To try to impress a woman ten years my junior, to avoid the loneliness and rejection of being left behind by Elspeth. I could hear the voices of the sour-faced Scottish aunties of my childhood mocking me with their barbed tongues:

"There goes young Donald again, Jean. You know what they say? Pride comes afore the fall."

"Right enough, Nell. Mind you, he's not so young anymore. He should ken better, but then there's nae fool like an auld fool, eh?"

The bickering going on around me made me weary. I tuned out and let it wash over me until I heard them discussing suspects.

I said, "Who do you think did the shooting?"

Tucker was scathing. "Stillwell of course. We know he was pursuing van Allen on Thursday night. Not that you told us, McLure, but in one of the endless reports that Pearson filed yesterday she mentioned that you thought it was van Allen who Stillwell was tailing on Thursday afternoon when you were playing action-hero in Burien. Maybe we would solve the case quicker if there was more cooperation from The Dell."

I turned to Walton. "I didn't know for sure what was going on the other night, Duane. I guessed it might be van Allen. I gave Katy the street name and number of the house in Burien that the guy emerged from."

Walton nodded. "She followed up. That house belongs to van Allen's cousin. The victim is van Allen. Mrs. Stillwell made the initial ID. Officer Pearson had already seen his face on the booking photographs from Texas and was able to confirm it."

"How many people have been tramping all over the crime scene?" I said.

"A guy called Brogan found the body at about nine fifteen. That's him over there. The big guy talking to Officer Sherbourg. Says he is a friend of the Stillwell family, was here to do some electrical work on the boat. He brought Mrs. Stillwell to look at the body. Sheriff

286

Pitman got the call right away and brought us in so Tucker, Pearson and I have all seen the crime scene. I oversaw it Donald. We avoided touching anything or stepping in blood, which is saying something. There is a hell of a lot of blood in a small confined area. We could make the ID from looking in through the doorway to the galley. He's lying face down with his head turned towards the door. We didn't need to disturb things too much."

"And you think it was Frank Stillwell and not his wife, Sonya or this guy Brogan who shot him? Or someone else?" I was clutching at straws.

Tucker prepared to speak but Walton overruled him. "Everything is pointing that way. We don't know the time of death. According to Mrs. Stillwell, Frank got up and left early. Well before seven a.m., she thinks. He was supposed to be working over by Hoodsport on some construction project today. He had mentioned to his wife that Jim Brogan would be coming by to look at the electrics on the boat. Stillwell may be responsible for this murder and the Garfield girl. And from what Pearson says in the report I read this morning he might even have done that Texas murder."

Tucker interrupted. "His gun is gone. The wife's not sure what kind but it's a handgun, not a revolver. A semi-automatic of some sort that they keep loaded and unlocked on a high shelf in a closet to keep it out of the toddler's reach, if you can believe that. She says that since Thursday night when he flushed van Allen out of the house in Burien, big Franko has kept his gun with him most of the time."

"Anyone else in the house?" I said.

Gary Pitman cleared his throat nervously, anxious to make a contribution. "Tami left even earlier than Frank, according to Mrs. Stillwell, to go to the nursing home for the early shift. Brogan showed up at nine and found the body. Mrs. Stillwell and the toddler were the only other people here at the time. I think she's relieved that Tami wasn't here to witness all this unpleasantness, after all she's been through this past week."

"Did Sonya or Starflame hear shots?" I said.

Pitman shook his head. "Mrs. Stillwell says she heard nothing until Brogan knocked on their door. The toddler is too upset to say much of anything right now."

I turned to Duane Walton. "It seems odd that Frank Stillwell would kill him and then leave to go to the construction site, knowing that Brogan would be coming by and would find the body?"

Tucker said, "Wouldn't surprise me. Maybe Stillwell arranged to meet van Allen here, ambushed him and then took off to leave his friend, Brogan, to take the heat. The bastard seems to be an expert at framing other people for murder. And we don't know that Stillwell went to his construction job, anyway. That's what he told his wife. He may have split."

Walton said, "Who knows? Maybe Stillwell was working on his boat and van Allen stumbled in. It will help if you do your part, Donald. Get us the time of death, confirm the mode of death. My guess is that the bullet is still inside the guy's brain. Maybe we can get a match to Stillwell's gun, if we find it. As far as I'm concerned Brogan and Mrs. Stillwell are definite suspects, also. But neither of them have blood on them or soot or powder residue. There's a lot of blood in the boat. You'd expect the assailant to have traces on him. We're asking both of them to let us examine their clothes. We're also looking over Brogan's car and the Stillwell trailer. One of your techs even suggested we unscrew the drain traps in the kitchen and bathroom sinks in the trailer to look for traces of blood there."

I said, "Good call. If the assailant washed hands afterwards some blood traces could get stuck in the junk in the U-bend of the sink. Who was it who made that suggestion, do you know?"

Tucker was getting impatient. "Bellagio. Mr. Enthusiastic! I think it's a waste of time. Stillwell is getting away, Captain, while we all pussy around here discussing stuff."

I said, "Where is the victim's car? Did Stillwell drive off in it? If it is the same one as he was driving the other night it's a blue Japanese import."

Tucker sneered. "Yeah? That narrows it down a lot, doesn't it? Problem is we don't know the make or license plate. It's going to be hard to put out an APB to State Patrol. The victim had no keys or ID on him."

Katy walked up and handed a piece of paper to Duane Walton. "The victim's car is a dark blue Nissan Maxima and here's the license plate number, Captain. It was rented from Budget Rent-A-Car in Houston three weeks ago to someone calling himself Kelly

Hudson."

"How the hell do you find all that out?" Tucker exploded.

Katy shrugged. I could tell she wanted to stick it to Tucker but was trying to keep her rage controlled. "It was a hunch. I spent time yesterday, checking the major car rental places that operate in the Houston area. Nothing was rented to van Allen so I assumed he had used an alias. This morning I called the prison where van Allen had been held and asked for the names of his friends and cellmates. Kelly Hudson is the name of a felon who is still incarcerated down there. He used to share a cell with van Allen. My guess is that van Allen used false ID when he got out."

For a few seconds no one spoke. I couldn't tell if Katy was enjoying the sight and sound of snorting bulls blowing hot air into the stillness of the morning. Was there sweetness in the air for her that overrode the reek of bad-tempered masculine sweat? Tucker snatched the note from Walton's hand and walked away.

"I'm done talking this thing to death. I'm headed for Hoodsport to see if we can't track down Stillwell."

The other three followed Jeff Tucker at a safe distance. Before she got into her car, Katy turned back and gave me a look that I couldn't interpret. The morning air just seemed to get colder by the minute.

XXI

Bloody Indictment

If anything it was even colder and less inviting inside the barn. Although messy, there had been some sense of order when I had looked inside the previous Sunday. But now everything lay in a jumble of violence as someone had waded through it overturning everything in a frantic search for something. Or someone. I picked my way carefully among rusting bed frames and broken vacuum cleaners. Toppled boxes spilled damp books and broken jam jars onto the floor. An ancient washing machine spewed its guts beside an unused spinning wheel. Cobwebbed fishing poles lay wearily against a bike with flat tires. The remnants of unfinished projects and unfulfilled hobbies lay everywhere. Pale watery light filtered through drafty cracks in the barn walls and glinted off a thick cloud of paint dust that hung in the air like toxic gas over a battlefield.

The bloated boat was at the back of the barn. It appeared to be floating in a sea of flotsam and jetsam from the Stillwells' shipwrecked lives. A rickety stepladder hung off the back end of the boat, secured to cleats and railings. I climbed gingerly up and stood on the deck.

291

From up here the lines of the boat were a lot more elegant. A thirty-five foot cabin cruiser with a single-screw engine she was probably built fifty years ago. The decking had been re-stained, new tar caulking applied between the planks. And although the varnish on the superstructure was peeling, I expect Frank Stillwell thought she would be a handsome craft sailing forth from a quiet harbor on a sunny summer's morning. Such are the dreams that keep sailors going on the long cold winter nights of renovation and repair.

A pair of swing doors led from the cockpit down to the accommodation below. Clipped to the top of one door was a portable floodlight attached to a large coil of orange extension cord. I switched it on with gloved hands and slowly descended the stairs into the belly of the boat where the harsh light exposed every detail of the ugly scene.

The main living area was about fifteen feet long and maybe eight feet across. A clear path ran from the foot of the steps towards the front where another small door showed the way to the toilet and bunk beds at the prow of the boat. An antique barometer with dust on its glass face hung above the door on the thick crossbeam at the far end of the room. Typical of boat design the main cabin was divided efficiently into intimate little functional areas. To the right a low oval table was bolted to the floor and farther forward there was a gas or oil-fired stove. Cushioned bench seats hugged the curves of the wall with recessed bookshelves above. It would be a cozy nook on a calm night with the stove on, a cup of tea and a good book.

The galley was on the left. A row of cabinets ran lengthwise down the center of the room for about eight feet, starting at the foot of the stairs. The cabinets were topped with a polished wooden counter top about eighteen inches wide. This gave an enclosed space for the galley between the row of cabinets and the port side of the boat. A two-ring propane cooker hung on gimbals. Net-covered storage areas and latched wooden cupboards covered the far wall. The varnished surfaces shone in the glare of the floodlight, smooth for the most part but speckled with blood. The source of that blood lay prostrate on the floor of the galley.

Clayton van Allen lay face down with feet at the bow end, and his head towards me. I leaned over the counter for a better look. His face was turned quizzically towards me. I recognized the gray crew cut and sallow skin drawn taught over his cheekbones. I had seen that grim unhappy face driving past me in Burien on Thursday night. Right on top of the crown of his head was a small neat hole from which dark blood oozed. He must have died instantly, like a frantic steer facing the humane killer in the slaughterhouse.

I clipped the floodlight to the side of the doorframe to free up both my hands, unslung my murder bag, and began photographing the scene. There were no real signs of struggle. On the table, stove and cushioned bench were the discarded tools of the remodeling project. The screwdrivers, hammers, wrenches and saws were free of blood. There was no blood in the center of the room, no bloody footprints leaving the scene. Blood was smeared on the far end of the counter top, splattered on the wall beyond that and in the galley to my left a large pool surrounded the body, spreading from van Allen's left arm.

I stepped round the far end of the counter into the galley and knelt to examine him more closely. He wore a long-sleeved denim shirt, matching jeans and scruffy cowboy boots, but no jacket, surprising on such a cold day. Sweat glistened on the skin of his hands and face. The fingers of his right hand flexed easily with no signs of rigor mortis.

Estimating the time of death is an imprecise science at best but it can also yield crucial information. Rigor mortis often begins within three to six hours but can be delayed considerably if the body is lying in a cold location. I placed a thermometer down beside the body to get the ambient temperature and debated whether or not to check the rectal temperature. It would mean disturbing the body and its clothing. In cases of possible sexual assault that is a no-no, but it didn't seem likely here. Besides, my morbid fixation on detail made me want to check something else.

I reached under the body and unbuttoned his jeans. They were a tight-fitting style but evidently he had lost so much weight during his incarceration that it wasn't too hard to ease them over his scrawny hips. He wore no underpants. I lifted his pelvis, rocked it to one side and inspected his shriveled genitals. Size may not have mattered to him during life but the fact that he was circumcised mattered to me. Lyle Newton, the sleazy Texan pathologist, had theorized that van Allen had masturbated onto Magdalene Reilly's dead body and that the presence of spermicide in her vagina was explained by him retaining enough spermicide from vaginal intercourse with his wife hours earlier. Perhaps it was a minor and unimportant detail now, but that scenario seemed totally implausible.

I gently prized his buttocks apart, confirmed that there were no signs of violence or trauma and inserted the thermometer deep inside his rectum. It is at times like these that my job seems particularly bizarre and unglamorous. I felt cold, shunned and friendless, the jester hiding back stage while the real show is happening elsewhere. While I waited for the thermometers to equilibrate I took a closer look at his left arm.

His denim shirtsleeve was soaked in blood with ragged holes front and back. It was a messy business rolling up the sleeve and wiping away the excess blood on the skin but this couldn't wait till I got him on the autopsy table. With a pencil flashlight held in my mouth I could see the details clearly. There was a small round hole just above the elbow on the medial and anterior part of the biceps muscle. The edges of the hole were smooth, the skin inverted with a reddish-brown abrasion ring at the margins. These are all characteristics of en entry wound from a bullet. About five inches farther up his arm, on the outer fleshy part of the muscle was a larger hole with ragged everted edges - the exit wound from the same bullet.

I stood up and held my own left arm out from my side, imagining the entry and exit wounds in the same locations as on the corpse. I tried crouching, stooping and swinging my arm in different positions. The only thing that made sense was that someone had fired at him from below as he walked past. He would have been walking down the middle of the room towards the bow end of the boat with his arm out to one side, maybe stretching over the counter top. His assailant would have been crouched down in the galley.

Blood spatter analysis has become a very sophisticated and

refined branch of forensic science in the past thirty years. I don't consider myself an expert but spending three weeks in Professor Herb MacDonell's laboratory in Corning, New York, has honed my powers of observation and deduction a lot. On the ceiling above my head was a fine mist of tiny blood droplets covering a wide area. The "dirt" I had noticed on the barometer glass was, in fact, more of the same. This was high velocity impact spray looking just like it did in Herb's demonstrations. It took me five minutes before I found the impact site for the bullet, embedded in the thick crossbeam to the right of the barometer.

There were plenty more droplets of blood on the side walls of the galley but these were bigger, tapered stains, elliptical in shape. Some even had "exclamation points" off one end, pointing back towards the stern of the boat. This blood had been thrown off as somebody bled profusely and turned back into the kitchen area. I followed the direction back to where van Allen lay on the floor. A picture was beginning to form in my mind but it was still fuzzy.

Both thermometers had cooked long enough. The ambient temperature was forty-one degrees Fahrenheit, or four point five degrees Celsius. It was barely above freezing whatever scale you used. No wonder it felt cold in here. The rectal temperature was ninety-one point eight; barely seven degrees lower than normal. My heart rate started increasing as I groped in my murder bag and extracted my laminated Henssge's nomograms. I estimated his weight at a hundred and thirty pounds and factored in that he was lightly clothed and the air was still. That put the time of death at about four hours ago, plus or minus three hours, which may seem a laughably wide margin of error but it is best to be conservative. It was still highly useful information. Van Allen might have been killed as recently as one or two hours ago, immediately before Brogan, the electrician, had made the nine-one-one call. Or he could have been killed as long ago as five a.m. But Clayton van Allen had been murdered sometime this morning, not during the night or yesterday evening.

This put a different complexion on things and got my juices flowing. The sooner you get to a crime scene after the event the greater the chance you have of solving it. The longer it goes the more time there is for the perpetrator to cover up the tracks and set up alibis. This corpse was still warm. I could almost hear the murderer's frantic breathing as he fled the scene.

The sequence of events inside the boat was still puzzling me. I squeezed into the corner beyond his head and squinted at the injury to his skull. It was a neat round hole the size of a dime with a rim of soot round it and a star-shaped tear in the surrounding skin. This would go in my report as a "hard contact wound with blow back." Someone had put the muzzle of a gun directly on top of his skull and fired into his brain. The high-pressure gas pushing out the bullet had gotten between the bone and the skin and lifted a dome shaped area of skin off the underlying skull causing the skin to rip under pressure. It was textbook stuff. But how could that have been done? The assailant would need to have been directly above him. There had been two shots fired, not one. The arm injury was caused by someone firing from low down. Were there two assailants? A husband and wife team? Could he have been dead already and lying down when the second shot was fired? The arm injury was serious but he hadn't bled to death from that. There wasn't that much blood around.

I crouched in the cold dark corner of the galley and tried to make sense of it. My joints ached and the smells of moldy seaweed, stale bilge water, blood, sweat and cordite played havoc with my thought processes. Smell is an unforgiving sensation. Unrelated episodes from my past flooded my consciousness and jostled for attention, distracting me from the here and now. I suddenly remembered a seasick sail up past Arran and Mull in my youth, with my uncle yelling orders as I retched over the side. That vision morphed into recent scenes of carnage down by the Seattle docks. And then my mind leapt back to a summer's morning in Loch Parton on the Isle of Stradday where I made love to Elspeth on the floor of my father's boat as the seagulls screamed with pleasure all around us. How far away from that time in my life I had traveled.

To the right, directly in front of van Allen's head was a small alcove under the counter top that I hadn't paid attention to before. It looked as though a cupboard or refrigerator had been removed, or was about to be installed. From where the floodlight was clipped to the doorframe above, this cubbyhole was in deep shadow. I found my pencil flashlight and probed the dark recess for a better look. There amidst some wood shavings, bent nails, cigarette butts and rat turds were two shiny brass cartridge cases lying exposed for anyone to see.

I pulled over the floodlight and rigged it up behind my shoulder to bathe the alcove in bright light so that I could photograph it. After that I picked up one of the cartridge cases. It was rimless, centerfire with clear breech markings and ejection marks, from a standard nine-millimeter semi-automatic handgun. I replaced it carefully where I had found it and inspected the second case, which looked identical in every way. Most common semi-automatic handguns that we see around here, like the Ruger, for example, eject the cartridge case to the right. The penny finally dropped.

There only needed to be one assailant who had been crouched down in the galley alcove when van Allen entered the room on the other side of the counter. As van Allen moved towards the front of the boat with his left arm out over the counter top the assailant had shot at him from behind and below. The bullet ripped through his arm missing bone but tearing the brachial artery before impacting in the crossbeam beside the barometer. Van Allen spun around in rage, with blood spurting everywhere. He turned back into the galley then slipped or dived at his attacker who backed into the corner alcove under the counter. As van Allen fell the murderer reached out, pressed the muzzle to his head and delivered the coup de grace. Both shots had been fired from the same area. Both cartridges were ejected into the darkness under the counter. When it was clear that van Allen was dead, the murderer carefully stepped over the body, avoiding the pools of blood, and escaped.

I stood to leave. I needed to clear my head. Besides, I could hear voices approaching through the barn, and I didn't want anyone else messing up the crime scene. My knees and back ached as I stretched to get loose. As I turned back to retrieve the floodlight I stopped and stared. I would never be able to hide myself under the counter in that alcove. And Frank Stillwell was four inches taller and fifty pounds heavier than I was. Looking back at the tiny space in which the murderer hid and from where the shots were fired it suddenly became clear. Neither Frank Stillwell nor his friend Brogan would be able to fit into that small of a space. The perpetrator who had murdered Clayton van Allen was someone who was nimble, athletic, ruthless and determined. And small.

XXII

Straggling Hound

"Stand back! The mad professor is emerging from his lair."

Keith Jepson and Rusty Bellagio stood at the foot of the stepladder preparing to clamber up onto the boat. Jepson's quip was meant to amuse the younger man. I must have looked a fright with my hair sticking out in sweaty spikes and my eyes wild with the excitement that comes from being the sole possessor of critical information on a murder still warm.

"What are you doing here, anyway, Donald? I'm meant to be on-call today. Didn't dispatch tell you?"

"The thought never occurred to me," I said. "Katy Pearson called me directly. I already knew about van Allen – that's the guy in the boat - so I came straight here."

Jepson winked at Rusty. "She must like something about you, Donald, if she's calling you in as a personal favor."

"Hardly. I think she is rubbing my nose in the fact that I messed up." I climbed down to join them on the floor of the barn. "I need to talk to Sonya Stillwell."

Rusty said, "You just missed her."

"Missed her? Have they taken her to the station?"

"No, she said she had to take her kid to see a psychologist in Seattle. I think she was going to swing by the police station to give her statement while the boy is being seen at Children's."

I raised my voice. "You mean no one is accompanying them? Don't they consider her to be a major material witness? Do we know if Tami is still at the nursing home?"

Rusty shrugged. Jepson was clearly puzzled at my intensity. "So what still needs doing on the body, Donald? Let me take over from here."

I gave them both a summary of my interpretation of the crime scene, leaving out only my suspicion about the height and size of the perpetrator. I told them my estimate of the time of death, and suggested that van Allen's body could be bagged and transferred to The Dell for autopsy that afternoon. Removing the body would free up space for Rusty and the rest of the crime scene response team to catalogue the findings inside the boat. I pointed out where he should look for the buried bullet in the crossbeam, the cartridge cases in the alcove, and described my preliminary blood spatter analysis.

"Did you find any surprises in the trailer?" I asked Rusty.

"Sure did. That's what I was coming to tell you about. We didn't find any traces of blood in the drain traps under the sinks, I'm afraid. I tested with Luminol. It would have been cool to show that. But I thought you might like to see what I found in the medicine cabinet."

He held out a large bottle of Phenobarbitone capsules. "Mrs. Stillwell says she has been taking these since she was a little girl. She got a head injury or something. Says these are the only thing that keeps her epileptic seizures at bay."

"Did you tell her why you were interested in them?" My question came across as an accusation.

"Of course not, Donald. I'm not that naïve. Actually, she seemed pretty relaxed about it all, considering. She was real cooperative with us. Kept telling us that it just couldn't be Frank who did the murders."

"I think she is right about that," I shouted as I strode out the barn.

My truck was cold, damp, and smelled of eight-years' worth of dropped food ground into the floor mats. It coughed and grumbled as I tried to get it going to warm myself up and gather my thoughts. I was the old unloved hound left to straggle in the rear while the exuberant youngsters kept up with the pack. But it seemed to me

303

that the pack was careening enthusiastically down the wrong trail. This was the second murder in a week in which Frank Stillwell could easily be implicated but where the details argued otherwise. And this morning, for the first time, I had clues that did more than rule him out, as far as I was concerned. They suggested someone else specifically. My self-confidence climbed a few inches out of the mud. Perhaps my professional judgment wasn't so useless after all. My pulse was still racing. I wanted to move fast but I needed to make doubly sure.

I called Linda's house on Vashon. There was no reply. I tried her Seattle house and got a foreign sounding maid who said that neither Mr. nor Mrs. Covington was at home. She was unwilling to proffer any more information. When our conversation began she had sounded quite articulate and fluent in English but the more I pressed her, the more she retreated behind a shield of Pidgin English with clipped sentences and grammatical butchery. I hung up and tried the back-line that Linda had given me for Sebastian Covington's office.

"Thank you for calling Covington's. Joni-Arlene speaking. How may I direct your call?" The receptionist had a silky Southern drawl, which made me think she might be a long term valued employee who had transferred here when the firm moved from Houston. This warranted a different approach.

I exuded deferential concern. "Good morning. I'm so sorry to bother you on the weekend but I'm trying to track down Sebastian. Covington," I added as if as an afterthought, conveying the impression that the great leader's first name was the more common usage for me. She wasn't buying.

"Whom shall I say is calling?" she said with careful neutrality.

"Oh sorry, it's Professor McLure here. Donald. I'm a long-term friend of Sebastian and Linda. I've been helping them with the awful…" I hesitated to demonstrate my consummate tact in such a delicate matter, "…problem that they have had at their Vashon house, recently. I'm sure you know what I'm talking about."

"Excuse me, Sir, but I'm going to have to put you on hold for just a minute, okay? Now don't you go away, now."

There was anxiety in her voice. She was probably scanning her notes to see if I was on either the "Put-through-immediately" list, or the "Stall-indefinitely" list. My guess was that I would be on neither. Last night, Covington had treated me as though I was unimportant chaff in his life. I rehearsed my next lines silently while I listened impatiently to the dull, on-hold music on the phone. Some days Mozart's exuberance is just irritating.

"Professor McLure I'm sorry to keep you waiting but I don't believe I can help you right now. Could I take a message? And could you spell your last name for me, please? Is it spelled M-C or M-A-C?"

I turned the deferential tone up a notch. "That's quite all right Joni-Arlene. I won't waste your time with that. I believe that leaving a message with you would be too late. You see I am over on Vashon right now and I have reason to believe that Linda and Sebastian may be in some personal danger. I'll just try some of our mutual friends and colleagues and tell them that you weren't able to help me. Maybe Kenny Jaratto will know where Sebastian is. Sorry to have troubled you."

The change in her manner was impressive. She almost tripped over her words in her hurry to keep my attention before I hung up. "Why Professor McLure I would be happy to help you if I could, I surely would, but Mr. Covington has left already and I am having trouble getting hold of him. He's not answering his cell phone. But he said he was going over to Vashon Island, himself. To see his mother-in-law. Perhaps you'll bump into him over there."

"He was going to visit Agnes? That surprises me. I got the impression they didn't get along and that he hadn't been to see her for months," I said.

"It surprised me, too. He came in for some scheduled meetings this morning, as he usually does, but after he checked his mail he told me there had been a change of plan and that he had to go to the nursing home immediately."

"When did he leave?"

"A little before nine."

If any of that was true it meant he probably caught an earlier ferry than I had. I thanked the flustered receptionist, hung up and headed for Goldentide nursing home.

• • •

Two yellow school buses were parked outside. The foyer was teaming with energetic middle-schoolers from West Seattle and Vashon school districts preparing to perform a play for the old folks. A clean-cut couple of teenagers holding hands in the gift shop explained that it was part of a cultural outreach program to celebrate and honor old age across cultures. They were doing performances in eight nursing homes in the Seattle-King-County area over the next two weeks. The play was both funny and touching, they assured me. I would be welcome to attend the performance, starting in the dining hall in less than an hour.

Mrs. Burley, the nursing director for Goldentide was holed up in her administrative office, scowling. A bustling round woman with a severe gray bun in her hair and a face to match, she clearly didn't remember me from our brief encounter the previous Monday. When I reminded her that I had witnessed her conversation with Linda concerning the altercation between Agnes Munro and Patricia Klein, she became cool and defensive. When I added that I was a friend of the family and a Professor of Medicine at the University of Washington she became a little more forthcoming. I didn't think it advisable to specify which branch of medicine I specialized in.

I said, "I was hoping to catch Sebastian. Has he been here today? His secretary said he was planning to."

"He left here an hour ago. It was quite a surprise to see him at all, actually. He has only been in twice in the past year, to my knowledge, and then only with questions about the billing statements for Mrs.

Munro."

"Did he visit Agnes today?" I asked innocently.

"I couldn't say. He burst into my office and asked for a letter that he had been told was waiting for him. I had no idea what he was talking about but I took him to see Betsy at the information desk. She knows everything that's going on around here. It turned out that she did have a package for him."

"I wonder if that is the package Linda told me about." I bluffed. "Was it a letter? Did you see it?"

"Yes, I took him out to the foyer and Betsy handed it over. It was a thick brown envelope. A nine by eleven."

"From Agnes?"

"I assumed so. It might have contained old photographs or some other mementos. Something of that nature. It didn't say who it was from. Betsy just said that Tami left it for her to give to Mr. Covington if he showed up today."

"Tami Stillwell? Why would she have given it to Betsy? I didn't think Tami had had much to do with Agnes until the scratching incident with Mrs. Klein last Sunday."

I kicked myself for bringing up that episode again so bluntly. Mrs. Burley's litigation antennae were back on alert. "Where did you get that idea? Tami and Agnes have a very special relationship.

Tami often stops by Mrs. Munro's room even when she has been assigned to other patients. Agnes probably gave her the letter and Tami took it from there. She's a very thoughtful young woman. She has a real affection for Agnes."

"That's sweet of her. Linda hadn't mentioned that to me. It must be nice for the old lady to have more company. I know that it is difficult for Linda to get over to the island as much as she'd like."

"She has a house nearby. Agnes, I mean. I believe Tami has even been there once or twice to bring Agnes things that she wanted. I assumed that Mr. and Mrs. Covington approved." Mrs. Burley looked suddenly troubled and unsure, as if she sensed a potential breech of protocol. When she was interrupted to answer her telephone I waved my thanks and slipped away.

The foyer was quieter now, with muted giggles and squeals echoing from the corridor leading to the dining hall. I found a bright-eyed elderly woman wearing a pink volunteer smock, and sitting at the information counter. She scanned her territory hungrily, eager to be helpful to any unwary passer-by. The name on her heart-shaped Goldentide badge said, "Betsy."

"Busy day you're having with all the school children," I said in my most endearing Scottish accent. "I used to love singing for all the old folks when I was in the school choir in Edinburgh. It's nice to see that they still do that kind of thing."

She beamed with pleasure. "Yes, isn't it? You hear so many bad things about young people nowadays but this group had such wonderful energy. Are you staying on the island? You're Irish aren't you? Are you staying for the performance?"

Her eyes pinned me to the wall, searching for weak spots in my polite façade. Half an hour with this woman and she would have extracted my entire life history.

"I'd love to stay but I'm running late, today, I'm afraid. I was hoping to talk to Mr. and Mrs. Covington. Or to Tami, maybe, if she's still here."

"You'll be here to see Agnes, then. Of course! That's a Scottish accent, isn't it, not Irish? I should have known. Agnes used to live in Edinburgh too, you know." I shuffled my feet to convey urgency as delicately as possible. "Everyone is in such a rush today. You are all missing each other. Tami left at about nine thirty." She looked at her watch. "She may have gone to Agnes' house to change but I don't expect she'll still be there. She was going off for a picnic this afternoon." Betsy waved to a middle-aged couple trying to slip out the front door unnoticed. "Bye bye Mr. and Mrs. Courtney. I hope those painters work out for you. See you tonight."

"Did Tami often go to Agnes' house?" I asked.

Betsy's voice dropped to a conspiratorial tone. "Most days, although I don't tell Mrs. Burley that. I doubt if she would approve. She only goes on her lunch breaks. Tami's a nice quiet girl. Likes to get away from the crowds to read a nice book. Agnes' house is very handy for her. It's much closer than her own house, you see. Just up the road here. I remember when that house was first built. John

310

Morgensen built most of it himself. He was a fine strapping man, back then."

I could see her eyes beginning to stare off into nostalgic reminiscences. I couldn't afford the time.

"Agnes lived there before she came to Goldentide, didn't she?" I said.

"Mmm? Yes, but only for a few months. The house was vacant for years before that. I was surprised that none of the Morgensen children wanted to buy the place. Those boys must have climbed every tree in that place, growing up. They even brought an old railway carriage over on a barge from Tacoma and winched it half way up the bank to be a guesthouse. That was in 1963, the same year that President Kennedy was killed. There must have been twenty men helping get that caboose up the hill that day. It was quite the event. I live next door, you see. Well, across the street, actually. I don't have waterfront but I used to enjoy watching all the comings and goings when the Morgensens lived there. Hello ladies. Are you not going to watch the play?"

A hunched up trio of female patients, in quilted dressing gowns and flip-flop slippers, shuffled past us on their way to the gift shop. They linked arms for extra balance and reassurance. I paid them no attention and was about to take my leave of Betsy when one of the geriatric trio peeled away and gripped my wrist with her bony hand.

Agnes Munro's wild vacant eyes scrutinized my face. "You're

not David!" she said in disgust.

I patted her hand absently and tried to make sense of the new details that I had pulled from Betsy's blizzard of trivia. Tami Stillwell had lied to Katy and me about knowing Agnes. She had developed a close relationship with the old lady and apparently had access to her house. Linda seemed to be unaware of any of this. It was odd. And then there was the altercation between Patricia Klein and Agnes last Sunday, in which Tami had intervened. Something about that didn't ring true either. When Tami had explained her involvement to Linda and me she had not acknowledged any special closeness with Agnes. She portrayed herself as the well intentioned referee, a helpful outsider breaking up an ugly scene, pulling the combatants apart and getting injured in the process.

As I gently lifted the old lady's hand off my wrist it finally dawned on me what had struck me so odd about her hands when I had given her the box of chocolates on Monday. Agnes Munro's fingernails were bitten down to the quick. Not only is that an unusual sight in someone of her age, it had a more specific relevance to what I was thinking about, right then. Those hands were incapable of being used for scratching anyone.

XXIII

The Culb Hut

I'm not sure what I expected to find at Agnes Munro's empty house. Sebastian Covington torching the place? Tami Stillwell trying on the old lady's clothes? Nothing made much sense. On impulse I had turned left instead of right after leaving Goldentide, just so that I could drive past. In the event the house was as quiet and lifeless as it had been when Linda brought me there the previous Monday.

There were no cars in the driveway. I walked slowly around the house wiping away the grime and cobwebs to peer through tattered lace curtains at the rooms beyond. Nothing was ransacked. No bodies lay on the floors. Instead, mismatched furniture stood listlessly around in dull conventional arrangements. There was dust on the dining room table. The pendulum clock in the kitchen stood motionless. It was mundane and unimaginative; a house that had never become a real home for a disorientated and sad old lady.

A leaden sky brooded over the sea below. The wind carried a few spots of rain with the promise of more to come. I stood on the front lawn looking half-heartedly for footprints or recent activity. I wasn't sure what to do next. I thought about calling Katy Pearson with my latest theory on why Frank Stillwell was not van Allen's murderer, but I decided against it. She wouldn't believe me anyway. I turned up the collar of my jacket, hung my head, and slouched back to the truck.

If I hadn't been so dejected I might have missed it. Lying among the sticks on the ground below the bushes at one corner of the front lawn was about six inches of dark green electrical extension cord. The cord itself was caked in dirt but the three-pronged plug was bright and shiny from recent use. I bent to look at it with idle curiosity. The front porch of the house was fifteen feet away. I could see an electrical outlet at one corner, next to an outside faucet that was wrapped in insulation. I tugged on the cord to see if it was long enough to stretch to the house. To my surprise it pulled out easily. It didn't get snagged in a tangle of grass, brambles and moonvine. I plugged it in and followed it back to the bushes. The dark green could hardly be seen in the grass. Parting the lower branches, I found a few more coils of green cord, which then attached to a thicker orange extension that disappeared down the steep bank. When I pulled on this it quickly tensed and held firm, as if caught in a branch. I might have let it go at that, but for one thing. When I stood and followed the line the cord was taking down the slope it pointed straight at the rooftop of the old caboose, thirty yards below me and obscured by blackberry brambles.

The entrance to the path down to the caboose was blocked by several large fir branches that might have fallen from a nearby tree. On the other hand they might have been placed there on purpose. A

314

rotting wooden sign nailed to the trunk said, "Culb Hut" in clumsy, boyish wood-burning from a childhood long ago. The first eight feet of the trail were overgrown but beyond that a path had been cleared leading to a wooden staircase built into the side of the slope. Some of the steps had rotted away and the railing was loose and shaky, but the brambles and nettles had been hacked back indicating some recent attention.

The caboose itself was secured to the hillside by massive creosoted pilings driven into the ground. The wheels of the carriage were long gone but the rusting axles protruded out into the damp air like stumps of leg bones. A small wooden porch had been built at the end where the door was. A dim yellow light shone from within, which gave me a jolt until I remembered that I had plugged in the cord up above. I could see the other end of the orange plastic snaking out from the undergrowth and disappearing into a crack in the window next to the door.

I tried the door handle but it was well and truly locked. My polite calls and knocks went unanswered. The place had probably been taken over by some of the neighborhood kids as a secret base or a hideout. At least that seemed to be the most logical explanation until I took my hand off the door handle and saw the smear of blood on my palm.

It took three hefty shoulder charges to break the old doorframe and send me sprawling inside. I regretted my brashness immediately. The place felt distinctly occupied. In addition to yellow light coming from beyond a half-opened door the air felt warm with a low steady whirring from within. I scrambled to my feet and braced myself for action but none was needed. No furies came forth to meet me. I moved slowly forward and pushed open the door to the main compartment of the caboose.

The furniture was sparse to say the least. This was a kid's den, no more. On the walls were narrow wooden shelves with little metal railings on their front edge, originally intended for keeping suitcases in place during bumpy train rides. A few faded posters hung of the ceiling showing bikini-clad surfers and blonde-haired ski-bunnies from the nineteen-eighties, relics from the Morgensen boys' teenage years, perhaps. A makeshift coffee table occupied the center of the room, fashioned from driftwood on short stubby legs. Some cushions and sacks did for seats. An antique table lamp cast a golden glow over the table on which folders and books were scattered. On the floor next to the table a small fan heater was blasting hot air with gusto. The orange cord supplied both heat and light. Somebody had created a cozy lair for secret study.

A battered suitcase in one corner contained a few T-shirts and some sweatpants in the baggy one-size-fits-no-one style favored by young people. There were no bras, tampons, shaving kits or magazines to even hint at the gender or size of the occupant; no sleeping bag and no food to suggest that the place was really lived in.

A loose scrap of paper fluttered off the table, blown by the current from the fan heater. I picked it up and recognized Linda Munro's writing straight away. I remembered the curvy round shapes and the way she put a circle instead of a dot over her "i." On a piece of University of Washington Memo paper she had written, in blue ballpoint pen, a list of nine names and telephone numbers. They were girls' names but I recognized none. All the phone numbers were local; Seattle or Bellevue mostly, though one had a Tacoma prefix. The names had all been crossed out in red felt tip pen and some additional notes were scribbled in the margins in different handwriting. This ugly script was not Linda's. Some of the phone numbers had been changed, with new ones written above. It didn't make much sense. Linda claimed she knew nothing about this place and had never been down here.

Two old shoeboxes were piled at one end of the table, each secured with well-used ribbon. The faded logo on the bottom box said, "Saxone," a shoe company prominent in Scotland about thirty years ago and probably long since defunct. Had old Agnes found her way down here in the months before she was moved to Goldentide? I carefully undid the ribbon and looked inside. Both shoeboxes were stuffed with letters and postcards organized roughly chronologically. They were all addressed to Agnes, in Edinburgh, in Linda's handwriting. They had been sent from all over the world although the majority came from the USA. The earliest ones were postmarked from Portland, Oregon, with dates corresponding to Linda's emigration to the USA over twenty years ago. The envelopes were fat and the letters frequent. The most recent ones were thinner and stopped a few years ago when Agnes had been moved out here. Those two shoeboxes contained a lifetime of treasured correspondence from a dutiful daughter to her doting mother.

I eyed the early, fat letters with some discomfort. From what Linda had said to me in recent days I wondered how much angst about me she had shared with her mother, how much regret, soul-searching and passion those pages contained. I replaced the lids firmly on the boxes. Whatever she had written was private, ancient history and of no interest to me now.

Most of the papers scattered on the table were in the same angular handwriting as the red felt-tip pen. It was ugly scribbles for the most part along with disturbing cartoons of skeletons, nooses and wilted flowers. Underneath, I came across several more of Linda's letters. Letters that had been removed from the box and examined in detail. They dated from the time when Linda was getting to know Sebastian. She was sharing her innermost anxieties, daughter to mother as best friend and confidante. Somehow knowing that someone else had already defiled them made it easier for me to glance at what was written on the pages. They confirmed what Linda had already told me of those early times.

Sebastian was wonderful ... talented ... devoted to Linda ... the future looked rosy ... then another woman had appeared to spoil everything ... an old girlfriend ... pregnant, impoverished, desperate, demanding ... Sebastian didn't want her ... didn't want her baby ... she was being so unreasonable ... it was all such a mess ... what should Linda do? ... what did mother think was best?

Several sections had been underlined and circled in the same angry red scrawl. The original writing was touching, poignant and deeply personal. To see which sections had been highlighted was chilling.

I searched through the rest of the documents on the table looking for clues about the angry stranger who had pored over these letters.

It took me five minutes to find the birth certificate, in an official envelope from the State of Oregon. The name meant nothing to me but the date certainly fit. With mounting trepidation I picked up Linda's list of girls' names on the UW memo and began dialing the phone numbers. I got no reply at the first two but the third time was a charm.

"Hello, could I speak to Misty, please?"

"Sure, I'll go get her."

There was a youthful clunk as the phone was dropped. I could hear distant rock music blaring, a vacuum cleaner going, and several shouted conversations and slamming doors. The sounds of weekend college life in a large communal house are easy to identify. A cheerful young woman came on the line.

"Hi, this is Misty?"

"Misty, my names is Donald and I'm a friend of Linda Munro. Do you happen to be in her psychology class this year?"

"Yes! Is it on again or something?"

"Is what on again?"

"The trip to Kamagutsz. I was so pissed that she cancelled at the last minute. I'd made plans and everything."

"When did you find out it was cancelled?" I said.

319

"Just this morning. Her secretary just left a message on the machine to say there was a family emergency. I called some of the other girls in the group. Janice and Carol got e-mails last night saying the same thing. Bummer! It would have been so fun."

I hung up and crossed Janice Philipsen and Carol Hoskins off the list. I made myself call one more name on the list, just to be sure but I knew I'd get the same result. All of the young women who were supposed to be enjoying a private retreat at the Kamagutsz Hot Springs had been told at the last minute to stay away. Tami Stillwell's name was not on that list.

I grabbed the Oregon birth certificate and the marked-up letters, and headed out. Behind the door I found a crumpled T-shirt stained with blood. At that point I wasn't surprised but it increased my sense of urgency as I ran back to the truck.

• • •

The ferry trip to Southworth is a mere pirouette from the north end of Vashon. You drive up one side of the boat, swing around the back end, then come back down to face the way you've come. Before you have time to set your parking brake the ferry backs out, reverses direction and makes a single arc to the west to join hands with the Southworth pier. The whole dance barely takes ten minutes but it seemed nine minutes too long to me, today. Stuck behind a logging truck in the belly of the boat, I couldn't get a cell phone signal so had to drum my fingers until the ferry workers indicated that I could drive off.

The Kitsap peninsula is a convoluted mass of watery inlets and twisting roads. I hammered west on Sedgwick Road leaving my stomach in the air as I lurched from hillock to hollow like a roller coaster. Acid burned my throat to remind me that I had missed lunch yet again. The glove compartment yielded a brick-hard granola bar and half a packet of antacid chalk. I passed on both. The drive got smoother traveling north to Gorst where I did a U-turn onto Highway-3. I got no reply calling Katy, so contacted dispatch and asked them to get her to call me directly.

The drive round the base of the Hood Canal through Union is one of the prettiest you'll ever see. From the corner of my eye I could see the late afternoon sun shining on the mudflats, while cormorants stood sentry on skeleton pilings of old piers. It was wasted on me, today. With my eyes fixed straight ahead I swerved around potholes, skidded on black ice, sprayed gravel onto cyclists and cursed stray dogs and camper vans.

The light was fading as I picked up Highway-101 at Skokomish and turned north up the west side of the canal towards Hoodsport. By the time Katy's call chirped on my phone I was less than half a mile from her. I could see her ahead of me, standing beside a half-built condo on the water side of the outskirts of Hoodsport. The building site was empty, as was the blue Nissan rental car parked out front. If Katy Pearson was in the mood to be aloof she had picked a bad time. I leaned on my horn to get her attention as I pulled up beside her.

"No sign of Stillwell?" I yelled. "They must be at the Hot Springs.

Do you know the way?"

"Hot Springs? What Hot Springs?"

"The Kamagutsz Hot Springs. You know how to get there?"

"They are up towards Mt. Ellinor, I think but I don't know exactly. Donald what the hell is going on?"

"Follow me. I'll ask at a gas station."

The surly youth at the Texaco Minimart took his eyes off the TV just long enough to hand me a photocopied set of directions to Kamagutsz. I gave Katy the briefest summary of my findings over the past few hours while I filled up with gas, locked the front wheels and threw the old truck into four-wheel drive.

With Katy's Jeep bouncing in my rear-view mirror I plunged off into long abandoned logging roads that zigzagged up the stump-covered foothills between Mt. Washington and Mt. Ellinor. The directions were a masterful display of understatement.

"Follow the South Fork of Lilliwaup Creek for four miles of unmaintained, single-lane track to trailhead parking area."

Those last four miles were half an hour of bone-shuddering, axle-breaking hell. The old Ford slithered into potholes big enough to accommodate a pregnant hippo. Instead they covered the rusting remains of cars that hadn't made it any farther. Great chunks of the road had slid off down the mountain so that I had to forge new paths into the underbrush from time to time before regaining the trail beyond the landslide. At one point a long tree branch barred the path completely and brought me to a stop. I got out for a closer look.

Katy pulled up behind me and shouted helpful advice. "Did you take a wrong turn? Doesn't look as if anyone has been up this way for days."

I was inclined to agree with her until I noticed the scrape marks arching across the mud. Someone had dragged the branch across the roadway after they had passed. It swept away any lingering doubts I might have had. I grabbed the tree limb and dragged it back into the underbrush at the edge of the trail. Half a mile farther on we came to a gravel-covered clearing at the base of an avalanche chute. Boulders and fallen trees marked the edges of what had to be the trailhead to Kamagutsz. A covered bulletin board and box for trail passes stood beside the start of a walking trail on the far side of the clearing.

There were only two vehicles already here; Linda's Ford Explorer and an ancient Chevy truck with a canopy bolted over the truck bed. Both vehicles were locked and looked empty until I wiped the dirt off the back window of the Chevy. Tools, work boots and garbage littered the inside, partially covered with a tarpaulin. Just as I was about to turn away I saw one of the work boots move. I grabbed the tire iron from my own vehicle and forced open the tailgate.

Frank Stillwell was bound and gagged with about ten rolls of Duct Tape. For good measure he appeared to be only half-conscious and reeking of bourbon. Katy trained her revolver on him while I ripped the tape off his mouth. He exploded into life, writhing like a hooked shark. His flailing feet sent Katy's gun clattering to the ground as he made a lunging attempt to bite me. I threw myself on top of him and grabbed his hair to fend off those teeth. His eyes were crazed and blood shot.

"It's Dr. McLure and the police, Frank. We're here to help," I said.

"Gun!" he roared. "The little bastard's got my gun!"

Katy Pearson recovered her gun and her composure. "And so have I, Mr. Stillwell, so quit your kicking. Hold him down, Donald. I'm going to cuff him and secure him in the back of the Jeep, then call for back up."

Stillwell's fury was spent. If not bewitched, he certainly looked drugged, bothered and bewildered. He stared at us balefully, like a beaten hound, and offered no resistance as we dragged him across the gravel and into the Jeep. I was obedient and helpful to Katy. I waited until she was preoccupied with the police radio before I took off running up the hillside trail towards the Hot Springs. I was almost out of earshot when she started screaming at me to come back.

XXIV

Red Water At Kamagutsz

The Kamagutsz Hot Springs are one of the best-kept secrets in the Pacific Northwest. For centuries the Native Americans knew that in the high hills beside the thundering waterfall, where the forest never sleeps, the mountain was angry. Steam issued forth from twin caves like the nostrils of some terrible god. The site was rediscovered in 1923 by a Japanese craftsman who found that the water spilling out of the cave walls eased his arthritic pains. He bought the thirty acres that included the waterfall and the caves, and set about creating a quiet restorative sanctuary.

Using local slate, granite and limestone he walled off the lower half of both cave-mouths so that the warm healing powers of the springs could be contained within. On the sloping ground below the mouth of the main cave he built a series of shallow pools and catch basins, linked by decorative spouts and aqueducts. In the front wall of the main cave he fashioned an outlet so that the water spilled over after building to a depth of four feet within. The water tumbled out, laughing, over the rocks and sculptures, filling the pools and basins of the rock and water garden before dropping off the edge of the plateau to join the icy torrent of Lilliwaup Creek far below.

For two decades the Japanese family shared their heavenly hideout with friends and neighbors. It became a gentle retreat where the cares and troubles of life could be eased and erased, sitting neck-high in the mildly medicinal waters of Kamagutsz; waters heated by the passion of the planet's very core. From deep within the cave water, protected in the womb of the mountain, they could look out across the gorge to the thundering splendor of Desolation Falls crashing amongst the dark forested hills.

The springs were abandoned amid the humiliation of Japanese internment during the nineteen forties. They fell into disrepair and were ignored and forgotten by everyone until a small group of hippies set up camp near them for a few years in the late nineteen sixties. During those years the smoke issuing forth from the fabled nostrils of the mountain god became tinged with psychedelic purple and orange. The parties were legendary; the encampment grew until some feckless young man plunged to his death trying to fly after the gigantic crimson butterfly he thought he saw fluttering out across the gorge.

During the nineteen seventies, eighties and nineties the Kamagutsz Hot Springs became abandoned again. In recent years the area has been bought over by a private trust who have lovingly restored it and now issue a limited number of passes to preserve the natural beauty of the peaceful sanctuary. So once again enlightened individuals or groups can stroll among the towering old-growth cedars or bathe in the rejuvenating waters of Kamagutsz.

The wooded path from the trailhead gains 2,400 feet of elevation in less than two miles. As I pounded up the trail over crunching gravel, spongy moss and slippery wooden bridges, I wasn't entirely sure whom I would find or what I should prepare for. I tried to recall some of the details that Linda had mentioned. The geothermal water entered the caves in three places at a constant, near-scalding 119 degrees Fahrenheit, but cooled to a bearable 108 degrees Fahrenheit in the cave pool. The water was only mildly sulphurous and stayed at a depth of between three and five feet behind the retaining walls. The largest cave was ten feet wide and eight feet tall at the mouth, gradually narrowing as it curved back thirty feet into the mountain. Each of the two catch basins outside was ten feet in diameter and two feet deep, lined with smooth polished slate. The temperature dropped by four degrees in each pool so that people who found the intense heat and claustrophobia of the caves too much to bear could lie under the sky in one of the outdoor pools watching clouds, eagles or stars dancing above them.

The two cave entrances were twenty feet apart with a rocky promontory in between, like a warrior's battered nose. Access to each cave was separate. On the far side of the buttress some rough steps had been hacked out of the rocky wall leading to the smaller cave like pockmarks on the giant's face. All the care and attention was devoted to the main cave. A wide stone staircase curved up to this entrance, with a cedar handrail for added protection. A covered cabana had been built at the foot of this staircase so that bathers could disrobe or take refreshment in relative comfort before entering the spa. Food, alcohol and other drugs were no longer allowed within the cave.

The panting of my breath became drowned in the roar of the waterfall as I neared the summit and the path came closer to the river below. In the half-light of the afternoon the club moss trailed off tree branches like a veil of unreality. The air was cold and humid, the smells fetid and earthy. Giant mushrooms sprouted off the crumbling carcasses of nurse logs. The path weaved around gigantic boulders, tree stumps and over roots bigger than my aching thighs. The ground flattened out and dropped to a sheltered hollow below the caves. I slowed and crouched behind a tree. The place seemed deserted. Through the mist of the falls massive tree trunks rose stiff and tall like sentries guarding a sacred place. With the sun low in the sky, shadows threw the cliff into craggy relief. Steam curled lazily out of both caves, but as I descended toward the cabana the smaller cave mouth disappeared behind the towering overhang of the rock, and a sense of foreboding fell over me.

The cabana stood empty. A neat pile of clothes lay on one of the benches beside a wicker basket, two bottles of wine and a stack of ten empty plastic glasses. On the floor of the cabana were a large bath towel and a single pair of women's walking shoes. They were brand new and designer brand, probably Linda's. I crept closer but saw nothing suggesting danger.

Close in, away from the noise of the waterfall, I craned my neck to distinguish other sounds. On the way up the trail I had heard chattering chipmunks and cackling jays, but here those daytime sounds were gone in that eery silence that comes as the light is fading before the creatures of the night issue forth. I heard no twigs snapping; no metallic clicks as cartridge cases were slid into place. The only breath I heard was my own. Water tumbled over the wall of the cave mouth and onto rocky pools below in a cascade of gently mocking laughter.

I could taste salt on my lips and the sweet acid in my mouth that comes from exertion on an empty stomach. Sweat cooled on my scalp then fell in icy trickles among my hair and down my neck. I crouched, shivering beside the pool at the foot of the stairway. The ground had the loamy pungency of rotting vegetation that never dries out. There was the chemical tang of pine rosin in the air and something else that I couldn't place but made my skin prickle. The outdoor collection pool beside me was still and serene. I dipped a hand in and marveled at the heat, so startling to feel this high in the mountain. The whole scene was kissed with gentleness and romance. Even the water tumbling from the cave wall above was tinged red in the light of the setting sun.

Except that the sun was not yet setting. The sky behind me was still pale gray and blue. I turned quickly to look at the rocks, the falls, the tree limbs. Nothing else was tinged red. With mounting panic I tiptoed up the steps to see that it was the water trickling down from the cave that was red. With my head just below the wall itself I could hear voices and sobs echoing from within, confirming my worst fears.

I lifted my head above the wall and peered into the darkness but could see nothing. It was a fathomless chasm of sulfurous steam and blackness. I could hear at least two voices, both female, but not what they said. Angry whispers and taunts mixed with muffled sobbing goaded me into action.

"Linda, are you in there?" My voice sounded distorted and unreal.

There was frantic splashing as Linda screamed, "Sebby, help me. She's got a knife. I'm bleeding."

Another voice cut her off, shrill and defiant. "So you've come, finally. Come on in and join us, you heartless little bastard. Come and watch your fat little whore bleed to death like a … stuck … pig!"

It was difficult to reconcile that deranged voice as belonging to Tami Stillwell, but I knew it had to be her. Those last words were accompanied by grunts and lunges, splashes and squeals of terror from Linda. I couldn't hold back. I took off my leather jacket, balled it round my left hand as a makeshift shield and took a deep breath. Unsure if Tami had a gun in there or not, and aware that I was an easy target in the cave mouth with the light behind me, I hurled myself over the front wall in a swift decisive roll, and plunged into the pool.

Nothing could have prepared me for the searing painful heat that engulfed me. My skin was on fire. I let out an involuntary roar under the water and imagined my skin turning bright pink like a boiled lobster. With my ears ringing and my eyeballs bulging out their sockets I pushed off the cave floor to bring my head above the water. The pool was even deeper than I had expected, almost up to my neck. I surfaced at one side of the cave, trying to keep myself in shadow while my eyes adjusted.

The primal fear of dark and unknown places can render human beings paralyzed. I took deep rapid breaths and tried to stop my legs from trembling or cramping. It was like floundering in a muddy Amazonian river just waiting for the first bite of a piranha's sharp teeth. Except that the piranha in this cave was a triple murderer who had a firm grip on a knife blade but had lost all grip on reason. I could sense her moving closer with stealthy cunning, all advantage on her side. Linda's demented blubbering was a distraction. It made it impossible for me to make out other sounds. She sounded pathetic and weak, her lifeblood draining into the pool.

I had two things in favor of my defense. My now-sodden leather jacket offered some physical protection. If I could tangle the knife up in that I might manage to snap the blade or twist it out of her hand. The only other weapon I had was the fact that they had both assumed I was Sebastian Covington. If I could time it right, revealing my identity might catch Tami by surprise and give me the advantage for half a second.

I raised my left hand to the surface and waved it slowly back and forth as I moved towards the back.

"Hurry Sebby! I'm feeling dizzy." Linda's voice sounded deathly weak. Her hysterical squeals changed to choking, spluttering coughs as she fought to prevent herself from slipping below the surface.

The water erupted in front of me. I punched towards the darkness with my left fist and felt the jolt of resistance. I heard the leather rip but felt no pain.

"Give it up, Tami. This is Doctor McLure. I've done nothing to hurt you. I just want to stop any more deaths."

There was a screech of fury. "You tricky bastard. You're all liars and cheats. You shouldn't be here. He should be here … cowardly … bastard."

There was a blur of movement and my hand was knocked down into the water as she tried to get the blade beyond the leather wad to strike at my arm. I kept moving forward, pushing her back in the cave, trying to reduce her area of movement. Maybe I could pin her to the wall. I also wanted to reach Linda.

"It's over, Tami. The police are outside. We found Frank in the truck."

I could make out her shape better now, as my eyes became used to the darkness. The cave seemed to curve to the right as it went back. Tami was crouched against the inner curve of the wall, her head above the water, the arm and knife concealed. Linda's sobbing seemed to be on the outer wall, which was my side of the cave. I moved steadily to get myself between Linda and her insane tormentor. Perhaps it was my imagination but the light seemed to be getting brighter the farther back I went. Tami slashed and prodded at me but I was able to parry her blows more easily now. She screamed in frustration, took a deep breath and dived below the surface.

I stepped back a pace and plunged my protected left arm under the water to fend off an attack from below. But none came. The surface of the water remained calm and unbroken. A full minute went by. Then another. Surely she couldn't hold her breath that long? Was she moving closer to Linda? Linda sounded so helpless and weak it was a wonder Tami hadn't killed her already. But perhaps she was waiting for Sebastian Covington to show up and witness the torture and torment.

"Move towards me Linda. It's Donald. Stay awake. Move towards the sound of my voice."

Linda was crammed into the farthest recess of the cave, immobile and unresponsive. I couldn't tell if she was still conscious or not. The cave walls were narrowing, and the roof was lower here, but the light was definitely improving. I wanted to get Linda's attention but saw her eyes roll back as she slipped below the surface. I dived to catch her and heave her head back into the air. She was a slippery dead weight and did nothing to help. I managed to hook my arms under hers and pushed our heads above the surface again. The effort took all the strength from me. My head spun. My brain was overheated and muddled, my thinking unclear. I felt close to passing out myself. As I fought to get my bearings I thought I could see two cave entrances and wondered for a moment if I was getting double vision. But the cave mouths were not alike. To my right I saw the large hole where I had entered, but to my left the tunnel curved sharply back on itself towards a second smaller patch of light with the outside showing beyond that.

It was a horseshoe cave. The two nostrils in the mountain

were from one cavern. My tired mind struggled to incorporate the implications of this discovery. I was sure that Tami hadn't swum past me in the main cave but this gave her new possibilities. Was she crouched in the darkness of the second cave biding her time?

Linda had regained some consciousness and clung to me like a terrified kitten. My strength wouldn't hold out much longer. Hypothermia is a well-known hazard of the mountains but when the body overheats it can be just as deadly. I looked desperately down one cave and then the other, utterly unsure how to proceed. The light was fading fast but the contrast with the relentless blackness of the cave meant that the entrances stood out like half domes of pale gray light.

A stringy, bony silhouette reared up in the smaller entrance. It was a naked woman but she had no knife in her hand. As she swung her arm round to point at us I glimpsed the unmistakable outline of a handgun.

"Dive Linda! Big breath!" I yelled as I pulled her under the water and pushed off the wall towards the deepest part of the larger cave.

In the confines of the tunnel the noise of gunfire was deafening. The first shot erupted before my head dipped below the surface. The next three were fired while both Linda and I were under water. Two more were squeezed off before I got far enough beyond the corner of the cave to have rock wall between me and the shooter. My ears were ringing but I felt no pain. Linda was spluttering and retching. I couldn't tell if she had been hit or not. At least she was still fighting.

We were sitting targets, but surely the noise would bring Katy? And with adrenaline clearing my head I reasoned that at least we had physics on our side. Despite the lethal destructive force that handguns wield when fired in the air, even the most powerful handgun bullets will be brought to a halt and rendered harmless in four feet of water. At The Dell we use water tanks to test-fire guns. Those tanks measure five by four by three feet. The cave pool we were in now contained a hundred times more volume of water. Provided she didn't connect with an exposed part of our bodies we were safe from Tami Stillwell's deadly intentions, although safe was obviously a relative term.

My relief was short-lived. Running my hands over Linda's slumping body I could tell that she was bleeding from multiple places. She had several deep defensive cuts on her palms and forearms, a stab wound on her left deltoid and another low down on her left breast. The texture of the water next to her skin was thick and sticky. She was slowly exsanguinating.

I was suddenly reminded of Professor Coulter's awful sheep experiments from my physiology course in Edinburgh University Medical School, twenty-odd years before. It was a gruesome rite of passage for medical students. Every Wednesday afternoon during the spring term groups of twenty students had to spend a four-hour laboratory watching Coulter and his assistant perform a slow vivisection of a sheep. Visions of that day came back to me as I crouched in that dark pool.

* * *

Professor Coulter was in a feisty and disagreeable mood, complaining to his assistant about the poor caliber of that day's animal's arteries.

"I don't know what the hell this animal's been fed on, Brian. It's got the arteries of a tough old ram. Watch where you're putting the flow meter, man!"

Coulter's eyes glittered with mischief as he looked up to find the palest and most distraught among his students.

"Miss Gallaher, what will happen if the flow of blood returning to the heart is suddenly interrupted?" he bellowed gleefully as he clipped a bright chrome clamp over the animal's inferior vena cava. "Don't just stand there, woman, read the oscilloscope! What is happening to the pulse rate? What about the systolic blood pressure?"

I could tell that Marie Gallaher's own pulse and blood pressure were taking a beating. She tottered past me and stared hopefully at the oscilloscope.

"The pulse is rising, Sir, and the blood pressure is f-falling," she stammered.

"Of course it is!" he shouted triumphantly, releasing the clamp. "And now it is returning to normal, is it not?

"You are a deadly dull lot. Future doctors, I am told. God help us! You'll need to learn to think clearly and quickly in the face of a little blood, eh? You there, McLure, step a little closer! What do you think

336

will happen if the aorta – that's the great big artery coming off the left ventricle, sonny – what would happen if it were to ... rupture!"

With a single snip of his surgical scissors he severed the sheep's aorta. This was the traditional climax to the infamous "Sheep Experiment," and I had been warned to duck. A few of the students at the back of the group were too slow and got drenched in a shower of warm blood. One large farmer's son from Huntly fainted. Several girls fled, but Coulter wouldn't let me go. With his bloody gloved hand clamped on my arm he shouted.

"The heart! Look at its heart, man and describe it to your colleagues."

He really was a vicious old lunatic but I bit my tongue and reported the results as calmly as I could. I wasn't going to give him the pleasure of seeing me faint-hearted or squeamish. The blood pressure plummeted, the pulse rate rose and the electrical tracing of the sheep's heart became an illegible scribble. I stared at the animal's perfect little heart as it stopped beating in that beautiful coordinated normal way and began to fibrillate. That big strong muscle became a writhing bag of worms quivering ineffectually for a few minutes before it finally stopped.

The tall bearded professor stood and towered above me as he tore off his bloody surgical gloves in disgust.

"You'll need to be made of sterner stuff than this, laddie. You'll see far worse than this once you are out there in the real world."

*　*　*

Professor Coulter's words echoed in my ears as I sat helplessly in the Kamagutsz Hot Springs. I am not sure if this was what he had in mind when he talked about the real world. This one seemed a bit on the surreal side to me. I felt for Linda's carotid pulse. It was well over a hundred and twenty beats a minute. Those beats were thready and irregular in time and force. She was teetering on the brink. I couldn't tell where she was bleeding from most or what I could do to staunch the flow. She was naked and I was in soaking clothes. I couldn't rip any of my clothes off to make a tourniquet. It was taking all my strength to keep her from drowning.

She was unconscious again. I needed to get her out of the cave so that she could lie flat. I have heard of people dying from a simple faint, if it happens when they are crammed with other people in a rush hour underground train. If the body is forced to stay vertical no oxygen can get to the brain and the person strokes out and dies.

How much time had passed? Four minutes? Twenty? I desperately wanted to get outside but knew it could be fatal for both of us. I had to move back towards the apex of the cave to be able to see down both passages at once. Tami was probably putting a fresh clip in her gun, preparing to fire again. Did she have a flashlight, I wondered? Was she waiting for Linda to have a cardiac arrest? What if she tossed in a lighted emergency flare and drove us out with the acrid smoke?

I was staring down the tunnel of the smaller cave when the light to my right dimmed suddenly. The barrel of a gun protruded from the edge of the main entrance. This was not a semiautomatic handgun, but the long distinctive barrel of a revolver.

"Police!" Katy roared. "Are you in there, Donald?"

"I'm here with Linda. She's bleeding to death. Be careful, Katy. Tami Stillwell's at the other entrance with a gun." My voice sounded weak and distant, as if it already belonged to another world.

XXV

Desolation Falls

Katy Pearson's voice sounded strong and clear. She was talking on her cell phone.

"Got it! No, there's no one here now. Tucker and Walton are on their way with backup and medics." She turned to shout into the cave. "Donald, can you bring Mrs. Covington towards me on your own?"

With relief and renewed energy I plodded back towards the entrance with Linda's dead weight over my shoulder. Katy had her back to the outside wall, probing the darkness of the hollows with her eyes and gun, straining to catch any movement in the woods. The cooler air at the cave mouth felt delicious. I sucked down a lungful of cold crisp air, and then dived to get my full weight below Linda's body. Pushing off the floor of the pool I managed to flip her over the front wall of the cave onto the path outside. I quickly followed suit.

Within seconds I was freezing again. The air temperature was icy and a stiff breeze had come up in the past half-hour. My clothes stuck to my skin stiffly and my teeth began to chatter uncontrollably. I could hardly see Linda as she lay on the path at my feet but could feel goose bumps rising on her skin.

"Can you ask for a helicopter to come right up here?" I asked Katy. "I think they'll have enough room to land. I don't think Linda will make it back down the trail, even on a stretcher. I'll get her down to that pool where she can lie flat and stay warm."

I managed to get Linda into position for a fireman's lift, which gave me a free hand to cling to the railing. Even with that extra support I came close to collapsing as I tripped and groped my way down to the first of the collection pools. I was weak, hungry and had a headache. But although I was shivering and trembling so much I could hardly function I was aware that Linda was not shivering at all. That is a bad sign. I laid her in the shallow pool, so that she was lying flat with her head resting on the smooth slate edge, and then climbed in beside her. The temperature was more bearable here than inside the cave. I sucked in cold evening air hungrily and tried to clear my head. Linda and I were sitting targets, still, but I was too exhausted to worry about that. A silver moon had risen above the trees, bathing the hollow in a cold silvery light.

From where I lay I could see beyond the rocky promontory to the smaller cave and the bushes beyond that. A line of trees followed the slope down to the edge of the plateau where the ground fell away sharply to the river below. The white water of the falls shone clear in the moonlight, a sharp contrast to the darkness of the trees. For just a moment the illusion of peaceful beauty descended on me. I listened to the comforting drone of Katy's voice talking to dispatch on her phone above me, and watched the branches of the tress swaying in the breeze.

The trunk of the tree closest to the edge of the cliff suddenly seemed to split into two as a figure peeled away from cover and stepped into the moonlight.

"Step out of the bushes, Miss Stillwell, and throw your little handgun ahead of you. It's no match for this."

Sebastian Covington was wearing full army camouflage fatigues and had his face blackened. He had a machine gun at his shoulder leveled at some bushes adjacent to the smaller cave entrance.

"Do it now!" he yelled. "Your vicious little game is over. You wanted to tempt me here but maybe didn't expect this, eh?" His voice sounded harsh and cruel. His attention never wavered from the bushes.

I sensed movement behind me as Katy dropped to a crouch and slipped silently down the staircase and into the underbrush beside the cabana.

Moonlight sparkled off metal as a handgun arched through the air and clattered off the rocks near Covington's feet. The bushes parted and the slumped figure of Tami Stillwell crawled down the bank towards him on her hands and knees. She had pulled on T-shirt and jeans but her feet were bare. Her body wracked with sobbing.

"Why did you throw me away? You're my daddy. You're supposed to look after me. Why'd you leave me to be raised by a bunch of drunken crooks? Look at all the stuff you've got. I've never had nothing. You're supposed to love me. You're my daddy!"

She whimpered and groveled like a dog at his feet. He kept the rifle trained on her all the way down the hill. The only sign that her words were getting through to him was the quiver of the gun barrel as he fought to keep it steady. It was impossible to know what was going on behind the black mask of his face.

"Drop the rifle, Mr. Covington. We can take it from here." Katy Pearson stood on the cliff edge some ten feet to Covington's left. Her handgun was held in two hands, with practiced authority, and pointed at his head.

For a long moment everyone seemed frozen in place, unsure what to do. The air was silent. Even the waterfall seemed muted and distant. Then a low rhythmic shuddering seemed to grow from within the mountain behind the caves. A steady powerful drumbeat swelled like the spirit of warriors old. I turned my head to look up at the angry granite face of Kamagutsz and was suddenly blinded by a brilliant light.

The rescue helicopter rose above the hollow and flooded the scene with unforgiving exposure. Covington lowered his rifle and raised an arm to shield his eyes from the searchlight. In that same instant Tami's small figure uncoiled at his feet and launched herself at him in a furious rush. She hit him just below his chest, her head butting his abdomen in the solar plexus as she drove him towards the cliff edge.

"I hate you!" she screamed.

Caught unaware, and leaning backwards to ward off the glare of light, Sebastian Covington was at a fatal disadvantage. Even his superior strength and athletic training could do nothing to stop his momentum from dragging him out over the edge of the precipice. Katy dropped her gun and lunged forward in a frantic effort to reach the writhing couple. With a flying rugby tackle she grabbed one of Tami's ankles before it disappeared. I watched in horror as Katy began to be dragged towards the edge with Tami's free leg lashing and kicking at her face.

Linda was unconscious but breathing, her head reclining safely on the edge of the pool without my support. I scrambled out of the water and rushed to the cliff. A stunted pine sapling stuck out into the gorge at the place where Katy's body was slipping. I curled my knee round its trunk, leaned out and grabbed the back of Katy's jacket with my right hand, seizing Tami's flailing ankle with my left hand. The forward momentum stopped. The pine tree roots held firm.

Sebastian Covington continued to slide, now separating from Tami's grip. He threw his arms out and scratched desperately at the crumbling rock. Under the halogen glare of the searchlight above us I saw his eyes lock with Tami's as he slid away from her and plunged into the blackness of the gorge. The look in his eyes was unfathomable. In the months and years since then that image has become burnt into my memory. As I revisit it I find myself projecting an interpretation of what his eyes expressed. Part fear? Part hatred? But mostly just disbelief that his callous decision in Portland, all those years before, could come back to bite him like this.

Tami's demeanor changed the moment he was gone. She cooperated with me and even helped Katy to regain her balance and clamber back to safety. She offered no resistance as Katy handcuffed herself to the girl and led her away. I threw a blanket over their shoulders and stayed with them to make sure Tami wouldn't try one final piece of insanity. She seemed comforted by the blanket. Her energy was spent.

The helicopter pilot positioned the chopper so that the searchlight probed the darkness of the abyss to the foot of Desolation Falls. The three of us stopped and looked back down one last time. We found Sebastian Covington in the deep black pool just beyond the foot of the waterfall. His lifeless body was caught in the eddy of the whirlpool created by the falls. Spread-eagled facedown, his camouflage fatigues made him look like an autumn leaf. As we watched he danced a slow pirouette amid the carefree bubbles of the river.

SUNDAY

348

XXVI

A Bitter Road To Follow

When T. S. Eliot wrote that "April is the cruelest month," he obviously hadn't spent February in Seattle. The sky was the color of dirty dishwater and just as inviting. The late-morning view from the parking garage at Harborview Medical Center was a dreary cityscape shrouded in rain clouds. The temperature hovered a few degrees above freezing and a bleak sadness sucked all the cheer from my soul.

To the southwest, Alki Point was socked in, with Vashon Island well hidden from view. I could almost make out the roof of The Dell, where two new bodies would be awaiting my attention tomorrow morning. Clayton van Allen and Sebastian Covington had been about as far apart in life as you could get, in terms of social standing, wealth, or education. But now they might well be lying side by side, in adjacent drawers, or stacked on top of each other, stiff as boards in the huge refrigerated body room with tags on their toes.

We would be lucky if the body count from yesterday's tragedy stayed at two. I had just come from the MICU where Frank Stillwell was being treated for alcohol and sedative poisoning. His conscious level had fallen after Katy and I left him. He was flown to Harborview in a coma to get his stomach pumped. When I saw him this morning the staff handed me a sample of the stomach contents for Rusty and colleagues to analyze. Big Frank was on a respirator but would probably pull through. He was a vigorous man.

Linda's prognosis was a lot more uncertain. The stab wound below her left breast had pierced the chest cavity, causing a pneumothorax and collapsed lung. By a miracle the knife had failed to puncture her heart or large blood vessels. I found her in surgical intensive care, sedated, intubated, on a respirator, with the fourth of six units of blood dripping into her arm. She hadn't passed any urine overnight, which raised the specter of acute kidney failure. The nursing staff was a bustling parody of cheerful efficiency, but I could tell from their body language that Linda's outlook was still in major doubt. She was surrounded by several other medical and social disasters with tubes coming out of every orifice. The suck and hiss of the ventilators made me think of Darth Vader, and of Callum safe at home watching Star Wars videos.

I felt like a fraud for only needing a few stitches in my forearm where Tami Stillwell's blade had found its way past my bumfled leather jacket. Apart from that and a few bruised ribs from Frank Stillwell's knee in the back of the truck, I was hale and hearty.

It was almost noon when I pulled away from Harborview, headed down Boren and onto Aurora Avenue going north. This afternoon was to be a surprise party for Harley – the unveiling of the new cold frame. It was probably too late in the season for it to be of much use to him this year but I hadn't said that to Callum. He was justifiably proud of his accomplishments, and Harley would be thrilled.

I saw no one tailing me as I crossed the Aurora Bridge, dropped onto Stoneway, and was equally oblivious going along Forty-fifth and into the QFC parking lot. I dashed inside for a quart of fresh-squeezed orange juice and a tray of extra-gooey cinnamon rolls, which I lugged back to my truck. I found Katy Pearson leaning against the driver's side door waiting for me. She looked tired, weary, and thoughtful. Wet hair, neatly combed, suggested a recent shower. She wore a red turtleneck sweater above black corduroy pants with a stylish jacket to match. Her smile was guarded, as she probed my face for signals.

"How is she?" she asked.

"Linda? They are handing out the usual bullshit clichés that her condition is critical but stable. I'm not too sure but I'd say her chances are better than fifty-fifty, now that she's in Harborview. She's got a collapsed lung, and may be going into renal failure, but I expect she'll recover. Physically, at least."

"She wasn't trying to blackmail him, you know."

"Who?"

"Tami. She wanted a real father. She had been searching for him, then stalking him, for years. Ever since she turned eighteen and could find out the names of her birth parents. The envelope she left at the nursing home to lure Covington to Kamagutsz was still in his car. It explained a lot."

I said, "I found her birth certificate in the caboose at Agnes Munro's house. The name of the female child was given as "Baby Jane," but the father was listed as Sebastian Covington. I didn't recognize the mother's name."

"Marilou Kendall. She died of a heroin overdose about three years after giving up Tami for adoption."

"It said that in the envelope stuff?"

"Yes, but Tami gave me more details in person. I got her statement this morning. She seemed eager to tell the whole story."

I said, "I feel stupid that we didn't have her as a prime suspect in Myra Garfield's case from the get-go. We have some DNA evidence in the lab from material found under Myra's fingernails. That would probably have clinched it, but we should have got onto Tami sooner."

"Don't be so hard on yourself, Donald. She did a great job of manipulating Aaron Klein into taking her to the Covington's Vashon place on Sunday and making him think it was his idea and that she'd never been there before. And her alibi for Friday night seemed solid."

"I've been thinking about that," I said. "It's easier going back over it, now, of course. Her alibi was only solid for the later part of

Friday night. Both Aaron and Mosh said they remembered seeing her dancing right in front of the stage at the end of the concert. We didn't pin them down to say when they thought she had arrived."

Katy gave a grim smile. "Not till eleven, actually. After they had started their second set. Tami had had a busy night by then. She was on the bus driving through Vashon town on her way home when she saw Aaron Klein going into Zoomies. Frank, Sonya and Starflame had left by the time she got to her own house so she took Frank's truck and drove back to Zoomies hoping to give Aaron a nice surprise. She was crushed when she saw that he was sitting with Myra Garfield. Tami followed them to the Covington's place and watched from the bushes while they fooled around in the hot tub. Her anger and jealousy were obvious when she told me about it this morning. And scary, too. She kept flipping between two personas, the insecure gentle waif and the ruthless, bad-ass nutcase. It was spooky to watch."

"Did she follow Myra home?"

"Yes, then she went back to her own house again to get a bunch of Sonya's Phenobarb. Capsules. She enjoyed telling me about this part. Said she was excited to try it again. It had worked so well on Magdalene. When she got back to the Garfield residence Myra was pretty bombed. She answered the door in her bathrobe and was really surprised to see Tami. Tami didn't let on that she had seen them earlier in the evening. She put on a show of tears, and told Myra she was falling in love with Aaron and wanted Myra's advice."

"From what I've heard about Myra Garfield she was probably

loving this."

"Absolutely. Tami said she lapped it all up and invited Tami in for a drink and a chat, eager to continue the deception with Tami and then gloat about it with her friends. Girls can really be bitches, sometimes. Anyway, Tami played her like a fiddle, feeding her ego, then breaking down and crying. She waited for Myra to leave the room and then drugged her drink."

My professional curiosity was piqued. "How many Phenobarb. Capsules did she use? Did she say?"

"She cut open about half a bottle's worth, maybe thirty capsules, and tipped the powder into an envelope before she arrived. She said it was easy to slip it into Myra's drink and watch her "suck that baby down." When Myra passed out Tami took her back to the Covington's Hot Tub in the back of the truck, pretty much the way you figured out."

"But she didn't know what clothes Myra had been wearing?" I said.

"She had seen her wearing Clayton's suede leather jacket but that was all. She was running late, too, by this time. It was taking longer for Myra to pass out than she expected. She wasn't sure when Frank and Sonya would be back. She also wanted to make sure she had been seen at the Skunk Bucket concert, so she rushed and threw some plausible clothes in the truck and then went back to lift Myra into the back. Myra began to regain consciousness when Tami dumped her into the hot tub so Tami held her head under the water.

That was when she scratched Tami. The rest of it you know."

"Was she trying to frame Aaron, then?"

"No, she hoped that Frank Stillwell would be arrested. She wanted Aaron to be frightened and upset, to pay him back for two-timing her. That was how she put it. Her real target was to shock and hurt Linda and Sebastian Covington."

"You said she admitted killing the Reilly girl in Texas, too," I said.

"Yes. She described it with a kind of cool detachment, as if it belonged to another time, another world. Very matter of fact, as though it was perfectly natural and that Clayton van Allen and the girl had it coming. She couldn't stand Magdalene. A "bible-thumping little bitch" is how Tami described her. Always niggling Tami about Sonya's drinking and Clayton's foul language. Tami felt a bit protective of Sonya but couldn't stand Clayton. I asked her about sexual abuse. She said, "No, not yet," but she thought it was only a matter of time. She knew that Clayton beat up Sonya pretty regularly and Tami could see that he was looking at her with more than paternal interest."

"So what happened the night Magdalene was killed?"

"Tami had been gone for a week in Portland. Not Eugene like she told her folks. She had been tracking down details about her real mother, and how she had died. Tami got back to her house in Houston three hours earlier than she told the police. She found

Sonya drunk and bleeding. Magdalene came over to gloat and told Tami that she had heard the fighting. She said she pitied Tami because her parents were just white trash who didn't belong in the neighborhood. Tami dumped barbiturates into a jug of lemonade and took it over to share with Magdalene by the Reilly's pool. Once she had passed out Tami went back, got some semen from Sonya's diaphragm, spooned it into the girl's vagina, then drowned her."

I was having a hard time reconciling this cold, heartless behavior with the Tami Stillwell I had met. "When did she turn her hatred on Linda?" I said.

"That came a whole lot later. At the time of Magdalene's death, all Tami knew was that Sebastian, this glamorous and successful businessman, was her real dad, and that he had been living in Houston for several years without her knowing it. And then, just when she could have contacted him she discovered that he was moving his company headquarters to Seattle. She found out that he had a house in Seattle and a summer place on Vashon, so she worked on Sonya to move the family up here. For a couple of years she enjoyed stalking the Covingtons, living a fantasy life vicariously, imagining that she was their real daughter."

"But she never approached Sebastian?"

"No, she began to enjoy the deception and the fantasy too much. She said she thought it would be scary to contact him and be rejected. She kept putting it off, waiting for the perfect time. It was after Linda's mom appeared on the scene and was admitted to the nursing home that things went sour for Tami. She got hold of a key to the old lady's house and found boxes of letters in which Linda tells her mother that she encouraged Sebastian to ditch his girlfriend and make her get an abortion."

"Had Tami planned her revenge for a while, then?"

"She was vague about that. She convinced herself that Sebastian was a victim, like herself, and that it was Linda who was the evil woman. Tami started seeing herself in the role of Sebastian's guardian angel. She took the psychology course at the University of Washington just so that she could keep an eye on Linda."

I said, "It's creepy thinking that one of the students out in the audience during your lectures might be acting all sweet and innocent but deep down is a psychopath. Like a terrorist sleeper just waiting to be activated. So then van Allen reappears. Was that what made her come unglued?"

"That was part of it. The clincher was when Myra humiliated her on the Friday night. It was bad enough that Tami had seen Myra screwing Aaron Klein. Myra then taunted her about Frank Stillwell coming on to her. Tami says she lost her temper and told Myra that she didn't care. "He's not my real dad, anyway. Sebastian Covington's my real dad!" Tami said that the moment she said it there was a silence, followed by a gleeful intake of breath from Myra. She laughed at Tami. "I've screwed him, too. Lots of times. Wait till I tell him he just fired his bastard daughter's stepdad!" Tami had already decided to kill Myra but hearing all that destroyed the fantasy she had invented about her real dad's noble character."

"So she decided to kill both Linda and her father," I said.

"Linda gave her the perfect opportunity when she invited Tami to Kamagutsz. A remote location, near where Frank was working, anyway. It couldn't have been better. Except that Clayton van Allen showed up out of the blue."

I said, "Did he know it was Tami who framed him in Texas, or did he think it was Frank?"

"Tami's not sure, but she had hoped that Frank would deal with him. Then yesterday morning, after Frank had already left, Tami stepped out of the trailer and saw van Allen getting out of his car. He ran towards her. She retreated inside, grabbed Frank's gun and fled out the back door of the trailer. Van Allen followed her into the barn. She hid in the boat, but he found her. She shot him in there, took his car, drove to the caboose to clean up, prepared the envelope of stuff for Sebastian, and then left it at the nursing home before she drove over to Hoodsport."

I said, "She called all the other girls who were invited to Kamagutsz, without telling Linda, so that Linda would be there alone when Tami arrived."

Katy nodded. "She drove the rental car to where Frank was working, and then got him to drive her to the Kamagutsz trailhead in his truck. Linda's car was there already. Tami forced Frank into the back of the truck at gunpoint and made him drink a bottle of bourbon laced with..." She consulted her notes.

"Phenobarbitone?" I said.

"No, Lorazepam, actually. She said she was disappointed at how slow and incomplete the Phenobarb had been on Myra. They use a lot of lorazepam at the nursing home. When Frank had nearly passed out she gagged him and tied him up with duct tape."

"I'm surprised she didn't just shoot him," I said.

"I don't know why she didn't. She planned to shoot him later, making it look like a remorseful suicide after he had supposedly killed Linda and Sebastian. At least that's what she said. Her thinking was becoming less and less clear and rational towards the end. She was hell bent on revenge against the Covingtons."

I said, "I think she planned to go over the falls along with her father, last night. She would have, too, if you hadn't caught hold of her ankle."

"And so would I, if you hadn't grabbed us both. It doesn't seem enough just to say thanks, Donald. I owe you."

"Och nonsense. I was just trying to make up for some of the daft mistakes I had made earlier in the week. I was trying too hard to impress you."

I blushed the moment I said it.

XXVII

Something To Celebrate

Callum was lying in wait for me behind the door. He snatched the cinnamon rolls from my hands and dashed back inside.

"Harley liked the cold frame, Dad, even though it's not perfect. It's asymmetrical."

I followed the smell of coffee and the sound of Taffy's happy wheezing to the kitchen. Jennifer and Harley were crouched down inspecting the freshly stained cold frame with its clear plastic top that lifted on bright brass hinges. I knelt beside them.

"Will it work for you, Harley? Callum says it's not quite right."

Harley could barely keep the tears at bay. "Amazed is what I am. It's just wonderful. There's nothing wrong with it. One of the hinges is not quite square, so it's a little stiff when it opens, is all. Far as I'm concerned it is perfect. He's a fine young gentleman, Donald."

I tried lifting and closing the front flap a few times. It was a little squint, but worked adequately.

I said, "Sometimes an imperfect symmetry is as good as it gets. It certainly looks functional."

I winced as I rose stiffly to a standing position. Jennifer pounced on me.

"Which is more than can be said about you, Dad. What on earth were you doing chasing after criminals? You're supposed to leave that to the police. You could have got yourself killed."

There was nothing I could say that would appease her. Harley had turned his back to give us a moment of privacy. He had attached paper clips and string to my soaked and crumpled dollar bills, and hung them above the stove to dry along with some wet business cards and credit cards.

I said, "Thanks for drying this stuff for me. I didn't think to take my wallet out my pocket before I dived in the pool, last night."

Jennifer scoffed.

Harley winked at her. "I think your dad's starting a new career. Or a new trend, anyway."

I said, "No jokes about money laundering, Harley."

"That's not what I was thinking. You don't make enough

money to be worth laundering. Now I've heard of lawyers chasing ambulances looking for new clients, but here we've got a pathologist chasing after crooks before they ever turned into dead bodies. Are you just making sure you got job security?"

I held up my hands in submission. "Okay, I apologize. I was reckless and stupid. What else is new? It certainly hasn't given me any job security."

Callum ran from the kitchen to answer the door, and returned a few moments later with Katy Pearson. She had a large plastic bag in her hand. The mood in the kitchen improved immediately. Jennifer smiled warmly at her.

Katy said, "Sorry, I forgot to give you this when we were in the parking lot, this morning."

From the bag I pulled out the sodden remains of my leather jacket; crumpled, ripped, and with white salt stains in places where it had begun to dry out.

Katy said, "I found it by the cave entrance, last night. We are not going to need it as evidence. I thought you might like to have it back."

The jacket looked about as good as I felt, right then. I held it up for inspection.

"It's beyond salvation, I think. I guess this is another piece of my suave, sophisticated image that I'll need to give up."

Katy and Jennifer exchanged mischievous looks.

Katy said, "If you want my opinion, Donald, the leather jacket didn't suit you anyway. A bit too slick and corporate for my taste. If I was going out with you I'd rather you wore one of your old Harris Tweed jackets… in case you're interested."

Printed in the United States
39805LVS00005B/1-78